The Memory Stones

Righteous Love is a Narrow Path (Book 2)

By
Lewis Pennington

622 Brush Creek Road
Fairview, NC 28730

ISBN: 978-1-7364239-3-6

For little peanut.

Chapter 1

"Are you ready?"

"Of course—are *you* ready?"

"Don't be a smart aleck," the man replied, placing a bear-sized hand on her slim shoulder. "I'm serious. This one's a certified killer."

She began bouncing on her toes, bobbing left then right, craning her head around the hulking man standing between her and the redheaded wrecking ball she was about to battle.

"You good with the plan?" the man asked.

"Yes, sensei," she said in the tiny voice of a child wishing to please a parent as she peered up from under brunette locks.

The man chortled through a crooked grin then jerked the black belt around her waist into a knot. Using his massive frame to partition her from the auditorium's eight hundred spectators, he bent over her. "Just remember the plan." He hesitated then sighed, placing a pink eye patch in the palm of her hand. "Are you sure about this?"

"Yes," she said.

The crowd's dull murmur slowly rose as the clock on the wall counted down to zero. A quick blast of an airhorn catapulted them to their feet, and she emerged out from behind the hulking figure and onto the spongy mat, her gait toward the center circle steady and unflinching. She gazed past a man with "REFEREE" across his shirt and fixated on the robed figure of the person the match had billed "the Red Assassin"—a rock-solid female warrior with a fiery auburn ponytail and an undefeated attitude.

As the referee motioned them to square up, she brushed a strand of hair behind her ear while pulling the pink patch over her left eye. The crowd exploded with undulating shouts of "Lef—ty! Lef—ty! Lef—ty!"

"Remember the plan," the big man yelled from the mat's edge.

With a wink from her uncovered eye, she blew him an exaggerated kiss.

"For heaven's sake, would you please focus!"

The second she turned back, the referee commanded, "Fight!"

In an instant both combatants were on their toes, bouncing, circling one another, waiting for the other to make the first move.

The Red Assassin struck first with a lightning jab that grazed her left cheek and pushed the pink eye patch to the side. She bounced backwards and gave her opponent a quick smile, acknowledging what could have been a fatal blow.

A sense of quick victory gleamed in the Assassin's eyes as she delivered a series of jabs followed by a sweeping left foot.

Nothing landed as she ducked, bobbed, and weaved her way through the flurry in a silky, singular move that appeared more appropriate for ballet than martial arts.

The redhead snarled, flicking her ponytail to the side and narrowing her gaze on the pink eye patch she was set on turning crimson.

As she adjusted the patch, hundreds of hours of training, along with an uncanny instinct for visualizing her opponents' next moves, suddenly channeled through her. Instantly, the crowd's roar was gone. She watched, as if in slow motion, the telegraphed blow she knew was coming. A misguided straight left hand passed her right cheek, leaving her challenger unbalanced for a split second. It was all she needed. As if a thousand pounds of pressure had been released, her left leg whipped around her body, landing the top of her foot square upon her foe's jaw, sending her to the mat, absent all her faculties.

Suddenly all sound rushed back as half the crowd howled in delight while the other half stood dumbfounded by how quickly it had all taken place. Moments later chants of "Lef—ty! Lef—ty! Lef—ty!" filled the auditorium.

With no need to calculate score cards or confer with judges, the referee grabbed her hand and lifted it over her head. The chant of "Lef—ty! Lef—ty!" slowly morphed into "Zo—ey! Zo—ey! Zo—ey!"

The massive man on the edge of the mat beamed up to the jumbotron that read, "Winner by KO: Zoey Antonelli."

When she entered the NYC *Chronicle* office building the following morning, Zoey was met at the elevator by a wiry little doorman in a royal blue suit with a silver skull pin attached to the lapel. "A little early for Halloween, isn't it, Bert?" she said, nodding to the pin.

"It's October first, Miss Antonelli, and it's never too early to celebrate my favorite holiday. Speaking of celebrating," he said, stretching out a little black book toward her, "would youz please sign this for me?"

She cocked her head. "Come on, Bert—really?"

"Absolutely! My nephew was at yesterday's match and he said youz was something special, that youz knocked out that gal with one shot, and that youz was quicksilver, that youz was going to the Olympics, and that…" he paused to provide a quick wink, "… and he says youz a hottie!"

"Okay, okay—I don't know anything about going to any Olympics, and I certainly don't know about being a hottie, but sure, where do I sign?"

"Here," he said, pushing the book toward her and flipping a couple pages. "Right there, next to the GOAT."

"Goat?"

"The GOAT, Miss Antonelli. The greatest of all time! Come on, Miss A, you know… Floats like a butterfly, stings like a bee?"

She puckered her lips, slowly shaking her head.

"Ohhh man," he said, laughing, "youz don't even know it, but you're going down next to *the king*. That there's Muhammad Ali, Miss A!"

"Well then," she said, bobbing her head, "I guess I'm in a good neighborhood." She scribbled down her name and with a polite mock curtsy backed into the elevator.

"T'anks, Miss A," the little man said before disappearing behind the closing doors.

Twenty flights later the elevator opened to a hushed lobby. Her office's foyer was strangely void of the typical chaos—the usual hurried, panicky atmosphere—that had grown to aggravate her more with each passing day. All that resembled the same old, same old was the expressionless gaze of the receptionist, Claire, a twenty-year veteran of answering phones with the same deadpan "NYC *Chronicle*, how may I help you?" Regardless of how chipper Zoey was or how clever a quip she threw at her, Claire's response was never more than cursory.

"Top o'the day to ya, Miss Claire!" she said, clacking her heels in an abbreviated Irish jig.

Nothing. No smile. No frown. *Maybe no pulse*, Zoey often thought.

Resigning herself to yet another failed attempt to crack the Mount Rushmore of stoicism, she politely nodded and headed to the door. Just then a dozen coworkers burst into the lobby, surrounding her with balloons and showering her with high fives and slaps on the back. Her jubilant friends tossed confetti while horns and whistles replaced the dull silence from before.

"Congratulations!"

"Way to go, champ!"

"You rock!"

Cheers, handshakes, and hugs transformed the foyer into something it had never been—a happy place. One by one, coworkers stepped up to express how proud they were of her victory in the previous day's match. Even Claire emerged from behind her marble fortress to express her admiration.

"I got you something," she said, with a curt nod of the head. From behind her back, she pulled a small plastic statue of a fist with the words *You Pack a Punch* written on the base.

"Aww, I love it!" Zoey leaned forward and gave her a hug, which although stiff in return was nonetheless pleasing. Mount Rushmore had been cracked.

"What on earth is this!" came a booming voice from the elevator. Now completely bald and twenty-five pounds heavier, Zoey's boss, Greg Eniss was more than ever a tyrant among tyrants. "Here it is ten after eight and nobody's at their desks. Can somebody explain why?"

"Zoey just won the karate championship, Mr. Eniss," Claire squeaked out.

Greg shot the mousy receptionist a vicious stare, sending her backpedaling into the crowd.

He turned to Zoey. "You won what?"

"Yesterday. It was the finals of the regional karate championship." She tilted her head down. "I just got lucky is all."

The room filled with contradictions to her modesty. "No way, Zoey, you ruled the mat. No luck to it. You're the real deal."

"Knocked the top seed out in less than a minute," crowed an elderly man shuffling past with a mail cart full of manila folders. "And did it all with just one eye."

"That's right, Greg," a tall man in the rear chimed in. "Lefty's going to the Olympics."

"Going to the Olympics?" Greg said, rearing his head back. "Where she's going—where you're all going—is back to work!"

The crowd fell silent.

"Now!" he bellowed.

In an instant the lobby was almost vacant, leaving just Greg and Zoey facing one another while Claire cowered behind her desk.

"Come with me, Antonelli," he said in a huff.

Without a word, she followed her portly boss through a maze of cubicles. Along the way, her office mates pretended to be hard at work—until Greg passed. Then they grabbed her attention, miming a high five or a thumbs-up while silently mouthing, *Congratulations*.

When they finally arrived at Greg's office, his bald head was beaded with sweat. He flopped down into his oversized leather chair and wiped his forehead.

"Sit down, Antonelli," he panted.

"You okay?" she asked, disregarding his command to sit.

He waved her comment aside. "Listen, I know you're some sort of hotshot kung fu fighter and all but—"

"Karate. Not kung fu," she said.

"Whatever. I really don't care what you do in your spare time but what I do care about is you finishing that dad-blame manuscript I hired you to write. It's been eight months now and all I have is a disjointed outline and two measly chapters. You ought to be finished by now."

"Yes, sir, I know, but I'm still working on the crime expose and then my normal workload is—"

"You keep saying that, Antonelli, but remember it was you who came to me about the idea. And as far-fetched as it was, I took the chance and forked over the advance."

"Yes, sir, I know. You see, I… I—"

"And now you're going off to the Olympics?" He threw up his hands. "How on God's green earth are you ever going to finish this thing?"

"Greg, there's no going to the Olympics. I'm really not that good. It was just the regionals. And besides, I'm thirty-two. I'm too old and—"

"Stop!" He held up his hand, his voice simmering to a low growl. "Listen, I'm actually glad for you. And I do know how good you are. You've been training like a mad woman for a decade now. So please spare me the false modesty. But—" he added, his tone climbing to a thunderous peak heard throughout the office, "I—want—that—manuscript!"

She pursed her lips as her stomach churned.

"By next week I want to see at least—and I repeat, at least—three new chapters! Do—you—hear—me?"

"Yes, sir, three chapters. But what about the crime piece and my regular assignments?"

Closing his eyes, his fingers curled into pudgy little fists. "Do them!" Veins in his neck bulged over straining tendons. "For Pete's sake, we're paying you good money to do a job and now you've got the chance to make more on the side with this book." He glanced around the room then back to her. "Don't pull a stunt like that lunatic, Paul Talbert, either. I swear, Antonelli, if you come in here with three hundred pages of gibberish like he did, I swear I'll—"

"No, sir," she said, shaking her head. "That won't happen. I promise. I'm on it." She began slowly inching her way to the door. "Okey dokey then," she said through a plastic smile, "I better get on it."

"And, Antonelli, when are you ever going to get a proper haircut and ditch the pink stripe?" He zeroed in on the tattoos on her right arm. "And when are you going to get the rest of those removed?"

She pulled the door open, started through it, then paused, giving him her best Vogue pose as she ran her hand through her long silky brunette mane, twirling strands of her signature pink stripe that ran down the left side. "I guess I could change it if you really want me to, but then I'm afraid the quarter million readers following my column might just decide to migrate over to the *Times*. As for the tattoos… getting rid of the left arm was enough. The right stays as is."

His glare remained fixed on the door as it closed behind her.

On the other side she took a deep breath, counted to three, then continued to her office where she shut the door and burst into tears. Several minutes later she reached into her pocketbook and pulled out her phone. Two numbers appeared at the top of her favorites, Dr. Peter Atwell followed by Paul Talbert. She held her shaking index finger over them as her tears returned.

Chapter 2

At ten thirty the next morning, Zoey entered a beige prewar brownstone and proceeded up the three flights of stairs she had become so familiar with. Instead of a dozen adoring fans from the previous day's office celebration, she was met by a single lady in horn-rimmed glasses coming down the steps.

"Hey, Zoey, he's on a call right now but should be off shortly. The door's open so go on in. Oh, and check out the new beanbag chair. It's to die for."

A minute later she was taking off her jacket and hanging up her purse while pondering the giant striped marshmallow in the corner.

"What do you think of my new zebra beanbag?" came a gentle voice from behind her.

She turned, smiling at the man who had helped her through so many tough times. "I think it's superb, absolutely superb," she said with a tiny bounce. "My good Dr. Atwell, where do you get your taste?"

"Hello, my dear," he said, taking her hand in his. His skin was wrinkled and thin, but it was warm, familiar, and safe. "Come on in, honey. Let's talk."

For the first fifteen minutes of her session, the elderly psychiatrist prodded her into describing every detail of her victory on the mat. Her voice was low and deliberate as she began, but her speech accelerated as she painted the picture of how her opponent became the aggressor and how her instincts took over, giving her the advantage that resulted in her win.

"And with just one kick you knocked her block off." His eyes twinkled as he vicariously took it all in. "I'm curious though. Why the patch? You don't have a problem, do you?"

"No problem—with my sight, that is."

"Then why the patch?"

"Just to... well... make it more interesting."

"So it's not because of the article this summer, the one about the little girl—the kickboxing prodigy—who lost her left eye and her will to compete. It was about that time I think you started wearing the patch... in what I believe was her favorite color. Pink." He scratched his chin. "It wouldn't have anything to do with that article now, would it?"

"I thought all you read were textbooks and medical journals."

He laughed. "Pink patches aside, did you celebrate?"

"Kind of. My office threw me a little ten-minute shindig in the lobby the next morning." She straightened in her chair. "There were balloons, confetti, noise makers and someone even gave me the cutest little statue. It's the first time in that place that people were actually laughing and having fun."

"And how did that make you feel?"

She took a long, easy breath. "Wonderful," she said, slowly exhaling each syllable, savoring the memory. But as quickly as it had come, her smile turned downward, and her head soon followed.

The doctor pulled a box of tissues from a side table and held it to her as tears welled. "And that's when things took a turn?"

She nodded.

"You know your boss's tirade you mentioned to me about on the phone was only a trigger, don't you?"

Her head slowly rose and fell.

"Why do you keep working there? You're an award-winning writer with a readership Hemingway would have envied."

She chuckled.

"Don't laugh, missy. You know it's true."

"No, Doc," she said, a tear rolling down her cheek, "that's just something he would've said."

He leaned in. "Who?" He examined her face. "Oh, do you mean Paul Talbert?"

Her eyes squeezed together as she fought back more tears. "Yes."

"My dear girl, you must let go. It's been ten years. It's simply not healthy to—"

"I know, I know, but I can't leave the *Chronicle*. I *have* to stay."

"But you don't. You could go anywhere."

"No," she said, pounding the chair's armrest. "I told you, I have to stay."

"But why?"

"Because he got me the job." Her voice grew louder. "He's the reason I'm where I am today. He made me."

"Come on now, no one made you. You've made it on your own. You've become a successful writer and you're even a black belt." He scanned the dozen tattoos running the length of her right arm. "And more importantly, you've learned to deal with the reason for all those."

She folded her arms, trying to hide all the ink—all the attempts to mask the pain of a child beaten and abused by a drunken father bent on taking out his frustrations over his own failed life. She slowly began rocking back and forth.

He put his hand on her shoulder. "My dear, what else do you need to tell me?"

"I-I promised but I can't. I just can't."

"Can't what?"

"I can't write the story he wants me to."

"What story? Who?"

"My boss. He wants me to write Paul's story."

"You have a story about Paul?"

"I have a journal from him that I was going to turn into a novel. I know I shouldn't have, but I sold my boss on the idea and he took me up on it. Now I can't."

"But that's good. Writing is therapy. Whatever it is you're dealing with, your writing will help. You know that from all our past sessions."

"I-I thought it would, but now…" She buried her face in her hands.

"My dear girl," he said, his voice softening, "if you feel it's too personal or it's too difficult to write about, then don't. Forget about your boss, forget the deal you made with him. Be honest and just tell him why."

She pulled her face from her hands. "*Why*?" Tears cascaded down her face. "You want to know *why*?"

"Only if—"

"Because…" Her face fell back into her hands, her tears seeping through her fingers. "Because I love him!"

The doctor pulled back. "You love your boss?"

"No, of course not." Slowly, she raised her head just enough so that he could see the glint of her eyes. With a tiny breath she said, "I love Paul."

Doctor Atwell blinked. "But he's been gone for so long."

"I know," she muttered.

"But… you never mentioned this before."

Her sobs came in waves. "I always loved him. I just didn't realize it. I was just too young, stupid and blind."

"Why didn't you tell him?"

"I couldn't."

"Why?"

"Because he was falling in love with someone else," she blurted. "I was too busy being his best friend." She pushed the chair back and turned away. "I thought I'd keep on being his silly sidekick until his infatuation with his Southern belle wore off and then he'd turn to me. I didn't have the nerve, but if he *had* made the first move, it would've worked." She arched her head back, then let it fall forward again to stare into the hardwood floor. "The funny thing is—she wasn't real. She didn't even exist." The muffled horns of the busy New York streets below provided the backdrop to an uneasy pause. She turned to the doctor and in a whisper said, "She wasn't—even—real."

"Zoey," he said, her name hanging in the air between them as he studied her, "are you okay?"

She continued gazing through him to another time and place, to a place she had read about in the pages of Paul Talbert's journal.

"Zoey—Zoey, do you hear me?" He took her by the arm. "Zoey!"

With a quick twist of her head, she was back, and in the present.

"Where did you go?" he asked.

"I-I'm sorry. I just…" She put her hand to her forehead. "It doesn't matter, Doc, I—"

"But it does. My dear, what I'm hearing is something that needs to be addressed. These hidden feelings you had for Paul need to be resolved. We need to get the old Zoey back. The one who always greeted me with a *Hey Hey* and a bounce in her step."

"I'm afraid the corporate world put a damper on that girl."

"Forget the corporate stuff for the moment. Let's concentrate on Paul for now and on resolving the issues around him."

She laughed. "How can we do that when he's not here? What're we going to do, have a séance to talk to his ghost?"

"That would certainly make my job a lot easier," he said. "No, we need to sit down and just start talking this through—like we've always done."

"I guess so."

He pulled a small, mangled notepad from his pocket. "I'm pretty booked for most of tomorrow, but I don't want to put this off. Let's do this, if you can get away for a long lunch tomorrow, we'll do an extended session from noon until one thirty. How's that sound?"

"Sure, I can manage that."

"Great, and between now and then I want you to do me a favor. I want you to think about one person in your life who makes you feel special—who's with us, who's *alive*—not Paul." He placed his finger under her chin. "Can you do that for me, karate kid?"

Her eyes brightened slightly. "Alright, Doc."

That evening, after typing out another incriminating piece for her mafia focused expose, she curled up on her sofa, wrapped a blanket around herself, then reached into the hidden pouch in her pocketbook she had made specifically for the one item that was always with her—the memory stone. As the nightly ritual proceeded, she laid it next to her, then slid her hand under her pillow and withdrew Mase's journal.

It was a scene she had repeated almost every night since Annabelle Lanier had given it to her nearly ten years earlier. Although she could almost recite it verbatim, she never tired of reading it, and as she did, the same emotions ebbed and flowed, just as they always did with each reading.

Her excitement rose when Paul described his return—as Mase—to his beloved Willow Creek Plantation. She bit her nails at the description of Juana and the retelling of her mystics. Her heart pounded faster with every harrowing scene of Spoon's rescue, culminating in Silas' death and followed by Spoon and Annabelle's journey into the future. She would then stop, trying to wrap her mind around how surreal these supernatural events were and why she was privy to them.

As she moved on, frustration and anger would envelop her when he described how his uncle's rule over the plantation had almost brought it to ruin. She grimaced at the horrific conditions of the South and how the now-freed slaves continued to be beaten, raped, and murdered. She mourned with him when reading of Lincoln's assassination, and she marveled at how he used his knowledge of the future to manipulate the business world into making his fortune.

Only the last page evoked mixed feelings in her. Unlike the other pages, this one was marked with several splotchy areas of blurred lettering, the apparent result of what she knew could only be tears. His opening paragraph caused her heart to flutter when he mentioned how much he missed her. She wanted to believe those tears were for her, but as he continued to describe the hardships brought on by having to conceal his love, she realized those feelings were not for her but for the slave girl that had won his heart through time.

Several passages later the stains increased as the text revealed a devastating illness that had swept through the county, falling hard upon the plantation, and infecting both him and Sissy. It was the last sentence, dated August 2, 1871, that troubled her the most—a single line of text that tormented her and that had ultimately brought her to seek Dr. Atkins' help. With no ending, the line simply trailed off into the margin.

My dearest is beyond any doctor's cure and I fear the angel of death is at our door.

Her heart ached for him while the bitter taste of an unholy desire rose in her as she envisioned a chance to gain his love. As always, her mind ultimately unraveled the emotional knot and twisted its way back to reality, leaving her disappointed in herself and her evil thoughts. She hated herself for it, and she hated that she had not acted sooner, when he was there with her.

Most of all, she hated that there was nothing she could ever do about it.

Chapter 3

The following morning Zoey awoke just as she had so many times before, Mase's journal on her chest, the lights still on, and a rude pain in her neck from maintaining an awkward reading position well into her slumber. Her familiarity with this routine also resulted in her skilled execution in a rushed prepping for the day that never failed to get her to the office ahead of her boss. Today was different.

At precisely 7:50 she opened her office door to find the diminutive tyrant sitting in her chair with his feet up on her desk, tapping his sausage-thick fingers together. "Well, well, well, glad you could make it in today."

She checked her watch. "It's not even eight yet."

"Eight's the start of the day for producers, those writers who make deadlines." He stood up. "But you're not producing, Antonelli. You're behind."

"But, Greg, I—"

"Didn't our little talk put any kind of fire under you?" His voice rose an octave. "I'm dead serious about—"

Just then a tall, thin man came bounding into her office. He had kinky red hair and wore a crisp button-down, ironed with enough collar starch to draw blood should he turn his head too quickly. "I heard about your win!" He stopped in his tracks upon seeing her boss. "Oh… hey, Greg. I'm sorry. I didn't realize you were in a meeting."

"Look at this. Another one of my slacker employees come to suck up more of your time," Greg said as he huffed past the man. "I'm serious, Antonelli," he said over his shoulder as he stomped down the hall. "Get me those chapters, or else."

The thin man rubbernecked his head out the doorway, waiting until the *Chronicle*'s most despised leader disappeared into his own office. Satisfied he was not returning, he rushed to throw his arms around her. "I'm sorry I wasn't there for your match. I heard you wore the patch again." He stuck out his bottom lip and lowered his head into a mock pouty position. "And I'm sorry for missing the surprise lobby party." He hugged her again, though her arms remained at her sides, refusing to reciprocate. The best she could offer was a taut smile.

"It's okay," she said, taking him by the elbows and pushing back.

"You okay?" he said.

"Yeah, yeah, I'm fine. It's just that—"

"Greg's a jerk," he said with a jittery glance back to the door.

"Well, he's—"

"A dictator, moron, soul-crushing beast. A—"

"Well, he's certainly not—"

"Listen, I've got us tickets to see *Two for Tea* tonight. It's Off-Broadway, the tickets were pretty expensive, and it took days to snag 'em but hey, nothing's too good for my girl."

"Oh, that's nice. It's—"

"And afterwards I've got us reservations at the Silver Marlin, that seafood place you love so much down at the

South Street Seaport. And you're going to love this—I've got us on a sailing cruise around the island. I know how much you love sailing."

She bit her lip. "Sam, I'm very appreciative of how much you've put into these plans—"

He put his finger to her lips. "No, no! It's all for my little karate gal. No need for thank-yous."

"Well, I really need to—"

"Oh snap," he said, swinging his head toward the clock on the wall. "Hold that thought. I gotta run to a quick copy meeting. I should only be about an hour. I'll be back afterwards."

"But, Sam, I really—"

"Be planning what you're going to wear," he said, bouncing out into the hall. "Just no kimono or whatever kind of bathrobe you ninja wear," he added, disappearing around a corner.

"Psst. Hey, Z. Psst—is he coming back?" Zoey turned to find Petra, her office confidant and bestie, peeking at her from around the doorjamb, as if trying to get her to come out and play.

Petra had come on board a month after Zoey. Spunky and without a verbal filter, they immediately bonded into a friendship that had continued over the past ten years. "Is carrottop coming back?" she said, muffling a snort that bordered on the verge of an outright belly laugh.

"Get in here, you little troll," she said.

"Sorry, Z, I couldn't help but hear your boy making all those dreamy plans." She raised her shoulders. "You think he's going to pop the question?"

"Shut your mouth."

"Wellll, it's been three months and he's telling everybody you're his girlfriend." She bounced her eyebrows up and down.

"Petra, we are not—I repeat, not—dating. Well, we're kinda dating, but it's not like that. It's not anywhere near that!"

"I know, I know, I'm just busting your chops. But you have to be prepared. That boy is pureed and smitten."

"Oh, for Pete's sake, I don't—"

"Well, who could blame him—or any of the stallions in these stables, for that matter? You've stolen the heart of every man at the *Chronicle*, not to mention the entire building and half the karate world. Face it, Z, the combination of beauty and brawn is an enticing tonic for boys. And the fact that you haven't dated anyone seriously for—well—ever, is pretty much sending him the message that you're in it just as much as he is."

"Wow, that's a juicy rationalization," she said, plucking her mail from the plexiglass box just outside her door.

Petra leaned across her desk and picked up a silver picture frame. "Now that's who you should've gone for."

"What'd you say?" she replied, head down, flipping through a handful of letters.

"Him."

Zoey looked up to find her friend holding a framed picture of her with Paul Talbert from a long-ago company party.

"I really liked him," Petra went on. "You two were always hanging out. Seemed like every time I came by his office you were in there, yuck'n it up." She turned her head. "Man, oh man, he was a handsome one too."

Zoey stood, staring at the picture.

"I always told you I thought he liked you, Z. How come you two never dated?" Her eyes twinkled, pressing her for dishy details. "Time to come clean. Did you and he ever—"

"Stop it!" she said, dropping her mail to the floor then snatching the picture from her.

Petra stepped back, bewildered, her hands held out in defense against the scolding. "What'd I do? I-I was just saying I thought you two made a nice—"

"A nice nothing!" Zoey said, placing the picture back in the exact spot from where it had been taken.

For a moment, neither said a word as Zoey concentrated on the picture and her friend stood, open-mouthed, wanting to speak but fearful of rebuke.

In a soft voice Zoey finally said, "I'm sorry. I-I don't know what's gotten into me lately."

Just then her phone's interoffice buzzer sounded, breaking the tension. Petra focused on the digital display. "Ugh, It's Greg."

Zoey glowered at the one name that could raise her blood pressure ten points.

"Aren't you going to pick up?" Petra asked.

Zoey continued leering at the flashing yellow light. On the fifth buzz she broke out of her trance, circling around Petra to the back of her desk where she pulled out a notepad and began scribbling. A few seconds later she ripped off the page and handed it to Petra.

"Do me a favor," she said, her voice vibrating with angst, "give this to Greg after I leave. Tell him it's part of the project and I absolutely had to go."

"That secret journal project you won't tell me about?"

"He'll understand," she said, pulling her laptop from her desk and shoving it into a small roller bag wedged into the corner of her office. "Sorry, P, I have to go."

"Go where?"

"I just have to go."

Her friend held out her hands. "I don't understand. What's going on? Is it part of your crime expose? Oh, please be careful. There're rumors all over the office that the mafia's got a contract out on you."

"There's not a contract and no—it's not part of the expose."

"Then why can't you tell me?'

"I'm sorry, I-I just can't."

"What do you want me to tell carrottop?"

Zoey fumbled through her desk drawer, grabbing a handful of pens and a cube of sticky notes. "Just tell him I… just tell him… oh shoot, don't tell him anything."

"Uh, okay, sure, I guess," Petra said, watching as she continued stuffing the little luggage case with various office items. She bent down below Zoey's chin. "You okay, Z?"

Stopping suddenly, Zoey replied through tight lips and in an even, measured tone, "Petra—I am fine." She zipped the case shut, pulled up the handle, and strode through the door, stopping in the hall just long enough to shoot her friend a wink and kiss.

Exiting through the building's revolving door, Zoey raced across the cobblestone entrance, almost twisting her ankle on the uneven surface. When she reached the curb, she adjusted her heel while waving for a cab. It had only been twenty yards from the door to the street, but she was breathing like she had just run a 100-yard dash. Seconds later she was throwing herself into the backseat of a cab.

"Where to, miss?" the driver said.

"Home! I mean, 225 East 95th Street. Normandie Court." She bent over, her head almost between her legs, her breath coming in a series of long, deep inhales followed by slow exhales. She placed her palms over her face and began to gently rock up and back, just enough to counter the pounding of her heart.

"You okay, miss?"

She held up one hand. "Yes, fine," she said and continued to rock.

By the time they arrived at Normandie Court, her anxiety had almost subsided, but it roared back when she got to her apartment on the 20th floor. She fell through the door, her wheely luggage bouncing against the doorframe. Seconds later she was pulling out her phone, ready to speed-dial Dr. Atwell. Just as she was about to press his number, she dropped the phone onto the kitchen table.

"What am I doing?" she mumbled.

She began pacing the floor then stopped and picked up her phone again, tapping out a frenzied text. She hit send, shoved the phone back into her luggage, then ran to her bedroom. From her nightstand she pulled out Mase's journal and slipped it into her custom-made pocketbook where her memory stone resided. A simple, canvas tote with straps that hung loosely from the shoulder to the waist, the pocketbook contained a hidden pouch specifically for the precious item. She reached in and pulled up its flap, running her fingers across the stone's smooth, cold surface, reassuring her of its presence.

In another second, she was riffling through her closet. She pulled out a sundress, a mustard-colored T-shirt with a huge smiley face emoji on the front, a pair of jeans, flip-flops, undergarments, and a small bag of toiletries. Quickly changing into the T-shirt and jeans, she threw on the flip-flops then crammed the rest into a wad in the bag. After scanning the room for whatever else she might need, she flung the bag over her shoulder, grabbed her wheely luggage, and was out the door.

At 12:10, Dr. Atwell poked his head out his office. "Mindy, is Zoey Antonelli running late? She was supposed to be here at noon."

"You didn't get the text?"

"What text?"

"I forwarded you a text from her. She had to cancel."

"Oh. No, I didn't get anything."

"You probably had the sound off again, Doc."

He pulled his phone from his pocket. "Yeah, I'm sure that's it." Swiping it on, he opened his messages and scrolled to the fourth entry that read: "From: Zoey Antonelli 10:03 a.m. *Sorry can't make appt. Have something I have to do. Going to see the person you said to think about. Will call later.*

Back at the *Chronicle*, her boss was fuming over a similar message delivered on the slip of paper by her friend Petra. The pale-blue notepaper vibrated in his hand as he read, *Sorry for the sudden departure. I'll be out of the office a few days. Have to do research for the project. Don't worry. All expenses are on me. See you in a few days.*

Driving through Manhattan had always been an ordeal for her, maneuvering through traffic with the timidity of an unsteady grandparent reluctant to give up their license. Today was different. She was dodging in and out of traffic, racing through yellow lights, and passing between cars and trucks with only inches to spare. When she finally exited the Holland Tunnel, she breathed a sigh of relief, but it wasn't until she was an hour outside the city that she began to settle.

As the odometer continued to tick off the miles, her calm slowly faded into a deep melancholy that she now knew, thanks to Dr. Atwell, had been brought on by her suppressed feelings for a man that had been out of her life for ten years. Through countless hours on his couch, along with a decade of therapy on martial arts mats, she had been able to cope. Now, for no apparent reason, Paul Talbert had come back into her life and she had to find out why. Atwell's advice was all she could rely on.

She looked to her dashboard. According to the GPS, if all went well, she would arrive in Beaufort, South Carolina, at 2:38 a.m.

Chapter 4

As Zoey passed through Charleston just after midnight, her eyes began to weigh heavier than she would have liked. Beaufort was less than an hour and a half away, but the day's emotional roller coaster had sapped her of the energy she thought would have propelled her on. Rather than risk an unwanted exit into a roadside ditch, she decided to stop at the next decent hotel she came across.

After another thirty minutes with no hotel in sight and on the verge of falling asleep behind the wheel, she decided she would stop anywhere with a bed and functioning shower. Ten minutes later that was exactly what she got.

The Gator Lodge, flush with an aboveground pool, pay laundromat, and ten roadside rooms complete with window-unit air-conditioning was all she needed. With its slumping-seventies décor and half-lit, buzzing neon sign, it was the type of place one would more likely rent by the hour than the day. She couldn't care less. Her head was now throbbing, and her eyes felt like grains of sand were grinding under her lids. All she wanted was sleep. And with only one car in the parking lot, she was assured there would be a vacancy.

With her handbag draped over her luggage, she stumbled across the gravel parking lot to the night clerk's office. The door was wide open, but all the lights except for a dingy glow emanating from a back room were off.

"Anyone here?" she announced upon entering.

The clank of a bottle toppling to the floor was followed by, "Hold yer horses." A minute later a greasy old man in baggy overalls appeared from the back room, the butt of a worn-out cigarette dangling from his chapped lips. The half-empty bourbon bottle in his hand was surely responsible for his bloodred orbs.

"You need a room," he said, spitting his cigarette out in front of her. "Scuze me," he giggled, "my bad." He placed his bottle on the counter, wiped his hands across his overalls, then picked up a nubby pencil and stared at her, the balance of his hospitality gone like his burnt-out cigarette lying on the floor.

"Yes." She pulled out her credit card and slid it across the counter. "One night, please."

The old man's head moved up and down her frame, stopping on the big smiley face on her chest. "That'll be fifty-three dollars," he said, swiping her card. The processing time lagged on forever, the only sounds coming from the buzzing neon sign and muted voices from the TV. Finally, he handed her card back, seeming about to say something, then stopped. His glassy gaze passed beyond her and out to the parking lot where a black Camaro had crept its way up to the last room on the far end of the lot.

Blindly he handed her a key while keeping his attention on the car. "Room 9." He pointed in the direction of the Camaro. "It's down at the end, next to—no, wait…" He turned and grabbed another key from behind him. "Take this one. Room 2. It's right next to the office."

"Thanks," she said.

"Lady," he called to her just as she passed through the door.

She turned her head halfway back toward him. "Yes?"

"I wouldn't be using the laundry tonight. You ought to go on to bed." He swung his head back to the black Camaro, the occupants of which had disappeared inside Room 10.

She had seen enough crime shows to know the bed linens in a fine establishment such as the Gator Lodge were breeding grounds for every nasty microscopic organism, bug, and whatever else could wreak havoc on even the healthiest person. She briefly considered the floor then quickly rationalized that flopping down on the covers was just as hygienic. Within seconds she fell into a deep sleep.

Not long after, she was awakened by the screams of a young girl. Had she dreamed them? The sounds of sobbing were real. As she pulled back the curtains, the muted light from the single streetlamp situated at the motel entrance loitered over the gravel lot past the black Camaro and into the room behind it, revealing the shadowy figures of two individuals. A small, panicked voice appeared to be pleading with a man with a thick Jersey accent. Although she couldn't make out the context of his words, they were rife with anger.

She cracked open her door and peered out at the room then back toward the motel's office where the old clerk was hanging onto the edge of the door. He held up his bottle of bourbon and motioned her to move back. "Nothin' to worry about," he said in a hushed tone. "Get on to bed."

"But something's wrong," she mouthed.

"Ain't my problem and it ain't yours." He disappeared for a few seconds then reappeared with a laminated sign that read "No vacancies." He hung it on a nail next to the door then slammed it shut. A second later the lingering glow passing from the office's back room through the curtains went black.

She furrowed her brow at the old man's cowardly retreat.

The smack of skin against skin penetrated the air, followed by a whimper that stopped amidst a mangled knot of curse words, then *whack*—another strike against flesh followed by more swearing.

She clenched her teeth, her fingernails sinking into her palms as she stepped out into the parking lot. The whimpering rose into a mournful, stuttering plea for forgiveness. "I'm s-s-sorry!" came the voice.

Zoey bolted across the lot until she was standing in the doorway of Room 10. Her blood boiled at the sight of a little girl sitting on the edge of a bed, the left side of her head a frayed mess of blonde hair, the other bunched into a tangled wad, clenched in the burly hand of a heavyset man in a silky burgundy jacket. His other hand was raised in the air, holding steady, awaiting the girl's response.

With his face inches from hers, he growled, "Where's that man's money?" The little girl's reply came only in sobs. The man yanked the girl's head back, a sliver of light glistening across her tearstained cheeks. Her head lurched back farther as the man reared his fist.

"Stop!"

The man spun toward the door, his grip on the girl's hair tightening. Her head snapped in tandem with a flick of his wrist.

Zoey's stance widened as she transferred the weight of her body to the balls of her feet. Clenching her fists tighter, she raised them ever so slightly. "Let—her—go."

"Who're you?" the man sneered as light flared off a pair of gold teeth.

The room went still.

Her fists continued to rise.

The man torqued his hand in a tight circle, twisting more of the girl's hair into his hand, then wrenched it downward, sending her face-first into the mattress. Sucking in the mildewed mist of the dank room, he sneered at Zoey. "I said—who are you?"

"Never mind who I am. Let the girl go."

The man rolled his head from side to side, studying her, the bridge of his nose bending into the snarling folds of an enraged bear. He suddenly opened his palm and released the young girl.

As he walked toward her, she surveyed his frame, his expression, and above all, the way he moved. It was a swagger that projected arrogance, the lumbering gait of a jock who had won too many mismatched battles based solely on size and strength rather than cunning and skill. Within three feet of her, he stopped. A foot taller and a hundred pounds heavier, he glowered down at her. She stood motionless.

He took a step back, examining her up and down, lustful lips etching skyward. "Hmm, you're a looker," he said, eyeballing her stripe of colored hair. "I think my clientele might enjoy a little pink." Captivated by its uniqueness, he reached out to touch it. When he did, she whipped her hand around his outstretched arm, locking it under his forearm and into his armpit while simultaneously throwing her other hand behind his neck. With all her weight, she pulled his head down into her knee that she was propelling upwards. The crack of his septum upon her kneecap yielded a stream of blood that followed him down to the floor.

She scrutinized the unconscious lump of lowlife at her feet. Blood oozed from his nostrils down his neck and onto a white flyaway collar, staining it in splotches that matched his burgundy jacket. She started to turn when a crippling pain, sharp and deep, penetrated from the middle of her back through to her sternum. White-hot, it burned from the inside out. Clutching her chest, she fell on top of her assailant. Either a heart attack or a stroke, she didn't know the difference but thought it had to be one or the other. It was neither.

The little girl she had risked her life to save stood with one hand covering her mouth, the other holding a six-inch knife dripping with Zoey's blood. "I'm sorry. I'm soooo, sorry! He would've killed me if I didn't…"

Zoey tried to roll over, but the pain was too great. She could only lie there, grimacing through a prayer for relief.

From out of the darkness, she awoke to another type of pain. The man in the burgundy jacket had her by the ankles and was dragging her across the gravel parking lot. She cried out for help as the jagged rocks raked across her back. The man dropped beside her, pulled out a bloody rag he had been using on his injured nose and jammed it in her mouth. When he hoisted her across his shoulder, she let out a muffled yell for help. Her head bounced against his back as the shoddy landscape of the Gator Lodge slowly gave way to dead branches and rotting foliage. Within several minutes dry land had transformed to swamp, and the man flung her to the ground. Her muted cries for help were cloaked by the thick croaking of bullfrogs in the backwaters of South Carolina, a mere hundred yards from the lodge.

The man knelt next to her, grabbed her face with one hand, and pinched her lips together. He leaned into her ear and hissed, "You messed with the wrong—"

A rustling from the direction of the lodge stopped him. Out of the darkness appeared the young girl from Room 10, towing behind her Zoey's luggage with her handbag draped over the top. She pushed them next to the man in a sacrificial offering. "This is all she had."

"You sure?" he barked.

"Yes, I'm sure," she replied in a small voice.

Grabbing the luggage, he ripped open its zipper and began pulling out its contents. One by one he threw everything into the brackish water. "Nothing. What about the bag?"

"I-I didn't check," the girl said. She stole a quivering glance at Zoey that begged for forgiveness.

The man dove his hand into the canvas opening, groping for anything of value. "Jackpot," he said, pulling out a small purse. Without opening it, he threw it to the girl. "Hold on to this." He plunged back in. Back and forth he ran his hand, searching the inside. "Hmm, what's this?" he said, fingering the hidden pocket she had fashioned for the one item that meant more to her than anything else. As he withdrew his fist, Zoey saw he held the memory stone. He turned it side to side, examining it, trying to attach some sort of worth to it. "You carry a rock?" He laughed, then turned to the girl. "You wanna make a necklace?" he said, tossing it to the side.

In a moment of clarity, Zoey realized her only hope lay beside her. As the man continued scouring her handbag, she inched her hand outward. Through the decaying leaves and mud, her fingers found the stone and slowly closed around it. With all her remaining strength she slammed it against his temple. The man reeled backwards then popped back up like a top, throwing his leg over her torso. Looking up, all she could see was his silhouette hovering above her, moonlight glinting off his gold teeth—and then flashing across the blade the girl had sliced into Zoey's back. Down it came, plunging through her chest and into her heart. Within seconds, she was gone.

Chapter 5

"Toss me that thar fork," the man said, bending over Zoey's body.

Lying faceup, her arms and legs splayed out like a starfish, her eyes were closed, and her expression showed neither a painful nor peaceful exit from the world.

The man stepped back, running his hand through a foot of dirty grey beard. The early morning sun illuminated a trail of tobacco spit running out the side of his mouth. Easing toward her, he nudged her side with his foot then jumped back as if he had just poked an angry hornets' nest. Pulling back the brim of a hat so tattered it was more holes than hat, he examined her and the emoji shirt. "I said throw me that dang—"

A three-pronged pitchfork came flying down from above, its prongs jabbing into the mud and pinning his foot to the ground. A haggard woman perched atop the bench seat of a dilapidated one-horse wagon howled with laughter. "How's my aim, old man?"

Behind her, hanging over the edge of the wagon bed, was a young, shirtless boy covered in dirt and smudged with the feces of the pig he had leashed to a rope. "She dead, Pa?"

"Cain't tell," he said, pulling back her pink strand of hair with the sharp prong of the pitchfork. "Looks like she mighta got shot. There's blood runn'n down her head." He squinted at the pink stripe. "Strangest colored blood I ever done seen."

"Jasper, ya best leave that dead girl be," the lady said.

"Hmm." He tilted his head. "She don't look all that dead though. She's got some color yet."

"Come on now, old man, leave 'er be. We gots to get Ulysses to market. Sides, take a gander at all them tattoos on that arm. Signs of the devil."

"Would ya shut up, woman," he said, positioning himself directly above Zoey's waist with one foot on either side of her hips. He tucked the pitchfork's handle under his arm and with the metal tips tapped the smiley face. There was no movement. He bounced the fork up to her neck. With the prongs hanging over her windpipe, he patted her throat three times. Again, nothing. Sensing more of the same, he pushed down, the prongs slowly pressing into her flesh, penetrating just enough to draw a dab of blood around each tip. "Yep, she's a goner."

As he was about to head for the wagon, a tiny moan pulled his attention back. Bending over her, he paused. "That weren't her, was it?"

All at once, Zoey's eyes popped open. For a hard second nothing happened, everything froze in place, then with the flash of a lightning bolt, she grabbed his pitchfork. Throwing it to the side, she flung her left leg around his knee, pulling it toward her until he collapsed face-first next to her. Snatching up the pitchfork, she was suddenly on his back, thrusting the implement at the nape of his neck, stopping an inch from delivering the final blow. Her eyes bore into the back of his head, filled equally with rage and bewilderment.

"Holy cow, Mama. Ya see that?" the boy howled.

The lady sat slack-jawed as the pig squealed and snorted back and forth, sensing the commotion below.

"Ma-ma-ma'am, I-I-wasn't fix'n to harm ya. I swear." The old man's words came out in a bubbling garble as his head teetered out of the mud. "Tell 'er, woman!"

"He's right, miss. He won't gonna hurt ya. He, me and the boy just happened on ya and he was try'n to—"

"Enough!" Zoey leaped up. "Turn over," she commanded.

"Ye-yessum," he said, rolling onto his back with his arms out and palms up in unconditional surrender.

She leaned forward, positioning the pitchfork under his chin. "Who are you—why'd you try to kill me—where'd they go—what's this—"

"Ma'am, I'll try answer'n them questions for ya. But ya ain't gonna kill me, are ya?"

"Depends. Why were you going to kill me?"

"He done told ya," the old lady began, "but youz—"

"Shut up, woman!" Zoey and the man shouted in unison.

She pressed the pitchfork up, forcing the man's head back. "Well?"

"Honest, we was just pass'n by on our way to market and we seen ya layin' off here in the mud and just figured ya'd been bushwhacked or somethin'."

She ran her hand across her neck, wiping away three small drops of blood, then opened her palm to him. "Then why this?" she said, displaying her three red fingertips.

"Cuz I thought ya was already dead. I was just check'n. Youz was bleed'n from the head so I thought it best I made sure."

"Bleeding?" She ran her hand through her hair, stopping on her pink stripe. "You thought pink was…" She stopped suddenly as a swell of adrenaline washed back on her. Her heart raced as she tried clearing her mind of the fact that she'd almost been murdered a second time. She could feel her pulse pumping in her veins, her jugular, her wrists, along her temples. Her knees felt like swivels as the ground beneath her began to sway, the wagon transforming into a blurry rectangle of browns and greys, a fuzzy silhouette of the lady and boy meshing into it. Turning back to the man, she dropped the pitchfork, fell to her knees, then collapsed face forward.

A half hour later she felt a nudge. A grunt, another nudge, and a slobbery swipe of thick tongue across her lips was more than enough to revive her.

"I think Ulysses likes ya."

She squeezed her eyes shut tight, then opened them slowly. Squirming a foot in front of her were two slimy nostrils centered in a mass of dirty pork snout. Another grunt, snort, and poke from the critter bolted her upright. "Get away from me, you-you filthy beast!" She backed her way through a pile of hay, kicking and pushing the animal into the corner next to the shirtless boy he was tied to.

"Ah, come on now, lady, she ain't gonna hurt ya," said the boy, wrapping his arm over the pig's back.

Suddenly the boy, the pig, and Zoey bounced into the air then smacked back down onto the rotten wagon bed. The thin layer of hay under them offered little cushion. "Ouch," she said.

"Sorry, ma'am," said the old man who had less than an hour ago been about to drive a pitchfork through her throat. "This here road's a plumb mess." He bounced the reins attached to a sweaty, slumped-back workhorse pulling the wagon.

The discomfort of being tussled about brought to light the agony of being stabbed twice the night before. Running her hand around to the middle of her back, her fingers searched for the entry wound delivered at the hands of the young girl she had tried to save. There was no blood, no hole, not even a tear in her T-shirt. She was pain-free with everything intact. She was healthy, filled with a sense of joy yet overcome by a head-spinning wave of anxiety. She began rubbing the sides of her head as she bounced back and forth in an unruly rhythm produced from the misaligned ruts in the road.

"How'd ya learn to fight like that, lady?" the boy prodded. "That ain't nothin' like we boys fight. And how come youz dressed like one and what kinda shirt's that? How'd ya get that face on it and them tattoos—"

"Would ya shush up," said the old lady. "Sorry 'bout that ma'am. My boy, Willy here, is a little chatterbox. By the way, I'm Sadie. Ya done met Jasper." Without turning, the man raised one hand from the reins, acknowledging himself with a tiny wave.

"What's yer name, missy?" the lady asked.

"Zoey," she said, patting down her legs, continuing her search of any kind of wounds. "What am I doing here? Where are we?"

"Ya fainted," the man said.

"Fell out like a sack o' tators," the old lady added, followed by an ear-piercing cackle that launched the pig into a frenzied snort fest.

"Stop it, Mama." The dirty youngster leaned over the animal, transforming his arm across its back into a full-on hug. "Ulysses's her name, miss. She don't much like loud noises."

"Ulysses?"

"Yessum. She's a she but Pa named her Ulysses count of he likes the general for all he done. Ya know, winning the war and such."

The old man handed the reins to his wife, pivoted to the back of the wagon, and leaned down, placing his palm over his heart. "Like I was tell'n ya, ma'am, we weren't gonna hurt ya."

She turned back to the pig. "Ulysses—really?"

The boy beamed. "Yessum, General Ulysses S. Pig."

"The S stands for sow," the old lady said, slapping her knee while stifling another laugh by covering her mouth.

Zoey's eyes left the animal to pan ahead of them then back to the road where they had come. Into the distance her mind took her to the spot on which she had been run through by the man in the burgundy jacket. There, bouncing about on the bed of hay, next to the boy and his pet, it played out—the last moments of her life, the glint of her murderer's gold teeth, the blade above his head just before he drove it into her heart, and the stone she had smashed against his face.

"Can you take me back to the Gator Lodge?" she said in a monotone voice. "Please."

The old couple looked at each other. "I'm sorry, miss," the man said. "I don't know a Gator Lodge. Is that somewheres near here?"

"I think it's where you found me."

"Ma'am, ain't nothin' 'round where we found ya. Nothin' but woods, a passel of thicket and more woods. The road we was on ain't much more than a sidewinder's trail head'n into town."

She brightened. "So are we heading into Charleston or Beaufort?"

The man reared back. "Sure ya didn't whack yer noggin somewheres, ma'am?"

She blinked, the foggy lens of her memory suddenly clearing, turning now to the stone. She remembered clawing her fingers through the mud and decaying leaves of the swamp to find it.

The wagon wheels continued gnashing through the ruts, careening off roots, banging against rocks, lurching sideways then bouncing up and down, jarring everyone inside. Her head jerked one way then the other, but she didn't utter a sound. She just sat, being tossed about, oblivious to the wagon's turbulent journey. Her mind ran through the events of the previous night, trying to match it up with what she had read in Mase's journal.

"Ma'am, ya alright?" the boy said.

She turned to him then drifted back to her visions of the storyline she had read through almost every night for the past ten years, the supernatural tale of how the stones had transported Mase, Sissy, Maudie, Annabelle, and Spoon through time. It was the story of how her Paul Talbert had come into her life but had gone back in time to become Mase Winslow. Scene after scene repeated with one common denominator—the stone. She could still feel the grip she had on it. She had not let it go. During the last second before she died, it was in her grasp and had done exactly what it was meant to do. Nevertheless, the results were still too unreal to come to terms with.

The boy nudged her elbow. "Ya sure yer alright? Ya kinda keep wander'n off like."

She pressed her palms over her face. "Ye-yes, I'm fine." She turned to the front of the wagon. "Where'd you say we're going, mister? Is it Beaufort or back to Charleston?"

"Didn't say either way, but, ma'am, I'm afraid I don't know nothin' 'bout a Beaufort. But when ya says Charleston, do ya mean West Virginia's Charleston, cuz we're a fer piece from yonder."

"No, Charleston, *South Carolina*."

"Oh lawdy! That's way down south."

"Then where are we?"

"Pert near into the city."

"The city?"

"Yep, just cross the bridge. That's where the market is."

"Can't you turn around? We have to be close to Beaufort. *Please*, mister."

The old woman tugged at the man's sleeve and mouthed, "Think she's touched?" Homing in on Zoey's emoji T-shirt and pink hair, her eyes bounced from one to the other. "Where ya from anyhow?"

Her mind was still a jumbled mix of emotions, all standing in the way of her coming to grips with what she could not rationalize. On paper, it seemed to make sense in Mase's journal, and it made even more sense when Annabelle Winslow explained it all those years ago. But now, after the memory stone had unleashed its powers upon her, she rejected it.

"Ya was talk'n 'bout South Carolina. Is that where ya from?"

"No, I'm from New York City."

"Well hot dang!" The old woman whacked the man on the shoulder. "Hear that, Jasper? Missy's from New York City. Well, Miss Zoey, from New York City, in about fifteen minutes yer gonna be home sweet home."

She went blank. "What?"

The lady turned and pointed dead north, past the horse and down the road. "Right straight on for fifteen minutes, the biggest darn city in the whole wide world—New York—home of the biggest steaks, best beer, fastest horses, most markets…" The old lady jabbered on, but Zoey heard none of it. She scanned the skies ahead, waiting for something familiar to appear. All that lay ahead was the continuation of the trench-riddled dirt road lined with pine trees dense with brush and thick undergrowth. Her mouth fell open.

"This-this can't be."

"What cain't be?" the lady said.

"This can't be New York. I-I was just in South Carolina. I was almost there." Wriggling nervously back and forth, she grabbed the side of the wagon, ready to leap out—out to anywhere but the nightmare of the wagon of delusions. "What's going on? I don't understand any of this," she cried.

The old man tapped his wife's hand. Her eyes followed the direction of his finger down to the revolver lying next to her feet.

"Where's the skyline?" Zoey said, trying to stand, only to have another bump in the road throw her back down. She scanned the top of the pine trees, praying to find the familiar concrete mountains she had left the day before.

"What's a skyline?" the old lady asked.

"The *New York City* skyline. All the buildings, all the skyscrapers! You can see them all the way from New Jersey." She turned to the lady, her voice dropping. "If we're near New York, then we should see a skyline. You hear me, woman? A skyline!"

The old lady locked on her while slowly reaching down. A moment later her fingers found the butt end of the revolver.

Chapter 6

A long minute passed with neither Zoey nor the old lady making any sudden movements other than those produced by the constant pitch and pull of the wagon.

"Missy," the old man said, "them fists and legs of yers are pretty fast, but the bullet in my woman's Smith & Wesson moves a heap faster."

She dropped her eyes to a fluffy fold in the old lady's dress. Poking out of the dirty grey fabric was the lethal end of a .44-caliber revolver aimed directly at her chest. With a huff she turned to the back of the wagon, pulled her knees to her chest, and wedged her head between them. Tears rained down between her legs and disappeared among a thousand straws of hay.

She rode for a while, wrapped up in a tight ball of denial, her head still tucked between her thighs, hoping when she raised back up the dream would be over. The boy, more eager to learn about her fighting skills and strange way of dressing, was held at bay by his mother's wagging finger. He kept his trap shut.

As they emerged from the forest, the old man tipped his tattered hat toward the horizon. A half mile out, rows upon rows of tents, lean-tos, and makeshift sheds lined the road. A large stockyard with corrals and pens comprised a quarter of the hundred-acre market. Hundreds of merchants, customers, pickpockets, and thieves mingled in and out of the bustling mecca of commerce. Behind it were the stone arches of the High Bridge, New York's engineering masterpiece and gateway into the city.

As they got closer, the air grew thick with the chattering of people mixed with the frantic sounds and pungent smells of livestock. In every direction there were customers locked in heated negotiations with haggling merchants.

Unable to hide any longer, she slowly lifted her head and looked through the masses, past the bridge and into the city. She gulped. The place she called home for the past thirty-two years was unrecognizable. The skyline of hundred-story buildings was no more. Not one rose higher than a meager nine floors. No longer did the sunlight shimmer across expansive walls of windows reaching into the heavens. Everything was low to the ground, shadowed, and drab.

"There it is," the old man yelped, gesturing high and to the right. "It's next to the bridge." With a snap of the reins, the wagon surged forward.

"Take it easy, old man. No need to kill us when we're almost sitt'n at Vanderson's doorstep," the woman said, fumbling to tie a silk ribbon in her hair.

The man ignored his wife's concerns as he tugged the reins back and forth, maneuvering the horse and wagon through the muddy market streets.

Zoey held tight to the wagon's plank siding as she examined the world she had been thrown into, one in which she wanted no part. There she was in jeans and a T-shirt while hundreds of women around her were all dressed in long, somber-toned woolen dresses. The type of shoes they wore was a mystery revealed only when they lifted their skirts to step over a mud puddle—black, high-laced, pointy boots. The majority of the men were clad mostly in dungarees, flannel shirts, and cowboy hats, and all had some form of facial hair. Whether it was a full beard and mustache or a pair of fluffy sideburns, they were all unkempt. The only exceptions appeared to be a smaller portion of men wearing top hats.

Like any other market, the merchants sold their goods and wares from canvas tents while horse traders and other beast peddlers made deals from foul-smelling stockyards. Tools, clothing, kitchen items, hunting supplies, and every fruit and vegetables indigenous to the region were for sale. It was a muddy cacophony of buying and selling set against the backdrop of the sepia-toned image of the greatest city in the United States.

She began to shake her head, slowly at first then faster, not knowing whether she wanted to scream or slink back into the corner of the wagon, refusing to accept that she had truly been transported to another place and time. From the pit of her stomach, despair rolled its way to the surface in an angry wave. Preparing to unleash her rage, she filled her lungs, flooding her nostrils with the stench of animal excrement that suddenly redirected her anger to nausea. She flung her head over the side of the wagon and threw up.

Minutes later the wagon rolled up next to a small drooping building at the corner of a large pigsty. A hand-painted sign arching over the door read, "Vanderson's Pork and Poultry." Hundreds of pigs snorted and grunted their way about the slop-filled premises while a few dozen chickens strutted amongst them.

The old man climbed down from the wagon, hanging onto the seat as his tired, worn-out body adjusted. He shuffled to the back of the wagon and held out his hand to the boy, who reluctantly handed him the rope tied to the pig.

"Everybody, say yer goodbyes to Ulysses," he said.

The boy wiped a tear away while Zoey stayed bent over the side of the wagon, arms folded tightly against her stomach, anticipating another bout of nausea. From the corner of her eye, she watched the man lead the pig into the tiny building. The door closed. Several minutes later it cracked open, a shiny black hat emerging. The body of the man wearing it, however, remained behind the door. The hat rotated toward the wagon then disappeared back inside. A minute passed, and the door opened again. This time Jasper hobbled out, followed by a tall man in a black suit, wearing a thick black bow tie and black stovepipe hat. With the hat, he appeared to be pushing six and a half feet tall. Unlike the rest of the men with their over-the-top facial hair, he had only a finely groomed five o'clock shadow that highlighted a cleft chin and deep set of dimples. His posture was straight, and he moved with a regal air.

"Good day, m'lord," the old lady swooned as he passed by.

He touched his finger to the brim of his hat then continued toward the back of the wagon. When he came to Zoey, he stopped. With her head still hanging over the side of the wagon, her stomach heaved again and out came another wave of bile along with whatever else was left in her stomach—splatting directly on the boots of the man with the tall hat.

She wiped her mouth then ran her hand through her hair, pushing it out of her eyes. They were puffy and bloodshot, thanks to the nausea coupled with the traumatic realization of her circumstance.

"Pleasure to meet you, miss," came a deep voice from directly above her.

She centered in on the boots she had just christened then slowly panned up to the outstretched hand of the man in the tall hat.

"Vanderson's the name—Boone Vanderson."

Her head swayed to the side. Tilting it upward, she took a labored breath. "I'm Zoey," she said in a hoarse whisper.

The man pressed his open palm closer.

She stared at it, then rubbed her hand across her shirt before swinging it up to meet his.

His reply was a small bow accompanied by a gentlemanly nod of the head. "Well then…" He paused, observing her ring finger, then began again. "Well then, Miss Zoey, might I offer you some refreshments?" His voice was warm, and although the offer seemed more appropriate for a garden party, it was nonetheless sincere. "I understand you've had a rather arduous journey."

Jasper appeared from behind him. "I told Mr. Vanderson how we found ya. He's a good man. He don't much like seein' people doin' poorly. He—"

Vanderson raised a single finger, bringing the old man's chatter to a halt. "Jasper has told me of your initial encounter." He began slowly shaking his head. "I truly am sorry. Awakening to the sight of Jasper certainly is no way for anyone to begin their day." He took her hand with both of his and bent down so he was level with her, his eyebrows falling at the corners in a sympathetic curve. "Truly,

I am sorry for whatever dilemma in which you have found yourself, young lady, but rest assured whatever that dilemma may be, it shall pass."

She wanted to explain that unless he possessed more memory stones, there was nothing he could do for her. "What's today's date?" she squeaked out.

The old man nudged Vanderson's elbow from behind. Vanderson promptly turned and brushed the man's hand aside. "Mind yourself, sir." He turned back. "Miss Zoey—"

"Antonelli. My name's Zoey Antonelli."

Like common livestock, he inspected her for a moment, scanning the tattoos along her arm, then panning from her T-shirt to her pink strip of hair. "It's October first. Do you have any relatives that—"

"I mean what year is it?"

His head slowly slanted back as a questioning stare emerged. "Why, it's 1871."

She gasped. "That can't be." She grabbed his sleeve. "It just can't be." Her voice rose as she began blurting out the events of the previous twenty-four hours, each statement growing more manic. "I left New York then I was in South Carolina. I was stabbed. I died—I think I died—no—I had to have died, I know I died, the stone brought me back—" She stopped, suddenly turning loose of his sleeve as tears rolled down her cheeks. "I-I don't have—"

"What don't you have, dear lady?" he said.

She threw her palms over her face. "I have—no one."

Vanderson turned to the old man. "Done," he said out the side of his mouth. Then turning back to her, he said, "Those things of which you speak, might we discuss them inside my office?" He scanned the market for prying eyes then leaned toward her. "I might be able to help you."

Her hands fell. In a small voice she said, "You can help me? But you don't even know—"

"I have my ways," he said softly.

"But you don't—"

"Come with me. Let's talk." He held out his hand.

"Seriously, you don't understand…"

The edges of his mouth inched upward. "Take my hand."

She turned to the old man.

"Go on now, missy, Mr. Vanderson, he'll help ya."

She swallowed before slowly moving her hand toward his. Hesitating, she glanced back to the old man before reluctantly placing her palm lightly on his. As he led her to his office, he motioned the man to leave. A few seconds later the door shut, leaving the old man thumbing through a wad of bills. With a craggy finger, his wife flicked over the first bill, then the second, then the third and fourth. "Holy mother!" she exclaimed. "That's a heap of money for a pig."

"Yep, pink pigs do bring the green."

The inside of Vanderson's office was basically a shed with a repurposed ship's porthole that shone a sliver of light across the room, illuminating a cloud of dust particles floating through the cramped space. A chest-high desk, filing cabinet, washbasin, one rickety chair, a cuckoo clock, and a tiny nightstand with a dusty flower vase next to a single bed crammed the space to capacity. The only vacant spot on the dirt floor was in the center, which was now occupied by Zoey, Vanderson, and Ulysses S. Pig.

She stood rigid, her hands across her chest, her face less than two feet from the top button of Vanderson's lapel.

"Pardon my less-than-luxurious accommodations, Miss Antonelli," Vanderson said. "This shoddy edifice is a mere outpost for one of my operations. A means to many ends, you might say. I assure you the rest of my properties are of a higher caliber."

Just then Ulysses, annoyed by the cramped quarters, spun around, swinging her rotund hindquarters into Zoey's legs, knocking her straight into Vanderson's arms. With the pig's enormous weight against her legs and no lateral escape, she endured being pressed into his chest.

"Oh, I'm so sorry." She twisted her body, trying to regain her distance from him but was pinned. Ulysses had marked her spot and was not budging, leaving Zoey helplessly in Vanderson's embrace. The animal continued her conniption, flinging all her weight into Zoey's calves. With no room to move and no way to balance themselves, they collapsed onto the bed, Zoey landing on top of him. Meanwhile Ulysses snorted joyfully as she rooted inside the top hat that now resided on the dirt floor.

Zoey laid with her chin just above the black crown of Boone's slicked-down hair. Through the stench of pig and dust, a whiff of lavender cologne filled her nose. As her eyes moved down, they fell upon his raised brow and curious smirk. Immediately she bolted to her feet.

Vanderson took a more relaxed approach to his rising. His grin now gone, he snatched his hat from Ulysses, grabbed her rope, and pulled the sow to the door. Turning to Zoey, he said in a matter-of-fact tone, "Please have a seat on the bed. I'll return shortly." The door closed.

She sat on the lumpy mattress, more confused, and frustrated than before. Her heart began to race as she realized how vulnerable she had become.

Ten minutes later Vanderson returned without Ulysses. Zoey remained seated on the bed, her legs pinched together, arms crossed tightly over her chest. Saying nothing, he pulled the chair directly in front of her and sat. The single ray of light coming into the room fell onto his back, transforming his frame into a soft silhouette. "Would you please place your hands on the bed?" His voice was calm and melodic.

She gauged his question, which came in the form of a request bordering on a plea rather than a demand. Rationalizing it to be harmless, she slowly lowered them to the edge of the mattress.

Vanderson watched her fingers clamp down on the bedsheet, then his eyes gazed up at her smiley face T-shirt—where they stayed suspended for an awkward moment.

She continued clutching the sheet, pulling the edges toward her.

"Is there anything I can get you?" he asked.

"Something to drink? I'm awfully thirsty."

"Oh, where are my manners." He reached into his pocket and brought out a tin flask. "I completely forgot my offer of refreshment." He uncorked the top and handed it to her.

"What is it?"

"Not lemonade, I can assure you. But I am afraid it's the only thing I have. At least the only thing sanitary enough to drink."

She took a sip, squinching her face as she fought to down the heavily alcohol-laced concoction.

"Mind your intake. That's a powerful mix."

As her thirst continued and with her taste buds numbing, she took another long swallow, followed by two more.

Vanderson's gaze ran up her shoulders and over her neck, fixing on her pink strip of hair for an uncomfortably long moment. His eyes moved back to her face, her cheeks, and her tongue as she licked the elixir from her lips. He laid his hat on the corner of the bed then slowly removed his coat, laying it next to the hat.

She held the flask with both hands, her dehydrated body soaking in the tonic, allowing its effects to instantly take effect. Her head began to feel light, and her thoughts softened into a hazy parade of random images. The wagon, the Gator Lodge, her packing to leave New York, her boss's tirade, her murderer's gold teeth… Finally, it settled on Paul Talbert with his laptop. Visions of him tapping away at the keyboard slowly dissolved into Mace Winslow standing on the banks of a beautiful pond, Spanish moss cascading from willow tree branches framing him in a tattered Confederate uniform. His arm waved her to him. "Come." He motioned again. "Come."

She blinked as Vanderson's image reappeared. The last things she remembered seeing were his dimples and his hands below his chin, loosening his tie. Her vision grew dimmer until all was dark. Although she could not see it, she felt his arm wrapping around her back.

"Lay back now…" His words trailed off as he lowered her helpless body onto the bed.

Chapter 7

As the first ray of light squeezed through Midtown across the East River and into the market, it triggered hordes of prized roosters to begin their morning alarm. Zoey's eyes opened by degrees then shut, her will to keep them open failing with every new attempt. The pounding in her head increased as the roosters' crows mounted into a crescendo of ear-piercing torment. All she could do was lie there, helplessly waiting for her throbbing headache to subside, praying for the sun to rise enough to silence the birds.

An hour later she awoke again to the sounds of the office door slamming shut. Her gaze shot to the end of the bed where her bare feet stuck out from under a heavy patchwork quilt. Taking a deep breath, she ran her hands under the quilt, across her chest, down her waist, and along her thighs. She was still fully clothed. With a long, slow sigh, she began to silently pray. For several more minutes she lay staring at the ceiling's rotting beams, trying to piece together everything that had happened before the alcohol had taken its toll. The images that played out were somehow fresh, the memory of Mase calling to her the most vivid of them all. The image of being lowered onto the mattress was just as clear—and made her skin crawl.

"Good morning, Miss Antonelli," Vanderson said, following his tall hat through the office door. I hope you—"

Crash. The flower vase from the bedside table smashed against the wall, just missing his head by inches.

Zoey sat on the edge of the bed, chest heaving, looking frantically for something else to throw. "You-you fiend! What did you do to me?"

Boone rocked on his heels. "Nothing! The only thing I *did do* was to put you to bed."

"You gave me that drink and then you tried to—"

"I didn't try to do anything, young lady. All I did was to lay you down before you fell on the floor."

"Well, you-you gave me that drink."

"Yes, and I did so at your request. And if you remember, which you probably can't, I told you to mind how much you drank."

"My clothes seem somewhat…"

"Intact?"

"Well, uh, I-I guess…" she stammered. "Well, you still shouldn't have given me that drink."

"I am sorry about that. But as I also mentioned, the sanitation in this place is poor at best. Alcohol is the only recourse when clean water isn't readily available. I apologize, I should have asked one of the other merchants for something fresh."

She puffed her lips, then mumbled her own half-hearted apology. "I guess I was a little hasty."

He handed her a mug. "Try this."

She peered inside the vessel, suspiciously swirling it around. "No, thank you."

"No, no, this is just the opposite of what you drank last night. This *I did* get from another merchant. It's fresh. I promise."

She flashed a rueful look at him, then took a sip. "Hmm, not bad."

"It's apple cider—*unfermented,* I promise." He pulled the chair next to her and sat watching her drain the mug dry. "Miss Antonelli, may I ask—"

"You can call me Zoey."

"That's a rather unique name. I don't think I've ever heard anyone called Zo—ey."

"And I don't think I've ever heard anyone called Boone either," she said coolly.

He lifted his chin and looked down his nose at her. "Ahh, sarcasm… very good, very good indeed." He pursed his lips as he concentrated on her T-shirt. "Tell me, what manner of dress is this? How does one put a child's drawing on one's shirt? Is it a child's shirt? And where is your dress? Do you often dress as a boy? And those tattoos and pink hair, what are—"

"Whoa, mister! Why the grilling?"

"Pardon me?" he said, leaning back from her.

"What's with all the questions?" She rubbed the sides of her head. "I'm nursing a hangover—brought on by you, I might add—and all of a sudden you're Sherlock Holmes."

"I don't know any Sherlock Holmes but I'm sorry if I upset you. And may I remind you—yet again. You drank of your own free will."

"That doesn't give you the right to be so nosy."

"I'll apologize again because I have no idea what your predicament is or what you've been through but given the circumstances, do I not have the right to ask these questions?"

The throbbing in her head continued. "You just need to mind your own business. Is that too much to ask?"

"Ma'am, I know you've been through something traumatic but—"

She rubbed her aching head. "Just please go back to tending your pigs."

Vanderson took a long, slow breath as he contemplated her growing anger toward him. "Ma'am, I'm trying to show you hospitality, kindness, and in good time, a possible solution to whatever trouble you're experiencing." He paused. "Maybe!"

"How? How can you help me? You don't know me. You don't know what I've been through. You say something like that, and you have absolutely no idea what's happened to me or where I've been." The combination of her headache, the roosters, her misperception of his failed seduction—everything collided. "You—have—no—idea!"

He sat calmly with his eyes boring into hers, waiting not for her to break the silence but in retaliation for her rebuke. A minute passed as they waged their war of wills. Frustrated, he stood up, brushed his lapel, turned, and walked out without another word.

She sat on the side of the bed, unhinged in thought, trembling, angry, and void of any ideas on what to do next. She could neither cry nor speak. All she could do was sit and wait—for what, she did not know.

Slowly the morning passed to noon with her falling back to sleep. The image of Mase at the pond returned. "Come," he said. "Come."

Just then, the door swung open and Vanderson walked in carrying a shovel. "How are you feeling?"

She opened her eyes. "Better."

"Good. Because I'm going to need your help. I'm down a man and I need someone to clean the stye while I do the books."

"You want *me* to clean your pigpen?"

"I'd do it but as I said, I have to balance my books, which can't wait. Consider it room and board. Besides it may help alleviate some of your frustration I can see building."

She looked out the tiny window onto the massive field of muck and envisioned walking across it, jumping the fence, and simply vanishing. But where would she go? What would she do? She knew there was no way he could help her navigate time, but he did offer to help, and she was pretty sure no one else would do the same. Lacking an alternative, she was tethered to him. She would bide her time and accept his offer, hoping that something would happen to lead her back home.

"What do I do?"

He handed her the shovel and walked her outside. "There," he said, directing her to the farthest corner of the pigpen. "Your friend Ulysses and all her new acquaintances have left you their special little gifts. You are to shovel them into the wheelbarrow leaning against the fence there in the corner and then deposit all your lovelies into the big box on the other side of the pen."

Sharp lines formed above the bridge of her nose as she huffed across the muddy field.

"Stop," he said. He held out a pair of worn-out high-top, laced boots. "It's not appropriate for a lady to parade around in her bare feet."

Neglecting the new attire, she sneered at him.

"Oh well, catch whatever disease you wish."

She snatched the boots from him, spun around, and headed for Ulysses.

Throughout the afternoon several small rain showers visited the market. They each lasted only twenty or so minutes, but never once did she stop. All the while Vanderson stood watching through the open door of his office, coffee in one hand, cigar in the other.

"Boone, who's the new lad you have working the pen?" asked a distinguished, grey-bearded man in a long topcoat walking through the gate.

"Not a man." He took a long drag from his cigar. "That's a woman."

The man placed a pair of spectacles on his nose. "Hmm, then why, pray tell, is she dressed like a boy—and what's that pink thing in her hair?"

Vanderson shrugged. "I'm not sure about either." His eyes narrowed on her. "There's something different about her. I can't figure out if she has an agenda or if she's truly without her wits."

"Touched in the head, is she?" the grey-bearded man said.

"I don't know."

"Well, good luck with her," he said, turning back to Vanderson. "Harper sent me to tell you there's an all-lieutenants meeting at seven tomorrow evening in the Five Points office."

"What's it about?"

"Don't know. Probably just an update." He turned and walked toward the gate then stopped and looked back across the pen. "I'll tell Harper you're bringing a gift," he tittered, holding a handkerchief over his mouth.

"No," he said. "Don't tell him anything."

"Too late, she's in the program now."

Vanderson tossed his cigar at the man's feet, then turned and walked to the fence where he watched Zoey stumble around the muddy field. Intrigued by her willingness to accept her task, he watched her for the next hour, amazed at how she carried herself, even as she grew tired and began to falter, never seeming to care if anyone was paying her attention.

After she finished filling another wheelbarrow and was pressing it forward, she lost her footing and ended up on her hands and knees.

"Enough!" he yelled. Quick-stepping his way into the pen, he fumbled toward her, waving his arms. "I said that's enough." By the time he reached her, she had managed to halfway right herself. Grabbing for the stability of the wheelbarrow, her mud-caked hand slid off its handle, propelling her into him, her chin colliding into his chest. Back he went, his arms groping for an imaginary lifeline. Flat on his back with her on top of him, they plunged into a puddle.

For several seconds they floundered about, finally flailing their way to their knees. Vanderson gasped for air while she remained motionless.

"I—said—enough!"

"Sorry, didn't hear you," she said nonchalantly.

"Didn't hear me?" He smacked his palm into the mud. "How could you not hear me?"

She tried to hold back the sudden urge to laugh at a man who had succumbed to a mud facial before they ever became popular, his lips slinging dirty brown droplets with every syllable. She couldn't help it. She tittered at him.

"Stop that," he demanded. Pulling up his top hat that had gone adrift in another puddle, he plopped it on his head. Streams of dark water cascaded across his forehead and down his cheeks. Two quick swipes of his dirty sleeve across his face revealed a contemptuous snarl. As he rose, he offered her his hand, pulling it back when their fingers touched.

"Ha!" he said, leaving her scowling in the muck.

"What're you doing?" she screamed.

Without turning, he replied in equal measure, "I'm going to my office. Stay here with your pet pig if you wish."

"No! *What* are you doing with *me*?" Her tone turning suddenly from demanding to pleading. "Why am I here? Why did that-that pig farmer just push me off on you? *What* do you want from me?"

He stopped, his head bent down in thought. "Just come with me. We have to leave in the morning, and you'll need to be rested."

Zoey watched him enter the tiny office, then gazed out past the pigsty to the hustling market streets. Again, she contemplated how easy it would be to jump the waist-high wooden fence to freedom, all the while knowing she needed to play out the Mad Hatter's game, using him for food and shelter. From here on out, she would have to keep her rants to herself—and certainly no more outbursts about time traveling. She slowly pulled herself out of the mud.

Upon entering the office, she found it empty. The only sign of Vanderson was his waterlogged top hat sitting on top of the filing cabinet. She sat down and unleashed a tiresome sigh, a product of shoveling pig feces for five hours with no breaks, no water, and no food. Her body ached from head to toe. Her karate practices had been tough but had never lasted this long. Her eyelids closed once with her head dropping only to have it spring back up. A moment later it dropped again.

"Well, there ya be!"

She lugged her head up. The fuzzy outline of a large woman in a frilly lace dress with an enormous bustle came into focus.

"You must be Miss Zoey," she said with the glee of a teenaged schoolgirl.

Blinking away her catnap, Zoey struggled for a proper greeting. "Hey," was all that came.

"Oh, m'dear," the woman said, swishing her bustle across the floor, "I believe I've roused ya."

"Well, uh—"

"I'd come back anudder time, but Boone's done told me to see that ya be washed clean and proper."

"He said to what?"

"Oh, where's me manners?" The lady threw her hand at her. "M'name's Darcy May Fallon, a lot of people calls me Miss Darcy. You can just call me Darcy if it pleases ya."

Zoey reached up and shook her hand, the lady examining the muddy fingers wrapped around hers.

"Oh, I'm so sorry," Zoey said, withdrawing her hand into her pocket.

"No worries, deary, that's why I come fer ya. Like I says, Boone's a want'n me to get ya shined up."

"I don't understand."

Darcy laughed. "Just come with me, deary." She started to grab her hand again, but Zoey kept it stuffed deep in the pocket of her jeans.

"Give me that dainty paw, missy," she said with a toothy grin. "It's just dirt and pig poop." She grabbed Zoey's hand and swung it under her arm, pulling her outside. "Come now. Time for a shine."

Chapter 8

The hubbub of the day's market had subsided into a twilight of vacant streets spotted with the occasional torches being lit along the dusty wooden sidewalks. The throngs of shoppers that had queued up in front of the storefronts were gone. Only a handful of merchants milled about the streets as they closed for the evening.

"Who are you?" Zoey asked.

"A short memory, haven't ya? I dun said, it's Miss Darcy."

"Yes, but—I guess I mean who are you to Mr. Vanderson?"

"I work for Boone. That's all ya be need'n to know."

"Who's the mud pie you tote'n with ya, Miss Darcy?" said a young man hefting a barrel of apples into the back of a wagon.

"Mind ya business, Neil," Darcy fired back.

"Don't look like much from here," the man continued.

"Shut ya trap, Neil, lest I cram a blarney stone down ya gullet. Don't mind him, deary," Darcy said, patting her hand. "Just a smidge down the way here and we'll be at Tula Rose's."

"Who's Tula Rose?"

"She owns the market's parlor. Boone knows Tula and—well, Boone he knows everybody here in the market—anyways, he's got Tula wait'n to put the shine to ya."

Tired of being jerked around, Zoey pried her hand loose from under Darcy's arm, stopping in the middle of the street. "Why do you keep saying I need a shine! What am I, a teapot? I don't need a shine. I need a cheeseburger and something to drink. I haven't eaten or had anything to drink all day." Crossing her arms, she stood fuming.

"Oh my, Boone did say ya had a tongue on ya." She put her hand to her mouth, tapping her lips with her finger. "That's good. Every girl needs a little vinegar in their veins." Darcy motioned her to follow. "If you'll come with me, I'll get ya that cheese thing ya said and something to quench ya thirst."

With her stomach grumbling, Zoey thought for a second then more than willingly followed. Several more yards farther down Darcy made a military-grade right turn into a side alley, Zoey following close behind.

"Here we be," she said.

Above them hung a whitewashed wooden sign with a purple rose hand-painted on each end. Between them it read, "Tula Rose's, Beauty Parlor." The wood-framed building it was affixed to was little more than a shed with a slightly sloped tin roof.

"Come on," Darcy said, opening the door.

As frustrated, hungry, and tired as she was, Zoey couldn't help but snicker as a tiny bell attached to the doorjamb jingled upon their entrance. The absurdity of having a bell alert someone's entry into a twenty-foot-square space was comical.

"Ah, I see ya be warm'n to the idea now."

Zoey frowned.

The doorbell jingled again, and in walked a beautiful young Asian girl carrying a bucket of hot water. "You early, Miss Darcy." She turned to Zoey. "Oh my, I bring more buckets." Then walking to an iron tub located along one wall, she dumped her load. "Have seat," she said, pointing to a chair surrounded by mounds of hair. "Tula back with last bucket in few minutes. Food under towel on table."

Darcy pulled off the towel, unveiling a two-inch steak next to a baked potato, piece of corn, half a loaf of bread, a dozen grapes, and a tub of butter next to a mug and pitcher of water.

"All for ya, deary," she said with a slight curtsy.

No sooner had the steak been uncovered than Zoey pounced at it with both hands, gnawing into it.

Darcy cleared her throat while rolling her eyes toward a knife and fork next to a barren plate.

Her cheeks bulging with prime rib, Zoey picked up the fork and used it to position the massive piece of meat onto the plate where she proceeded to devour it, along with the rest of the feast.

A few minutes later the doorbell jingled the Asian girl's entrance again. This time she was carrying two pails of water. "Thought she need more."

"Go on, deary. Ditch ya duds and dunk on in the tub that Miss Tula's fix for ya. Me and her'll be leav'n ya to be on ya own."

Zoey stood. "This is my shining? Taking a bath?"

"Tis part of it, for sure."

Tula nodded toward the tub. "You find bar of lye and towel on other side of tub."

"Take ya time, dear," Darcy said. "We'll be outside. Just give us a holler when ya feel all shined."

"Would you *please* stop saying that?"

"Come now, Tula, let's have the little mud dauber start her scrubb'n."

Zoey ran her hand through the water as the door closed behind them. To her surprise it was warm. With a full stomach and warm bath ahead of her, she began to think kindlier of her new acquaintance. Soon she was naked and easing her way into the soothing water. Leaning her head back, she took a long, easy breath. Miss Darcy was indeed growing on her with every relaxing second.

A half hour later three knocks came from the other side of the door. "Are ya decent yet, deary?" said Darcy from the other side.

"Just a second," Zoey said as she finished wringing her hair dry then combing it straight. When finished, she wrapped the towel around her and tucked in the corners over her chest. At her feet were her jeans and T-shirt, both unrecognizable from when she had left New York—when they had been clean, bright, and new. Now they were weathered into a miserable grey heap, a mirror to her own condition.

The doorbell jingled as Tula and Darcy entered. "We're coming in, ready or not."

"Oh my," Tula exclaimed.

"Land sakes," Darcy said, placing her hand over her mouth.

The two women stood gawking.

"What? I did what you said to do. I shined."

Darcy's mouth fell open. "That ya did." She turned to Tula. "Have ya ever seen a more beautiful creature in all ya livelong days?"

Tula continued to gape.

"Such smooth skin," Darcy said, running a finger across Zoey's shoulder and pulling it away before touching the first of her tattoos. "Get a load of these, Tula. The girl's done gone and got her a dozen tats the likes of a sailorman. Beautiful they are. Too bad you won't be able to be showing 'em."

"What do you mean?" Zoey asked.

"I like the cross, deary, but the others most likely'll be scare'n folks. They'll be think'n ya done been with the devil—or worse, been caught up with the injuns."

"Do you mean Indians? Native American Indians?"

"Whatever ya be want'n to call 'em, but you'll need to keep 'em covered." She turned her attention back to Zoey's face. "But the rest you'll be want'n to show." She sighed. "Oh, what I wouldn't give to have them high cheekbones and shoulders so firm and tight." She walked closer. "And them green orbs. Like gemstones, they be."

Zoey took a step back as Darcy reached her hand to her pink strip of hair.

"Easy, girl. Just take'n a gander. What might this be? A birthmark? A pink birthmark in ya hair?"

Zoey reared farther back. "No, of course not, it's dye. Don't you know about hair dye?"

"I've heard tell of it but never seen it."

"It's so common, how could you not have seen it? Everybody's doing it. In *Vogue* and *Cosmo*, you'll see tons of—"

Tula and Darcy ogled her in unison, stopping Zoey midsentence, realizing her monologue on hair dye wouldn't be relevant for decades to come. She had to remember to stop and think before speaking. She couldn't give anyone reason to think she might be "touched in the head," as Boone had said. Whatever she said had to relate to the time in which she now existed.

"What I-I meant to say is that I met this travelling medicine man who had this special paint for hair. He said it could turn it a different color and I was curious so I bought it and tried it and it worked but it turned this weird shade and—now I can't get it out. I'm not sure what's in the dang stuff but I haven't been able—"

"Oh, deary, don't be babbl'n on. That skunk stripe will just grow out in time. Besides," she said wrangling her hair into a bun, "it's got to go up. Can't have a proper lady wear'n her hair down." Darcy turned to Tula and rolled her yes. "Well then, all that's needed now is the wrapping."

Tula handed Darcy a small rectangular package bundled in tan paper. She undid the bow and handed it to Zoey. "Go on, deary, we'll be gett'n rid of them dirty duds of yours in the morn."

Peeling off the paper, Zoey watched a long, sage-green tea-party dress unfurl to the floor.

"Look! See, Miss Darcy," said Tula. "Dress match eyes some kind of good."

"And the sleeves cover the tats just fine," Darcy added.

Zoey turned it around. "It's actually beautiful."

"Ay, that it 'tis," said Darcy.

Zoey ran her fingers across the delicate, hand-embroidered heart-shaped neckline, down a whimsical floral pattern over tiers of gossamer fabric that cascaded from a narrow, gold-banded waistline all the way to the hem. Along the way, a glittering array of sequins, beads, and small rows of tiny pearls caught the light.

"That piece of beauty is for later, deary." Darcy handed her a pair of black leather lace-up boots with kitten heels along with another article of clothing. "This is what ya be wear'n for now."

Zoey unfolded the other garment—a remarkably boring cotton dress with a prudish, high-collared neck, puffy, ruffle-trimmed long sleeves, and an endless row of simple buttons running down the bodice all the way to a hemline that touched the floor.

"This is what you want me to wear?"

"Unless ya'd like to be shimmy'n into that mud pile on the floor."

"No, no, this will be fine."

A few minutes later Zoey stood in the middle of the room peering down the long line of buttons. "It's going to take me an hour just to close this thing."

"Let's see about the back, shall we?"

Zoey turned away while holding out her arms. Just as she did, the bell jingled and in walked Boone.

"Good job, Tula, I see we finally have a—"

Zoey slowly turned.

Boone's neck tipped forward. "Well, then. Yes, I-I see that all is in order with the shine."

She rolled her eyes again at hearing the word. "Must you keep using that phrase?"

"What we do now, Mr. Boone?" Tula asked.

His gaze held fast on Zoey. "N-nothing. I mean, just button her up and send her to the office." He turned and walked out.

"I guess he likes it," Zoey said with a shrug.

On the way back to the office, Zoey said to Darcy, "You never told me what your relationship is to Mr. Vanderson."

"And like I was tell'n ya, I work for him and that's all ya be need'n to know."

"Well, what does he do?"

"Lots of things. He's a man of commerce who just seems to know how to work with people. He's got people he works with all over the city."

"But he's just a pig and chicken farmer or trader—right?"

"Oh no, those are just some of the things he's into. He's got people of every kind of business com'n and goin'. But listen to me now. Don't ya be goin' pry'n in on his business. We women folk don't do that, especially with Mr. Boone and his people."

"What people?"

"Just people, deary." She stopped. "Like I done said, don't ya go pry'n. Just do as he says, and you'll be just fine. He can help ya."

Zoey grabbed her by the sleeve. "I know he said that but how's he going to do anything? Help me in what way? He doesn't have a clue about what I need, and I can assure you there's no way he can help!"

"First of all, I'll be thank'n ya not to be paw'n at me," she said calmly.

Zoey recoiled her hand. "Oh, I-I'm sorry."

Darcy's tone turned hushed. "Miss Zoey, these be troub'n times. With the war still going on in so many ways, there's people that'll do ya harm just out of necessity. I don't know anything about ya so I can't be givin' ya advice, but I can tell ya one thing—Mr. Boone Vanderson can help ya make a way in this here life."

When they arrived back at the office, no one was there. On the bed was a note that read, *Rest easy, Miss Antonelli. We will be leaving at first light tomorrow*. Next to it was a flask with another note. *Take two sips to help you sleep. No more!*

As she began the arduous task of unbuttoning her dress, she stopped to search the front door for a lock. Finding none, she buttoned herself back up, took one look at the flask, and placed it on the filing cabinet. There it would remain. A clear head, her martial arts skills, and dozens of buttons lining her dress were her only protection for that evening.

The next morning the roosters, once again, jarred her awake at the first ray of light. Along with their unwanted crowing was a loud knock at the door.

"Miss Antonelli, are you up?" came Vanderson's voice from the other side.

"Just a minute," she said, running her hand through her hair.

"Alright but five more minutes and then—"

She swung the door wide. "I'm ready."

"Good then." He extended his arm toward the street where there stood awaiting them a small, open carriage harnessed to a silky black stallion. A straight-backed coachman manned the reins.

"Where are we going?" she said, walking out the door.

He stopped. "The dress?" he said flatly.

"What about it?"

"You need the other dress. Retrieve it, if you please."

Growing tired of both his increasingly negative attitude and constantly being prodded, she started to launch a stiff retort but stopped short, remembering her self-imposed rule to remain compliant. "Sorry, I'll get it."

A moment later, they were in the carriage, the package under her arm. Slowly they moved through the market streets. Within a matter of minutes, every merchant appeared to be back on the streets prepping their merchandise for another day of haggling. Without exception, everyone they passed offered their greetings to Vanderson as if he were royalty on parade.

"Good day, Mr. Vanderson."

"May you have a blessed day, Master Vanderson."

Even a beggar bowed his head rather than raising his hands to plead for coin. In return, Vanderson provided a quick finger touch to the brim of his hat.

Although Zoey was intrigued, she was far from impressed. The surroundings were dirty, and the merchants were a filthy lot, most missing teeth and wearing ragged clothes that obviously had been worn for weeks on end. Anyone with a pinch of higher income would stand out among this sort. In her mind he was the same ten-cent millionaire—putting on airs with his top hat and carriage—as the twenty-first-century version with the rented Lamborghini managing a Ponzi scheme. She was a true New Yorker, after all, and could smell this type a mile away. Regardless, she would continue to heed Darcy's words.

Bide your time, she thought. *This man can possibly help.*

Chapter 9

As their carriage pulled away from the market, the tents, lean-tos, and sheds bordering Vanderson's Pork and Poultry began to disappear, replaced by a dense forest of huge oak, walnut, and maple trees.

Vanderson sat ramrod straight next to her, the expression on her face matching his growing indifference. The only thing providing any clue as to her mood was her left knee, which she was bouncing up and down frantically.

As the dim light of dawn faded away into the canopy of hardwoods, Vanderson broke the silence. "Don't be afraid."

She glared at him from the corner of her eye while calming her leg by placing her hand on her knee.

Thirty minutes later a small hazy cloud appeared a hundred yards in front of them. As they approached, the confines of the forest began to give way to a vast fog bank so dense the only thing she could make out was Vanderson's waistcoat and the back of the coachman. Suddenly the slippery swagger of the carriage over the muddy road transformed into a smooth roll of wheels on wooden boards. Zoey cast

Vanderson another glance. His stoic profile aimed in front of them continued to pay her no attention.

Soon their journey transitioned again as the clomping of the horse's hooves against wood changed to a clacking against something denser. With it came a commotion of sounds without images amidst a growing mist. Doors opened and closed, horses neighed, wagon wheels turned, and then, as if they had returned to the market, came the sounds of merchants haggling, along with the stench of manure and garbage.

"Pull over," Vanderson said. "There's too much fog. Let's hold up a bit."

"Yes, sir," the coachman replied.

She hung to the side of the carriage as it lurched up next to a curb.

There they sat, inches from one another with miles of rising tension separating them.

Zoey strained to see through the fog, trying to make out vague outlines of people passing, listening to their conversations and trying to uncover any clue as to where they were. Unable to determine their location, and with her frustration coming to a head, she grabbed Vanderson's arm. "Where are we?"

He leaned toward her ear and began to speak when suddenly a gust of wind swept past them, thinning the mist. Shadows began to form around them. Two, then ten, twenty, fifty. All at once grey silhouettes were moving about them as rays of light beamed down around them. One by one a spectrum of unsaturated colors began to replace the greys. A long steady breeze followed, sweeping the dull remnants of the shadows away. Another gust of wind lifted the remaining fog, revealing a long cobblestone street flooded with hurried people.

She sat thunderstruck at the revelation of this new world. Throngs of people meandered up and down the thoroughfare, in and out of alleys and side roads, while men on horseback trotted by amidst the comings and goings of wagons and carts. Many of the men were dressed in the same attire as those in the market, but the majority wore top hats and long black coats similar to Vanderson's. The women's garb was slightly more refined. They all wore dresses, but these had more lace and larger bustles, and unlike at the market, most all of them wore large floppy hats decorated with an assortment of feathers and bows. Just as Darcy had said, all of them wore their hair up.

Then there were the buildings. Gone were the sheds and shanties of the market. In their place bordering the sides of the street, they rose no more than two or three stories. Although the fog had lifted, it seemed to have been absorbed into the brick and stone they were built upon. The occasional ornate carvings outlining many of them were lost in a dismal pallet of dark greys and browns, a fitting backdrop to the subdued colors worn by the residents of this strange place.

Putting her hand to her mouth, she remembered what the pig farmer's wife had said as they approached the market. "Is this—"

"New York!" Vanderson said, a renewed brightness to his tone. "Isn't it grand?"

She swallowed hard as the final nail of reality was hammered into the coffin that was her new existence. There was no more denying it. Although it was more than a century and a half in the past, the memory stone had sent her home.

Her eyes glazed over as her thoughts faded to a place of indifference, a place void of reason, to a place she could escape.

"Miss Antonelli." Her head swayed with his nudge. "Miss Antonelli—Zoey!"

She blinked with a quick twitch of her head as the coachman snapped the reins, starting the carriage forward.

"Are you okay? You're a little flushed," said Vanderson.

"I-I'm fine."

With the lifting of the fog, it seemed that Vanderson's mood had lifted as well. Either the sun or the city had inspired him to suddenly want to converse. "I recall you saying something—in a rather odd manner, I might add—about the city when we first met. Have you been here?"

Knowing her response could make or break her case for being sane, she replied, "It's been so long that it all seems so… well, so new to me."

"That's easy to understand. This city seems to change overnight. How long has it been since you were last—"

"Mr. Vanderson, where are we going?"

"To Tweed's Five Points office."

"Tweed?"

"Yes, William Tweed, he's my employer."

She reared back. "William Magear Tweed—the one they call Boss Tweed?"

"That's right."

"Your employer is Boss Tweed, leader of New York City's Tammany Hall political organization?"

"Yes. Why, do you know him?"

She wanted to tell him that she had been working on a crime expose for the NYC *Chronicle* that stretched from modern day all the way back to his employer and how he had bought votes, encouraged judicial corruption, embezzled, and extorted millions from city contractors. She wanted to tell him that his boss was one of the crookedest politicians in U.S. history and that in a year he would be thrown in jail.

"I don't know him," she said, holding back the urge to unleash all the dirt she had on the man. She took a quick breath. "I've only heard of him."

"Well, now you'll get to know him a little better. You'll be meeting him this afternoon at the garden party."

"Oh no!"

"Excuse me?"

"I mean, I don't have anything to wear."

Vanderson chuckled. "My dear, you're holding it in your hands."

She adjusted the tan package in her lap. "Oh, the dress."

He tilted his head toward her. "You do have a way of confounding a man, Miss Antonelli."

"You had been calling me Zoey. You can call me that again if you want."

He studied her briefly. "Zoey it is. And you may call me Boone."

She tipped her head. "Then Boone it is."

As their carriage ambled through the city, she found herself increasingly appalled at its living conditions with heaps of garbage piled into corners and horses defecating in the middle of the street. She shifted in her seat as she began thinking how she would survive. Gone were all the necessities she had taken for granted—no sanitary toilets, no easy means of travel, no electricity, no cell phones—no phones at all. The only thing she had was the man sitting next to her, this strange man who, for whatever reason, had taken her into his care. A man who one minute was kind and generous while the next finagling her into cleaning pigsties. One minute he was pleasant and chatty, the next aloof and sullen. If she was going to use him, she would have to find out how he planned to use her.

Mustering her most pleasant voice, she said, "Boone, how much farther?"

"About forty-five minutes. Why?"

"I was wondering if... well... if we might get better acquainted. I was wondering if I might ask you some questions."

"Of course. And in return, I might ask you some and you won't get upset?"

"Deal. We'll alternate back and forth with one question each." She skewed her lips, pretending to think about a question she had already prepared. "What is it you do exactly?"

"I'm what you might call a go-between. I barter and trade goods. I buy things for less than market value, hike up the price, then sell them. It's rather complicated."

Her stomach churned at his suggestion she couldn't understand such a rudimentary business tactic, but she only said, "How do you know Boss Tweed?"

"During the war I met one of his associates, a man named Cody. When the war was over, he asked if I'd like to come work with him. I didn't have any other prospects at the time, so I said yes. Mr. Tweed just happened to be his employer. You might meet Cody at the party."

"You actually fought in *the* Civil War?"

"Yes, I fought in *the* Civil War."

"Were you ever afraid the Confederacy would win?"

He hesitated. "I was actually hoping they *would* win."

"Why would you want that when you're from—"

"Hold on a second! You just asked me four or five questions in a row. It's my turn."

"Oh, I'm sorry. I got going and couldn't quit. Okay, your turn."

He placed his hand to his chin. "Let's see now… are you married?"

She held up her left hand and wiggled her naked ring finger. "Do you have any relatives nearby?"

"I don't. What about you?"

"Me neither."

He cleared his throat. "Have you ever been in an insane asylum?"

There it was. She knew he had his suspicions. "As a matter of fact, I have."

He gaped at her.

"I was visiting an uncle who had been committed. He was an alcoholic who had lost his business, wife, and kids and things had spiraled out of control. He just lost his mind for a couple years, and being a good niece, I'd go see him."

He nodded. "I know it's your turn but since you asked all those questions in the beginning, I'd like to ask one more."

"I suppose that's fair," she said, relieved that they'd gotten past what she thought would be her biggest stumbling block.

"Okay." He tapped his fingertips together. "When we first met, you mentioned something about a stone bringing you back. What did you mean by that?"

Instantly she regretted agreeing to his next question. She had forgotten most of her rant, remembering only that she had sounded like a madwoman. Just as a plausible answer came to her, the carriage lunged forward then back as the coachman yanked the reins into his chest.

"What's the matter?" Boone asked.

"Up ahead, sir. We've got a bunch of young hooligans who look to make trouble."

Zoey clutched Boone's arm.

"Is the shotgun loaded?" he said.

"Yes, sir. But there's five of them. Can't tell, but I believe the biggest one has a bat."

"When we get close, raise the gun so they can see it. That should be enough to scatter them." He patted her on the arm. "Don't worry. This part of town is a little rough, but we'll be through it shortly. If they don't run off, my man will just race the carriage right past them."

She had not been paying attention, but as their game of Q&A progressed, so had the level of the city's destitution. She remembered from her research for her expose how desperate certain parts of the city had become and how, at that time, it had the highest crime rate in the world.

As they drew closer, Boone reached down and pulled his own bat from under the seat.

"For heaven's sake, does everyone in this city carry a weapon?"

Boone stayed squared ahead. "This isn't heaven, and my guess is yes."

When they were within fifty yards, the obvious leader, an older boy with a mop of sweaty platinum-blonde, shoulder-length hair covering his face like a veil, walked into the middle of the street holding a sawed-off bat in the air.

At the same time the coachman held up his shotgun, shouting down at him. "Tit for tat, young fella!"

The boy ran his hand under his nasty locks, sliding it upward across his forehead, pushing the greasy strands to the back of his head. Temporarily forgetting about the danger they were in, Zoey stared at a complexion so blanched, she could see his veins pulsing blood over his temples and across nonexistent brows. Wisps of white lashes wrapped around a mesmerizing gaze from eyes so faint in color they almost blended into the surrounding whites. Only a hint of blue provided any contrast. He zeroed in on her with a menacing snarl, leaned back, and howled. The other boys, all ragged and equally sweaty, split into pairs with each twosome maneuvering to opposite sides of the street. At the same time, from out of a side alley a smaller boy wheeled a long, narrow wagon behind the boy with the bat, in effect blocking them from passing.

"Tit for tat," said the bat-wielding thug.

The coachman pulled the shotgun to his shoulder and aimed it at him. "Boy, I'll have you move that wagon now, if you please."

Just then an empty whiskey bottle flew past Boone, crashing against the back of the coachman's head and sending him flopping face-first over the front of the wagon. The shotgun flew out in front of his unconscious body.

Boone and Zoey turned to find another gang member positioned directly behind the carriage, armed with a crooked grin and another bottle in his hand. "Wanna see me do it again?" he snarled.

"What do we do?" she said, tugging at Boone's coat.

"Just stay calm. We have to get to the gun," he said under his breath.

"Well, well. Looks like you and the missus are stuck," said the gang's leader, pounding the bat into his hand.

Zoey leaped from the carriage.

"What're you doing?" Boone said.

"What you said—getting the gun."

"For Pete's sake," he muttered and jumped down behind her.

As she moved toward the weapon, so did the gang's leader.

Boone caught up with her just as they all met in front of the wagon, equal distance between all three and the shotgun. Behind them stood the bottle thrower, while to their left and right, gang members slowly closed in. The leader remained steadfast, staring at her. She returned the same gaze to him with one exception. While she figured him to already be counting the money in Boone's wallet, she was calculating her next four moves. Her peripheral vision picked up on the position of the two members to her left and the two on her right. One was muscular with an air of confidence, another had a scar running across his face. The others were smaller, with meeker postures.

"Take the one behind us, then help me with the lead," she whispered.

"Do what?" he said.

"Just do it. On my mark take out the one behind us then help me with the bat boy."

"Are you daft? There's too many!"

Frustrated, the boy with the bat broke eye contact and sprinted head-on at her.

"Now!" she yelled. Vaulting forward, she raised her knee above her waist, recoiled it back against her torso, then unleashed it forward like a jackhammer into the boy's chest. Head over heels he flipped back onto the cobblestones.

Boone stood riveted in place, shocked at the precision and force of her sudden fighting skills.

"Don't just stand there," she said. "Take the guy in the back!"

He turned just in time to duck another bottle. With the boy off-balance from his throw, Boone punched the end of the bat into his gut, thrusting the other end up and driving it directly below his chin, propelling him onto his back. To his right, he caught the two smaller boys running down the alley from where the wagon had been wheeled out. He turned to her. "Where're the others?"

She angled her head down to where the other two boys lay sprawled at her feet. In front of her was the boy with the bat, his pale jaw muscles twitching with rage. "I'm going to split your skull."

"You'll do no such thing," Boone said, stepping up beside her. He tapped his finger on the top of his bat.

The boy took a half step forward and stopped, then puckered his lips, arched his head back, and flung it forward, blowing a spit ball inches from her feet. With a snarl he turned and disappeared down the same alley where his two cowardly friends had skulked off.

Chapter 10

A hand reached up and grabbed the carriage footboard. "What happened?" the coachman moaned.

"You're hurt," Zoey said, running to his side. Bending down, she placed her hand behind his head where the bottle had found its mark. His hair was matted with blood. Her voice was calm but concerned. "We need to stop this bleeding." She ripped a length of her dress off then wrapped it around his head. "This should stop it for the time being."

Boone stood in the same spot, spellbound by the way she had handled the attackers and taken control of the situation.

"We need to get him to a hospital or at least someplace to clean this wound," she said.

With a blink, he snapped into action. "Ye-yes. Let's get him up. I'll drive us the rest of the way." He grabbed the man by the waist, and with her on the other side, they hoisted him into the carriage.

After clearing away the wagon that had been used to block them, they were off again, leaving behind two of their assailants who had just begun waking from a beat-down at the hands of a twenty-first-century martial arts champion.

For the next half hour, they rolled through the city streets, free from any more attacks. Zoey sat in the back with the coachman's head on her lap while Boone manned the reins and guided them toward their destination. Occasionally, he would turn around to see how his wounded driver was doing—and gawk covertly at the woman who had suddenly captivated his imagination.

Just before ten that morning, the carriage came up in front of a small, two-story redbrick building that stood only three paces from the street. After tying the horse to a hitching post, Boone stepped to the edge of the carriage and offered up his hand to her.

"Where are we going now?" she asked.

"This is my home. This is where you're to get ready for the party this afternoon."

"What about your coachman?"

Boone leaned down and placed his hand on the man's shoulder. "Better now, ole chum?"

The coachman bobbed his head.

"He's going to be fine. In fact, I'm taking him with me to the mansion. Someone will take care of him."

"The mansion?"

"Mr. Tweed's mansion. I'll drop him off there, attend my meeting, and then I'll be back. In the meantime, you'll be using my house to freshen up and prepare for the tea party."

Grabbing the edge of the carriage, he pulled himself back into the driver's seat.

"Do you have a key for me to get in?"

"All you have to do is knock. When my man Gibson comes to the door, he'll ask who you are. You are to politely reply that you're a purple finch. He'll help you from there."

"A purple finch—what the heck? Wouldn't a key suffice?"

"Not today, young lady. Today, you're a purple finch."

Zoey stood on the curb, looking first at his house, then back to the carriage, then back to the house. "A finch?" she grumbled, planting her laced-up boots on the doorstep. Grabbing the door knocker, she rapped it three times. A few seconds later a small round metallic plate, located in the center of the knocker's opening, flipped up. A pupil floating within a hazel sphere twitched back and forth on the other side.

"Who are you?" came a voice from within.

She stood stiffly, holding her package to her chest.

"I asked, who—are—you?"

"Oh, I-I'm sorry. I forgot. I'm a purple finch," she said, shaking her head at the absurdity of it all.

The metal circle immediately flipped down, and the door latch opened, followed by some bumbling about from the other side. "Come in, please."

She poked her head around the door to find a tiny man in a tuxedo pushing a step stool away from the door.

"Are you Mr. Gibson?" she asked.

The little man turned and clasped his hands together. With his equally angular chin and ears, he possessed an elfish quality. His eyes sparkled as they ran up and down her body. "My, how the finches do get prettier every season."

"Excuse me?" she said.

The little man stepped toward her, straightened himself, and clicked his heels, pronouncing, "I am

Kenworth Gibson, valet to Mr. Boone Vanderson, here to serve you."

"Well, Mr. Gibson, I'm Zoey Antonelli and I'm not certain what I'm supposed to do here other than get ready for a party."

"Yes, ma'am, the Tweed garden party."

"That's right," she said.

"Your room is upstairs and to the right. You have full run of the house while Mr. Vanderson is away. Regarding the garden party, I suggest you acquaint yourself with your room where you'll find fresh linens, towels, and toiletries."

She looked down the hallway to the end of the house. "I see there's no back door. Would that mean you have an indoor restroom?"

"If you mean a water closet, we certainly do."

"With a toilet?"

Gibson beamed. "Yes, indeed. Down the hall, past the dining room and Mr. Mase's office."

"Oh, I could just about kiss—"

The tiny man bounced forward. "There is a bell in your room. Feel free to use it if you need me. Is there anything else I can do for you?" He closed his eyes and puckered his lips. Hefting his chin up, he opened one of them. "You mentioned something about a kiss."

She laughed. "No, I think I'm good right now. Thank you." She started toward the stairs then turned back. "Actually, there is. I'm writing an article on merchants like Mr. Vanderson and I need a little background info. Can you tell me a little more about—"

"No, ma'am. I'm sorry," he said. "I'm afraid I have no information I can provide you." With a quick bow he disappeared down the hall.

As Zoey ascended the stairs, she took her time, noting what appeared to be a hundred black-and-white photos on the walls. Surely, they would provide some insight into the man. One after the other showed him shaking hands or standing stiffly erect next to other gentlemen all dressed in the same dignified suit and tie of the day. All but a few wore top hats. With twenty or more apparent ribbon-cutting ceremonies intermingled with the others, it was obvious he was indeed a man of some stature and not the ten-cent millionaire she had previously thought him to be. The hallway showcased a definite business acumen but nothing of family. Not one picture included anyone who could be construed as a wife, child, or other relative, unless of course that person happened to be a business owner or colleague. What appeared on those walls was a man devoted to one thing only, the pursuit of currency.

The room she was to occupy was small with elaborately appointed feminine touches. From the finely hand-crocheted doilies on the nightstand and dresser to the matching lace trim on the curtains, it was obviously a space meant for a woman. A small brass bed stood in the center with a two-foot-thick mattress that beckoned to her as her whole body recalled all the hardships of the past several days. From the arduous wagon rides and painful nights on wafer-thin mattresses to a full day of pigsty cleaning, she was exhausted. Tossing her packaged dress into the corner and bouncing up onto the oversized mattress, she sank down into six inches of heavenly goose-down bliss. With a long exhale she fell back, her arms spread wide. Lying motionless, Zoey let her aching muscles and joints revel in the feathery cloud of relief. For several minutes she eyed the curtains gently rolling as the cool morning breeze wafted through. The hypnotic rhythms of the lacy fabric, along with the murmuring of passing wagons and carriages on the streets below, soon demanded sleep.

With her mind and body finally at rest, a soft voice whispered its way through her dream. "Come," it called to her. A shimmering light faded in from the dark with the silhouette of a man walking toward her. He stopped as streams of Spanish moss unfurled from the crooked branches of large oak trees. Behind him a beautiful pond appeared as his shadowy figure came into view. Mase was once again at the water's edge. "Come." He drew his hand to his chest. "Come to me." She tried to move but her legs would not budge. All she could do was reach out to him. She tried to speak but no words came. "Come to me. All you have to do is—"

"Miss Antonelli!"

Hey eyelids flew open.

"Are you up?" Gibson said from outside her door.

From her slumber, she struggled to gain her bearings as her mind hung on to the vision of Mase beckoning to her.

Three loud bangs on the door filled the room with greater alarm than the roosters who had rudely awakened her the day before.

"I say, Miss Antonelli, are you—"

"Yes, yes, I'm up," she replied.

"I'm sorry for the intrusion, but I wanted to inform you that Mr. Vanderson should be arriving within the hour. You'll need to be ready."

"How long have I been… Oh, never mind. Alright, I'll be ready."

As the pitter patter of the little man's feet faded away, she wiped her forehead. The gentle, cool morning breeze had been replaced by the stagnant air produced by a muggy New York noonday sun. Still thinking of Mase, she rolled her head toward the lifeless curtains. Hoping for the breeze to return, she walked over and pulled them back. There, framed in lace were the room's harshest features—four wrought-iron bars crisscrossed the window. Suddenly, Zoey found meaning for "purple finch." Her thoughts of Mase calling for her vanished, as she dropped onto the bed, glaring at the metal bars.

The scampering of the light-footed valet coming up the steps was vastly different from the heavy-hoofed clamor that announced Vanderson's arrival. Upon hearing him climbing the stairs, she rushed to finish fastening the last button of the dress she had been commanded to wear.

"Are you ready?" Boone said when halfway up the stairs.

"Just a minute." With no rouge or any other makeup on hand, she pinched her cheeks for color. Picking up a pearl-handled mirror from the dresser, she immediately put it down. *Why bother?* she thought. *There's no one to please.*

"I'll be downstairs," he said.

She walked to the door then turned back to the window and bars that tainted the sunlight entering through them. Her lips drew tight as her hands balled into fists. She turned back to the door, took a slow breath, and with a long exhale let her fingers stretch out by her sides. As she had done so many times with her boss, she channeled a facade of happiness. With a smile, she pulled the door open and walked outside to the upstairs landing.

Boone had just made it to the bottom step when she called down to him. "I'm ready."

"Very good," he said, spinning around, "because we have—"

Transfixed, he stood gaping up at her. The light from her room fell across her back, illuminating her body in a glow that accented every curve that had been hidden by the drab garment that had replaced her T-shirt and jeans.

Silently he leaned forward against the banister, studying the beauty that appeared above him. "I, uh, I have something for you," he finally said.

Remembering the barred window, she bit her lip, vanquishing the urge to address why he persisted with chipping away at her freedom while pretending to care about her. With every good turn he took there was a misstep that she forced herself to remain silent about.

"Whatever could it be," she said with a syrupy cadence that caused her stomach to churn.

"Come down and I'll show you."

"Then I shall." She resisted rolling her eyes, wanting to scream at how ridiculous she sounded to herself.

When she reached the bottom steps, Boone pulled a long gold satin scarf from his pocket. "Tula and Darcy thought it would accent your dress," he said.

"Why, it's beautiful." She tied it around her waist, then forced her arm out to him. "Shall we go?"

Tucking his arm around hers, he led her through the hall to where Gibson was holding the door open. "I trust you enjoyed your room, Miss Antonelli," he said.

"I did. Thank you. The view from the window, however, is..."

"Is what?" Boone asked.

The emotional restraints within which she had carefully wrapped herself suddenly began to fray. She could feel her blood pressure rising as his hand seemed to tighten around her arm. “It’s… it’s incredible.”

Chapter 11

Stepping onto the busy New York street at noonday was a different experience than when they had arrived that morning. Maybe she had not noticed before due to the harried circumstances, but just like the market, every other person seemed to know Boone, and they all wished him well.

"May you have a wonderful day, Mr. Vanderson," said an elderly lady inching her way by.

"Good day to you, Mr. Vanderson!" shouted a merchant, hanging his head out his shop window across the street.

A young lady approached, twirling her parasol in front of her, then tipping it back at the last minute to reveal a sheepish grin. "Lovely day, is it not, Mr. Vanderson?"

Zoey snickered to herself, watching the girl blush then sneak a peek back to see if he had noticed her.

On it went as he readied the carriage. She mused how many paparazzi would have been snapping pics if they were in modern-day New York.

Oblivious of the fanfare—or else so accustomed to it—he helped her into the carriage. "It appears I will be your coachman today," he said with an exaggerated sense of pride.

"Oh, how is..."

"James."

"How is James?"

"Fine. In fact, I think he's rather enjoying his convalescing. The last I saw of him he had a whiskey in his hand and a silly smirk on his face. And he definitely wasn't annoyed by the attention the two doting young ladies at his side were paying him."

"See you at the party," said a stately gentleman on horseback trotting by. "You'd better hurry if you're going to make it in that carriage."

"I'm afraid I won't be much of a conversationalist until we get there," Boone told her. "I'm going to need all my faculties to navigate these absurdly packed streets today."

With the image of the window bars fresh in her mind, she replied, "That's quite alright. I don't feel like talking anyway."

Forty-five minutes later, Boone was pulling back on the reins in front of a sprawling two-story château-style mansion. With steeply pitched roofs, turrets, sculptural ornamentation, and a circular three-story entrance tower on the far end, it occupied a full city block. Surrounding it was a menacing, seven-foot-high wrought-iron fence with gargoyle statues on each corner. Capping it all off was the pomp and circumstance of the entry procession. Lined up around the block were both open and closed carriages drawn by either one or two well-groomed horses.

One by one the carriages pulled under the tower's opening where a team of footmen attended to each occupant, escorting them out onto the cobblestone courtyard that led to the backyard. There they were met with a host of waiters and staff rushing about three acres of manicured flora and greenery. Centered in a stand of finely cut grass was a large marble fountain with stone dolphins spouting water above them. Beside it, holding court, was the man himself, Boss Tweed, all three hundred pounds of pure corruption and deceit. Zoey knew from a distance exactly who he was. The mere fact that he was surrounded by bootlicking sycophants was itself a giveaway, but it was his commanding mannerisms and physical swagger that truly gave him away.

"Come," Boone said. "I'd like to introduce you to him."

She reared back.

"What's wrong?"

"Give me a minute," she said, composing herself to meet the real-life version of the political devil she had spent months studying. Even though she knew every aspect of his downfall, she was nevertheless taken aback at actually being in his presence. After all, if demons could possess others, then she was a likely target. She wrung her hands together. "Okay, let's go."

Boone took her by the hand. "Don't worry, my dear. He's just a man—a man with a whole lot of wampum."

Recalling from her research that *wampum* meant money within the Tweed circle, she let loose of his hand. "Go on then. Lead away."

"You'll be fine," he said. "You'll see."

As he began walking, she lowered her head and followed quietly several paces behind, muttering, "Yea, though I walk through the valley of the shadow of death, I will fear no evil, for thou art with me…"

"Were you saying something?" he asked.

"Just keep going," she replied, waving him on.

Thirty yards away from Tweed, she grabbed Boone's arm, turning him back to her. "You really work for this man?"

"Yes. I told you that." He sighed. "I know all the rumors and the talk about his business dealings and his politics but—"

"But what? Boone, this man is a monster. He's as bad as—" she stopped short of declaring him as evil as the mafia bosses who had supposedly put out a contract on her for writing the expose that had helped land some of their members in jail"

He pulled at her. "Come now."

She flung his hand away, and they scowled at each other.

"Tell me," she said, her voice rising, "why am I here? What're you doing with me? None of this makes sense. Tell me. Why—am—I—here?"

"Now is *not* the place."

"And who might this be, Boone?"

Together they turned to find Boss Tweed behind them. Zoey swallowed hard, examining the balding head, large nose, and ruddy complexion. Everything matched the descriptions she had pored over for so many hours—down to the huge 10.5-carat diamond stickpin he wore on his lapel.

"I heard you were bringing a guest," he said. His eyes roved over her in a lustful manner that would have elicited an immediate rebuke in modern times.

Boone cleared his throat. "Allow me to introduce Miss Zoey Antonelli. Zoey, this is Mr. William Tweed. All this is his estate," he said, sweeping his hand over the grounds and back to the mansion.

"And what a magnificent one it is. I would venture to say it puts all those silly shanties in the Hamptons to shame." Her voice was suddenly full of wonder, as if her spontaneous tiff with Boone never happened.

"Thank you, Miss Antonelli. Boone, this young dove has good taste." Without a pause he moved on to her hair. "What an interesting shade of dye. My, wouldn't the ladies in Paris be jealous?"

"Oh, you know the technique, Mr. Tweed?"

"I have heard of it." He rubbed his broad, slick forehead. "If I had anything to dye, I might be inclined to venture a similar shade." He laughed with Boone following suit. "Where are you from, my dear?"

"Where am I from?" She hesitated. She had to say something based on either sound reasoning or solid facts—either that or divert the question away from her. Suddenly it came to her. The perfect place she could speak about with some reasonable knowledge, all compliments of Mase Winslow's journal. "Why I-I'm from South Carolina, a plantation called Willow Creek."

Boone rocked back on his heels. "I thought you said—"

"You know what's much more interesting than little ole me?" she said, channeling her best Scarlett O'Hara. "It's that bronze statue we all want erected of Mr. Tweed. I'm sure it's a heap of wampum, but I do believe every one of your patrons would say it's more than worth it. Don't you think, Boone?"

His stare intensified as Tweed slapped him on the back. "Well, count me flabbergasted. If she were a man, I would put her on the payroll right here and now."

Zoey bit her cheek, fighting to ignore the comment.

Tweed summoned a waiter. "I want you to take special care of these two. Especially this one," he said with a wink to Zoey. "Make sure their glasses are always full, and if they need anything, make sure they get it." Taking her hand between his meaty palms, he brought it to his lips and kissed her fingers. She tasted blood as she bit down harder on the inside of her mouth.

"I'm sorry, Vanderson, but I need to go make the mayor feel as if he has some friends. Take care of our little dove."

As soon as Tweed turned, she bent forward, exhaling with her hand pressed to her chest.

"What was that?" Boone exclaimed.

"That was me surviving."

"I don't understand you, Antonelli. One minute you're berating my employer then the next you're fawning all over him."

"Isn't that what you wanted?"

He shook his head. "And you told him you're from a plantation in South Carolina. You told me when we first met that you didn't have anyone."

"And—I—don't!" she shot back as tears began to form.

Noticing several bystanders eyeing them, he stopped his questioning, tucked his arm under hers, and pulled her begrudgingly behind a secluded cypress tree. "Then why did you tell him you're from South Carolina?"

"Be-because I am. I'm from *Beaufort,* South Carolina." She turned away, full of the angst that came with knowing that now she would have to stack lie upon lie.

"Then why did you not just tell me that in the first place rather than go on with that insane rant about being stabbed and dying and being in New York, then South Carolina—"

"See, I did mention South Carolina!"

"That doesn't mean anything. Can you not see how crazy you were sounding?"

"I'm not crazy." Her lower lip began to quiver. "I'm just from another…"

"Another what?" He leaned in, tilting his head down to hers. "I'm not here to hurt you. Why do you think I asked if you had any relatives nearby?"

"I don't have any that are close. But that doesn't mean I don't have any."

He wiped a tear from her cheek. "I don't know what your story is or what you've experienced but I'd like to. Will you trust me?"

"I don't know if I can. I've already seen things that aren't…" Her voice trailed off.

"What is it?" he said.

The edges of her mouth slowly curled upward.

"What're you thinking?"

She held up her hand, silencing him so she could think clearly. Her mind churned through her sudden revelation. It was 1871, and Mase was alive. He was where his diary told her he would be. He was at Willow Creek. In her dreams, he had been calling her to come to him. All she had to do was convince Boone that she did indeed have relatives and that Mase Winslow was one of them. Whatever she concocted would have to be clever enough to explain why she had not told him sooner. Harder still would be explaining away his concerns that she was insane.

"How much longer are we staying?" she asked.

"I'm not sure. I only wanted you to meet my boss, so I'm fine with leaving anytime."

"That would be nice. I have some things I need to tell you."

"Alright then. Just allow me twenty minutes to make my rounds. I need to glad-hand some of the dignitaries, and we can go."

"Take your time. I'll be next to the fountain across from the carriages where we came in."

As she waited, a continuous parade of young gentlemen, along with a handful of elderly curmudgeons, strutted by, puffing their chests in a manner to rival the proudest of peacocks. Unbeknownst to them, the smiles she reciprocated were not for them. She smiled, anticipating seeing Mase again. For the first time since the memory stone had thrown her into the past, she was happy. Time was now on *her* side. Whether it was a day, a month, or more than a century in the past, she could now do what she had wanted to do—profess her love to him.

"I see you're here with Mr. Vanderson," came a voice from behind her.

Zoey turned to find a man of about Boone's age and stature. He was even dressed like him, the only difference being his empty right coat sleeve that was folded and pinned across his chest.

Having picked up on the mannerisms of the day, she curtsied. "Yes, I am."

"Allow me to introduce myself. My name is Cody Armstead."

"I'm Zoey Antonelli. You're a friend of Boone's?"

His face brightened. "Indeed I am."

"Do you work for Mr. Tweed as well?"

"I used to." He turned to her. "I'm sorry, may I get you a drink?"

"No, thank you. We were just about to leave."

Spying Boone in the distance, he said, "I see our Mr. Vanderson is doing his usual rounds of hobnobbing."

Her voice fell. "Yes, he and the boss are doing their thing."

"You have a very unique way of phrasing things, Miss Antonelli."

"These are unique times."

Several silent minutes passed between them as they scanned the crowd, watching Tweed and Boone weave their way through the crowd shaking hands, patting the men's backs, bowing to the ladies, and smiling their way into the hearts and wallets of everyone they met.

Zoey swung her head back and forth.

"I take it this party is not to your liking," Cody said.

"Tell me, Mr. Armstead, did you enjoy working for Mr. Tweed?"

"Yes." He hesitated for a second then added, "In the beginning I did. But then times, as they often do, changed."

"Aren't you just being polite now?"

"An astute observation," he snickered.

"Did you and Boone start work together at the same time?"

"Actually, I was working for Mr. Tweed first. It was after the war that I got him a job."

"Oh, I do remember him mentioning something like that. So you were in the war?"

"Yes. In fact, he and I were in the same regiment."

Her eyes traveled to his empty sleeve.

"I didn't even feel it when the cannonball took it off." He froze for a second, the pang of the ordeal flashing back across his face. "Boone saved my life that day. I would have probably died on the field or in a Yankee prison camp had he not pulled me into a thicket then carried me back behind Confederate lines."

"You mean you and he didn't fight for the North?"

"Why, no, ma'am. Did my Southern accent not give me away?"

"I guess it didn't occur to me," she said, watching Boone chatting up a couple of bloated dignitaries.

"He's a good man, Miss Antonelli."

"There's my handsome corporal," said a lovely young girl, sashaying her large hoopskirt up behind Cody. "I'm sorry, miss, but I'm afraid I must steal this gallant gentleman away." She plunged her arm under his only one. "Finnigan and his wife are leaving, and I wanted you to see their baby."

Cody produced a quick grin. "I'm sorry, Miss Antonelli. I'm afraid there are infants to be doted upon. Would you please tell Boone I'm sorry I missed him?" With the young lady beside him, he began walking away, then suddenly turned and quick-stepped back to her, leaving the young lady alone with a frown.

"What is it, Mr. Armstead?" she said.

"Boone is my friend."

"Yes."

"He's a dear friend." His voice took a desperate turn. "I owe everything to him. I owe him my life. He…"

"He what?"

"I only say this because, well…"

She leaned forward.

"There're dark forces at play," he whispered.

She searched his face, awaiting further explanation.

"Cody, please hurry," the lady urged.

"I'm coming," he yelled back. "Just know that, Miss Antonelli."

"Would you hurry up," the lady said, stomping her foot.

He spun around and rushed back to his lady's side. Grabbing him around the waist, she tugged him forward, only to have him stop again and turn back. "Please be careful, Miss Antonelli."

The minute Boone left Boss Tweed's side to return to Zoey, the distinguished, grey-bearded gentleman who had visited him at the market took his place, asking, "What do you think Mr. Tweed?"

"Oh, she's a beauty all right. Much more beautiful than you described her, that's for sure."

"What do you want to do?"

"I want her in the program, of course," Tweed replied.

"This one's a little different, sir. Vanderson's got her under his thumb."

"Don't worry about Vanderson, he'll let loose. Besides," Tweed said with a growing smile, "I've already got the ghost on it."

Chapter 12

By the time Boone returned, Zoey had been approached by a forgettable number of men offering a drink, a dance, or a stroll about the gardens. As she politely rebuffed them and thought about Cody's departing words, she had not noticed that Boone's twenty-minute leave of absence had turned into an hour and a half, most of which she spent scheming a way to Willow Creek.

"I am so sorry. Time tends to get away from me during these things. Between having to listen to the exaggerated rhetoric of want-to-be politicians to negotiating passage for business prospects on my clipper ships, it's a drain on one's disposition."

Her eyes widened, the connection coming to her like a bolt of lightning. This man she once thought was a fake, who had offered to help her, could actually do just that. "Did you say you own ships?"

"Among other things."

Her face was suddenly aglow.

"Why, Miss Antonelli, I do believe you've started to finally enjoy yourself."

"I think I am. What was that you said about your boats?"

He laughed. "First of all, these *boats* are ships. They carry cargo up and down the East Coast."

"And passengers? You said something about passage for business prospects."

"That's correct. They also carry the type of people I like."

"Which is?"

"Wealthy," he said, extending the word gleefully.

On the ride home she refrained from asking any more questions about his ships for fear of jeopardizing the beginnings of a strategy she had yet to flesh out. Instead, she turned to a more benign subject while she plotted how to use the man she still felt was using her.

"I met someone who knows you. A man named Cody."

"You met Cody Armstead?"

"Yes, he was very nice. He said you and he were in the army together."

"That's right. I told you that Cody is the one who got me the job with Tweed." He began laughing. "You know what we used to call him in camp?"

She couldn't help but laugh, watching him becoming amused ahead of the punchline. "What?" she asked.

"Cooties Cody."

"Oh no, do I really want to know why?" she said, feigning disgust.

"No, no, it's alright," he said, wiping away a tear. "You see, for some reason every bunk Cody bedded down in seemed to have bedbugs—or the beds would have them by the time he woke up."

"Tell me you didn't. Tell me you didn't sneak bugs into that poor man's bed."

"No, of course not." he said, his cheeks puffing up in anticipation of the finishing point of interest. "I didn't, but two privates, a sergeant, and one lieutenant did!"

Zoey whacked him across the shoulder as he burst into laughter. "You're a terrible man, Boone Vanderson," she said, laughing along with him.

"Yes, Cody Armstead is indeed a good fellow."

"He said the same of you."

"We were so close at one time. Almost like brothers."

"You're not like that anymore?"

"Unfortunately not."

"What happened?"

"We were just on different paths."

"How so?"

"Our temperament for doing business was a little different. You might say I was more ambitious. Boss Tweed took a liking to me because I have an affinity for getting things done, and I believe that upset Cody. He also just wanted different things out of life."

"Like what?"

"Like a wife and kids, a little house in the countryside with a picket fence." He laughed. "He started off wanting a few chickens. Now he has a couple hundred. No kids yet but a coop full of cackling toddlers."

"And you didn't want those things?"

"Chickens? I have chickens and pigs and—"

"No, the other things."

"I know what you meant."

"So. You don't want a family or a quiet little place full of serenity, happiness—love?"

"No," he said nonchalantly.

"No to all of them?"

"That's correct."

She infused her voice with passion bent to persuade. "But don't you feel you're missing out? Life is meant to be shared. Forget the little house with the picket fence. Forget the chickens. Material things don't bring happiness. But what about love? Don't you want *that*?"

Casually he turned his head. "No."

"Oh, Boone," she said, throwing her hands in her lap, "you truly are impossible." She mirrored his erect posture and turned back to face the busy street. "You're going to go through life chasing things that don't mean anything." A moment passed. "You're going to be old one day, and you're going to be sad and lonely and, well, that's all I have to say." A second later, she added, "Sad and lonely, that's what you'll be—sad and lonely." She raised her chin and continued staring straight ahead.

"Are you quite finished with your lecture on happiness?"

"It's not a lecture. It's the truth," she said with a huff.

"Well then, tell me the truth—are you happy?"

"Well, not of late, given all that's… Well, I am now or at least I'm—"

"See? You don't even know. And what about love? Have you ever been in love?"

"Well, I…" She turned away.

He breathed in slowly. "Your truth, as you call it, is indeed that for some people. But for others it's a lie. Not everyone wants the same out of life, Zoey. Although it seems you have never experienced any of it yourself, you seem to subscribe to all those things you define as a fulfilling, joyful, wonderful life. For others," he said, repeating himself and shaking his head, "it's just a lie."

"But don't you at least want—"

"It's a lie!" He snapped the reins. The carriage jolted forward, and she grabbed the seat's railing.

"I'm sorry," she said, running her hands across her thighs, straightening her dress.

With her attention turned away from him and his eyes channeled on the road ahead, they sat isolated in their thoughts.

Upon arriving back at his house, Boone helped her down from the carriage. "I'll be back in the morning," he said, climbing back up.

"But I wanted to ask you something."

"It'll have to wait," he said with an icy gaze. The carriage lunged forward, leaving her on the curb.

As if on cue the front door swung open. Gibson stood in the opening, his feet wide apart. "Saw you froo the window," he slurred. He waved his arm inward. "Come now, little finch, dinner will be weddy in apwocksumwy one hour." The little man's alcohol-soaked breath lingered in the doorway, causing Zoey to wince as she walked through.

"Mr. Vanderson will not be here this evening," she said.

"I know."

"How did you know?"

"Because. He's always out and about the evening of a Tweed garden party." He turned with a tiny swaying motion and began to leave. "One hour—dinner will be swerved."

She withheld a giggle as she watched him wobbling away like a drunken penguin in his tiny tuxedo. As she turned to go up the stairs, she noticed a door across from Mase's office that was cracked open. Through it she could see the corner of a four-poster bed. She glanced back. The drunken penguin was nowhere to be found.

Creeping to the doorway, she peeked inside. In the center of the room, with its posts the size of small oaks, sat a bed fit for a Viking. An ornately carved wooden panel hung above it while burgundy curtains with gold trim framed each side. Overstuffed pillows in matching silk patterns lay upon a deep mattress. Mahogany paneled walls and a coffered ceiling spelled out that this was the master suite. Through floor-to-ceiling windows light flooded the room, revealing a row of mirror-polished black shoes in front of an opulent chaise lounge. On the opposite side was an open closet with at least ten identical black suits, the same as the only ones she had seen Boone wearing.

Turning her head, she listened for small footsteps. Hearing nothing, she tiptoed to a large teak dresser next to the bed and picked up one of the only two items on it, a small crystal bottle filled with a teal-green liquid. She pulled the stopper and raised it to her nose. It was a cologne, the same lavender scent of Boone's. Next to it, facedown, was a small silver picture frame. Placing the bottle to the side, she picked it up. A thick mat of dust and dirt covered the picture that lay hidden inside it. With a handful of her dress fabric, she wiped it clean. The grainy black-and-white photo was that of a tiny wooden house. In front of it, under a large tree, was the image of an elderly man and a young woman holding a baby. Behind them was a blurry image of another child sitting on a tree swing.

"Thirty minutes, Miss Antonelli," came Gibson's voice from some distant part of the house.

She threw the picture back onto the dresser and rushed out of the room and up the stairs.

A half hour later Zoey descended the stairs and headed down the hall to the dining room. Gibson awaited her, holding open a set of thick velvet curtains partitioning the room from the hallway.

"Good evening," he said with a raised yet somewhat unsteady chin, his glassy eyes indicating he had continued to indulge himself with the spirits of his master's single malt scotch. "Pweeze have a seat," he said, stretching a finger to a lonely place setting dwarfed in the middle of the massive twelve-seat mahogany table.

She waited as he clumsily pulled out her chair then pushed herself to the table. "My heavens, this is incredible." Spread in front of her was a full Cornish hen, baked asparagus, and a heaping mound of mashed potatoes with onion and mushroom gravy. "Did you do this?"

"Yes, ma'am. I hope it is to your liking. Will there be anything else, ma'am?"

"No, thank you. This really is lovely."

He made a quick turn toward the curtains. "Good then, I'll be down the hall if you need me."

"Wait," she said, catching him as he was about to leave. "Have you eaten?"

"No, ma'am, that was what I was getting ready to do."

"Would you please join me?"

"Oh no, ma'am. Wouldn't be approp—riate."

"Nonsense. Besides I hate dining alone. Pleeeeease."

The little man looked left and right, as if someone was monitoring his response. "Why not?" he said with a bounce. "I'll be back in a jiff."

A minute later he wobbled through the curtains, precariously balancing a plate of food in one hand along with a bottle of scotch and a glass in the other. "Mind if I sit here?" he said.

"Wherever you please, Mr. Gibson."

"Thank you, miss," he said, gently placing his plate across the table from her. He held the bottle out to her. "Would you like a dwink?"

"No, thank you, but a glass of water would be nice."

He slammed his hand on the table. "Gibson, what a fool you are. I'm sorry, miss. I'll be right back."

Zoey sat patiently waiting, smiling in anticipation of her impending dinner conversation.

A moment later Gibson sloshed a glass of lukewarm water across the table to her. "Sure you wouldn't like some wine?"

"Maybe later," she said as she began cutting into the hen. Upon the first bite her shoulders fell, and she let out a soft groan. "This is so good."

Gibson beamed as he took a swig of scotch. "Thank you, ma'am."

"Do you often dine with Mr. Vanderson?" she asked.

"No, ma'am, Mr. Vanderson prefers dining alone."

She leaned in, eager to pounce at the little man's sudden willingness to impart information on his employer.

"So he never comes home after the tea parties, does he?"

"No, ma'am, he's out cultivating whatever he's been up to at the party. He calls it bird-dog'n."

His known absence would certainly explain Vanderson's man helping himself to his liquor cabinet. *A perk of the job*, she thought. "And what exactly is bird-dog'n?"

"Lots of things."

"Like…"

"Like making deals on goods he sells. He's a trader. A man who buys and sells things."

"Is that all?"

"He's also a collector."

"A collector?"

Gibson smiled, his cheeks bloated with mashed potatoes. "Yes," he said out the corner of his mouth.

"What does he collect?"

"Greenbacks, lots and lots of greenbacks."

"Money? He collects money?"

"Yes, ma'am. He and one or two big fellas go out, and they collect it."

"He's a collection agent then?"

"Maybe that's it. I've only heard people call him a shark."

"Wait," she said, placing her fork down. "Does he also loan people money?"

Gibson took a sip of scotch. "Of course. Why else would he be collecting it?"

"Well, there's—never mind." Her mouth skewed. "Mr. Gibson, does Mr. Vanderson have any relatives nearby?"

"To tell you the twoof, I don't know."

"How long have you worked for him?"

"I believe it'll be five years this May." He jabbed his fork back into the hen, swerving a piece of meat into his mouth. "For such a little finch you sure do chirp a lot."

Fearing the food was sobering him up and that he would soon lose his willingness to answer more questions, she chose a temporary redirect. "I just ask because people fascinate me." After several minutes of benign conversation, she ventured back to her line of questioning. "So you've never met any of his relatives?"

"No, ma'am."

She grabbed the bottle of scotch and poured a shot of amber liquid into his glass. "Here, Mr. Gibson."

With a single gulp, he finished it. "I don't know this to be twue." His slurred speech indicated her actions were on target with digging deeper. "I've only heard it second-hand, mind you," he said, leaning forward, "but supposedly he lost everything at the beginning of the war."

"What did he lose?"

He swung his hand across the table, knocking over a small flower vase. "Everything!"

"Like what though—his business?"

"No, *everything*."

"But—"

"I think that's enough chirping for one evening, little birdie," he said, stumbling back from the table. "I'm tired and I need to clean up before he returns in the morning."

"I'll help you."

"No! This is my job and you're a…"

"A what, Mr. Gibson? What am I?"

"You're a purple finch," he said, staggering into the hall.

"Will you tell me one last thing?" Her question came in the form of a plea that brought tears to her eyes. "Will you—please?"

He stopped without turning. "What is it?"

"*Why* am I here?"

He stood swaying in the darkness.

"Tell me, Mr. Gibson. Please tell me."

In a soft, low voice, absent any slurring, he replied, "He's a trader of goods, Miss Antonelli. That's all I can say." He continued down the hall and vanished into the darkness.

Zoey stood peering into the void behind him. Her heart pounded as her suspicions grew into a realization that she had to do something quick or else she too would become another transaction.

Back in her room Zoey sat contemplating her next move. One minute she was heading for the door, ready to chance it on her own in a city she knew so well in the future but in which she was a stranger now, in the past. Next, she was walking in circles mumbling to herself, ironing out the details of a scheme that would end with her in Mase's arms. She needed a little more patience, a solid foundation of deceit, and good timing.

Chapter 13

She awakened the next morning to the sounds of lumbering feet outside her door. “Miss Antonelli, are you awake?”

“Yes,” she muttered.

“Good. Mr. Vanderson is already here. Breakfast will be served in one hour and he asked that you be ready to leave directly afterwards.”

“Wait, what about leaving?” she said, staggering to the door. She tried opening it, but the knob would not turn. She tried again. “Gibson, open this door!”

A short time later she heard keys rattle, then a click, then the door opened with a timid Gibson peeking in. “Sorry, Miss Antonelli.”

“You locked me in! You snuck up here last night and locked me in?”

“It-it’s customary.”

“How on earth is *that* customary?”

“I’m sorry, Miss Antonelli. I really must see to breakfast.” He backpedaled to the steps. “Re-remember, one hour, Miss Antonelli.”

Zoey stood fuming as she watched him scurry downstairs like a scolded dog. Turning back inside, she looked to the window, the bars appearing and disappearing behind the curtains as they rolled with the breeze. With a stiff, right-handed jab, she sent the door slamming shut, her defiance echoing throughout the house.

An hour later she reluctantly made her way downstairs to the dining room where once again a single place setting had been laid. Replacing the Cornish hen dinner of the night before were plates of ham, sausage, and eggs, along with a basket of biscuits, a dish of assorted fruits, and a large bowl of grits.

Gibson stood at attention behind her chair, eyes bloodshot but steady.

"Where's the scotch?" she said snidely.

"No scotch, ma'am," the little man said, shaking his head, indicating his desire to keep his previous night's indulgence a secret. "There is, however, coffee, tea, juice, and water. Which would you prefer?"

"Water will be fine. Where is Mr. Vanderson?"

"Mr. Vanderson does not eat breakfast, ma'am."

"Where is he then?" she said, sitting down.

"He's preparing for the day, I assume. It's Sunday, after all."

"What does Sunday have to do with anything?"

"It's the only day of the week he doesn't work."

"And there I was thinking he was a full-fledged workaholic," she smirked.

Twenty minutes later she placed her fork upside down on an empty plate. "Thank you, Gibson," she said, showing him grace for incarcerating her the previous night. "That was a nice breakfast."

"My pleasure, ma'am. I believe Mr. Vanderson is probably waiting for you out front."

As Zoey walked down the hall, she could see him through the window standing on the sidewalk with his back to the house. Her pulse quickened with every step. Placing her hand on the doorknob, she hesitated as she thought through the role she was now to play. Then she slowly opened the door.

Hearing her step out, he turned, his smile growing larger as she walked toward him. "Good morning, Miss Antonelli," he said with a slight bow.

"Good morning, Mr. Vanderson," she replied in equal measure.

He held out his arm to her. "Will you walk with me this morning?"

"Certainly," she said and smiled.

Unlike the day before, the streets were serene and sparce of activity. The gentle breeze felt good against her skin while the morning sun warmed her back. There were no merchants haggling with customers or the clamor of businessmen rushing to and from work, only the sounds of a few carriages click-clacking off in the distance. On they walked, neither speaking as the previous day's events lingered without being addressed. Several times Boone parted his lips to speak but stopped. Several times she felt the urge to bring up the bars on the windows, the locked door, or what she had learned of him but stopped. On they walked in cordial awkwardness.

As they approached the next intersection, there appeared to be a migration of men dressed all in black, wearing top hats as usual, and the women dressed in similarly subdued colors, wearing mostly bonnets and carrying parasols, all ambling reverently in the same direction. As they approached the corner, Boone turned with the procession and fell in line behind an elderly couple snuggled together. Halfway down the block, the line bottlenecked in front of a small, one-story building tucked behind an iron fence and several large maple trees. As they got closer, Zoey spotted, through the branches, the sharp angles of an elevated roof. Several steps closer the trees gave way, revealing a stone facade with stained glass windows on either side of an arched doorway where a man in a white-collared vestment stood greeting people as they entered.

She tilted her head. "We're going to church?"

"Shh," he said, mirroring the solemn manners of the line ahead of them.

When they got to the gate, he stopped. "I wasn't sure, but I thought, with it being Sunday, you might want to be here."

"Why, yes, actually I would. But how did you know?"

He reached down and pulled up her sleeve, tapping his finger on the crucifix tattoo on her inner wrist. "Just a hunch."

She stared at him, befuddled by his observation.

"I'll be back in an hour," he said, releasing her arm.

"You're not coming in?"

"No," he said, turning his back to the church. "I-I…" He stopped. "Don't worry, I'll be back in an hour."

She watched him quicken his pace back through the crowd that had gathered behind her. As she walked through the gate, she turned her head and tried to find him, but he was already gone.

An hour later Zoey filed out of the church along with the rest the congregation. Several people passed by, glaring at her pink-striped hair, mouths gaping, while a few others wished her a blessed day or told her they hoped she would come back next week. Across the street she spied Boone sporting a boyish grin.

"You missed a wonderful sermon," she said, stepping onto the sidewalk.

"Let me guess. Be good to thy neighbor as thy would be good to thyself. Oh—and all's well that ends well."

"Phhht! That's pathetic. You got some serious Bible learning to be had."

"I swear, your way of speaking continues to confound me."

"And you, sir, should not swear." She doubled her stride, leaving him flat-footed several paces behind.

A second later he was by her side, leaning into her as they walked. "Are you happy now?"

"Why? Was I not happy before?"

"No. In fact, you were rather cold."

There it was, offered up on a silver platter. He had brought it up and now she could freely list her grievances. She filled her lungs, ready to unleash, when something tugged at her from behind. She stopped to find a little boy looking up at her.

"Mama says she likes your hair."

Across the street a young lady holding a Bible against her chest smiled at her.

"I gotta go now," the boy said, ducking his head and racing back to his mother.

"Thank you!" Zoey yelled after him. Turning back to Boone, her urge to explode on him evaporated, and she asked, "What was it you were saying?

"Nothing." He watched the little boy leap into the woman's arms. "When we return to the house, I have a request."

"What is it?"

"Would you go upstairs and change into the new attire Gibson has laid out for you?"

"You know, all these dresses you're buying for me remind me of a scene from a movie I saw once. There was this rich guy and there was this—"

His face went blank, stopping her cold.

"I-I mean scenes that touched me. Things I've seen other people doing for other people. Th-that's what I meant. I saw this rich guy one time—"

"Can you feel it?" he said.

"Feel what?"

"The bubbling babble. When you start gibbering, can you feel it building up like a wave and just can't stop it?"

She watched as his mouth crooked upwards, delighting in her gaffe. She had recovered well enough, but her crimson cheeks reflected her embarrassment. She was at his sarcastic mercy.

"Oh fiddle dee dee, there I go again." That was it, whenever in doubt, she would call upon Scarlett O'Hara to bail her out.

"What exactly is a *fiddle dee dee*?"

"Nothing, just something I say when my vocabulary runs dry."

Boone burst out laughing. "Well, whatever it means, would you do me the favor of changing your attire?"

"Of course," she said, relieved at being let off the hook.

Several minutes later they were back at the house. He waved her inside while turning to the street.

"Where're you going?"

"To prepare the carriage. I have someplace I want to take you. Hurry upstairs and change. I'll meet you back here in twenty minutes."

On her way up the stairs, visions of another prudish outfit waiting for her in her room made her shudder. Would the button count be more or less than her current twenty? Could she possibly button all of them within the twenty-minute time frame allotted her? Pushing the bedroom door open, she gasped. "What the…?"

Spread out on the bed like a two-dimensional starfish were her smiley face T-shirt and pair of jeans—a little weathered and stained, but every bit a delight to behold. Next to them lay a pair of canvas slippers with silver buckles atop a tan bow. Not her first choice in footwear but a million times better than the torturous knee-high laced boots she had been subjected to.

Escaping the confines of her Victorian garb invigorated her. With a spring in her step, she bounded down the stairs and out onto an empty front porch.

"How do you like them?" said Boone, appearing from around the corner on a lean, muscular black stallion with a smaller chestnut mare in tow. Gone were his top hat and funeral-black dress coat and polished shoes. Instead, he wore brown slacks tucked into knee-high riding boots and a loose cotton shirt with the billowing sleeves of a pirate. With broad shoulders and sitting high atop the magnificent horse, he was a striking figure of masculinity.

"What's all this?" she said, stroking the mare's neck.

His eyes twinkled. "This is Mildred. She'll be your transportation today. Or at least some of it. Have you ever ridden?"

"Are you kidding?" she asked, her voice rising. "I'm a member of a riding club in Long—" She caught herself before expanding on her skills at the Long Island riding club, knowing it would bring disastrous results. "I mean I've been riding for a *long* time."

"Good. Then hop on up and we'll be on our way."

Zoey grabbed the saddle horn, placed her foot in the stirrup, and swung her other leg over Mildred's back. The horse suddenly reared, but with the poise of a veteran equestrian, she leaned forward, remaining upright, and pulled the reins downward, sending the horse into submission.

"Well, now. I truly am impressed," Boone crowed. "I believe you do know your way around these beasts."

"Hush your mouth," she said, leaning down and patting her horse on the neck. "He didn't mean it, Mildred. You're not a beast."

Boone wheeled his horse around in a circle to face east. "Follow me, you sympathetic softy."

"Where're we going?" she asked as they trotted off down the street.

"Don't worry about it. Just ride and enjoy the city."

Being on horseback on a cool autumn day and in the comfort of her favorite jeans and T-shirt allowed her to do just that. As they made their way through the city, her fear of the unknown began to melt away. With Willow Creek firmly in her sights, she would try and enjoy whatever the day had to bring.

Along the way, Boone played tour guide, pointing out different buildings and places of interest. And although the dirt and filth were there, she somehow began to find it fascinating. She had tolerated history in college, but now that she was living it, things had changed.

An hour into their ride he turned down a narrow alley. "Can you see it?"

"See what?"

"The water."

Zoey squinted. Growing bigger by the minute was a small, glittering patch of light dancing across the street's narrow horizon. The closer they came, the larger it got, the flickering light show changing to an open expanse of whitecaps.

"Are you seeing it?" he asked.

"Yes… is that what I think it is?"

"Yes, ma'am. The Atlantic. Well, Hudson Bay to be precise."

"I love this part of Manhattan!"

A few minutes later they were trotting through the South Street Seaport amid the hustling wagons coming and going, unloading crates, barrels, and containers of all sizes onto great wooden sailing ships. All along the waterfront men toted and heaved goods to and from the vessels. Boone, giddy as a schoolboy, rattled on about every ship they passed, explaining its origin and purpose.

"You see those three, way over there?"

"The ones docked side by side?"

He brightened. "Those are mine. They're what are known as tea clippers. They're clipper ships used for transporting cargo as well as passengers. They're the ones I mentioned yesterday."

Zoey brought Mildred to a standstill. Her heart soared. On one of those ships, her plan would set sail.

Chapter 14

When they reached Boone's three ships, he slowed his horse to a walk with her ambling alongside. "This first one is named the *Santa Maria—*"

"Oh, oh—let me guess, the other two are the *Pinta* and *Nina*."

"Nice try, but no. The second one is *Guinevere* and the last one is the *Lady Anne*."

"They're beautiful. How many passengers can they carry?"

"Depends on how much cargo is being transported, but usually there're fifteen to twenty-five crew members. As far as the number of passengers, we only allow ten at most. And they do pay a pretty penny."

"Where do you sail them?"

"From the tip of Maine all the way to Key West. *Guinevere* has even done several voyages to the Caribbean and the *Santa Maria* has been to Liverpool a half-dozen times."

"If you were going up and down the East Coast, say to Key West, where might you stop along the way?"

He drew his head back. "Are you truly interested or just placating my fancy for the sea?"

"Oh no! I told you, I love the seaport, including everything that comes with it."

A sudden smile appeared, matching a chipper tone. "So you really like sailing then?"

"Oh yes! Horseback riding and sailing are two of my favorite things."

"Well, let's go then," he said, prodding his horse ahead. "It's time we indulge your second fancy."

From fifty yards away she could see his smile growing larger. "Giddyup," she yipped, sending Mildred into a full gallop.

No sooner than she had pulled next to him than two spry teenaged boys sprang up from inside a small sailboat docked next to the *Lady Anne*. One remained next to the boat at an uneasy attention while the other rushed to help her off her horse.

"What do you think of this little one?" Boone said, swinging his leg over his horse onto the cobblestone street.

"This one's yours too?"

"Yes, indeed. She's my favorite."

The boy turned to Boone, his chin raised proudly. "Everything's in order, sir. Would you like us to attend to the horses now?"

"Yes, please," he said, handing him the reins and whispering something in the boy's ear.

"Understood, sir." The boy then turned to the man next to the boat. "Come on, Lawrence."

The other boy raced off the dock and up to Zoey. "May I, ma'am?" he said, holding out his hand.

She placed the reins in his open palm, and the boys mounted their horses and galloped down an alley and out of sight.

"Shall we?" Boone said, holding out his arm to her.

"We're going sailing?" Her face glowed as she placed her hand under his elbow, letting him lead her down the plank to where the little sailboat bobbed against the dock's broad beams.

Next to the *Lady Anne*, the sailboat was a bantam-sized dinghy, even though it was a good thirty feet long and could accommodate four people. The polished chrome, brass, and shellacked decking with strong rigging and a pristine white sail reeked of luxury for its time. It was easy to picture the vessel fetching at least a half-million dollars at a modern-day auction.

"And what is this one's name?" she asked.

"She's *Little Tess*," he said, helping her aboard. "Ah, they did remember." He turned to a large plate of food, a carafe of wine, and crystal goblets sitting on a tiny table next to a large wooden wheel. "Go ahead and help yourself while I cast us off."

As she watched him untie the ropes and adjust the riggings, an uneasiness swept over her, something she had not felt all day until now. *Just enjoy the day*, she thought. *Remember the plan and everything will be alright.*

Suddenly a gust of wind filled the sail with a loud *pharump.* Boone sprang to the wheel and spun it hard right, gliding the boat smoothly away from the dock. A minute later they were clipping through the harbor, wind tossing her pink locks back over her ear. She leaned her head back and breathed in the salty air, cleansing her lungs of the stench of the city streets. The sun radiated warmth on her skin while the breeze caressed it, vanquishing the sudden wave of anxiety she had just felt.

An hour later Boone began to ease the tension on the sail as they reached calm water. Two miles out he released the sail all the way, letting the boat slowly glide to a stop. "This should be a good spot for a picnic, don't you think?"

"What? No island? No grass?" she joked.

"No island, no grass. Just the beautiful Atlantic." He held out his arms and exhaled. "And no people."

"I thought you were a people person?"

"At times, I suppose, but for the most part I would rather be out here or deep in the woods." He sat down and picked up a tray of finger sandwiches. "I had my boys make these for you."

"Thank you. You said, 'my boys.' Are they yours?"

"Yes."

"So you have been married?"

"I'm sorry, that was quite misleading. I call them 'my boys' because they work for me, and you saw how young they are, so there you have it—they're my boys."

"You should be more accurate, Mr. Vanderson, in your narrative. Miscommunication could get you in trouble someday."

He laughed, stopping to gaze at her with an intense curiosity. "What is it about you, Antonelli?"

"What do you mean?" she said, her mouth full of a bite of ham and cheese sandwich.

"Your way of talking. It's just different. With the exception of a few comments at the garden party, you have no airs about you, no prudish mannerisms or character of the typical lady of the day."

"At least you didn't refer to me as a lady of the night."

"That's just it!" he said, half-smiling. "You jest and you're direct with nary a flinch."

"Does it offend you?"

"On the contrary. I admire it. It's—well, it's refreshing." He shook his head. "And the way you handle yourself. The fact that you can fight. I've never seen anything like that. Girls don't fight and if they did, they certainly wouldn't fight like you."

As he prattled on with his admiration, she eyed the carafe of wine, remembering how she had taken advantage of Gibson's drunken state to manipulate him for information. With an overt fixation on the bottle, she awaited his offer to indulge that in turn would start her strategy in motion.

"Oh, would you like a glass of Merlot?"

She perked up. "Only if you'll join me."

"Of course." He grabbed the bottle, poured each of them a full portion, then sat back, balancing his glass on his knee while staring out to sea, occasionally sneaking a sheepish glance her way.

"Is there something wrong?" she said.

"No."

"Why aren't you drinking then?"

"Oh, yes," he said, suddenly concentrating on the rim of his glass.

"Go on then," she said, bringing her glass to her lips.

He followed suit, raising his with hers, then he surpassed her effort by downing half his glass.

"Well done!" she said, refilling his glass to the brim and raising hers again. "A toast. Here's to the mighty Vanderson sailing fleet."

"Here, here!" he said, then downed another half portion while she registered a single sip.

He extended his glass toward the open sea. "And here's to new beginnings."

After several more toasts Zoey sat holding her goblet between her knees, contently waiting for the wine's effects to begin. With several minutes of small talk behind them, her head began to sway in time with the easy rolling of the boat.

"You know what?" he chortled. "I think I'm rather tipsy."

"Really?"

He laughed. "I do believe I am."

Realizing the trigger point she had been waiting for had arrived, she began her questioning. "I do find your sailing fleet fascinating. Can you tell me more about it?"

"What would you like to know?"

"You mentioned they go up and down the East Coast. Do they ever stop in Charleston, South Carolina?"

"Sometimes."

"When would that be?"

"Usually on the longer runs when we're going farther down, like to Florida. But occasionally we'll do short runs there and back for special cargo schedules."

"Florida, you say. I've never been to Florida. Is it nice?"

"Too humid for my taste, but it's beautiful."

"Do you have any long trips down there anytime soon?"

"Unfortunately, with the exception of the *Lady Anne*, my ships are docked for the next couple months for repairs and upfitting."

She squeezed her glass.

"Every day they sit idle is another lost opportunity."

Zoey sat listening, crestfallen. "Yes, another opportunity lost."

"At least I have the *Lady Anne*'s junkets to keep me afloat. Sorry for the pun."

"What do you mean?"

"I said, 'keep me afloat.' It was a pun when I said—"

"Yes, yes, I got the pun. What did you mean about the *Lady Anne*'s junkets?"

"Those short trips I mentioned. She still has a full schedule of those."

Zoey patted her fingers together. "Any of them go to Charleston?"

"As a matter of fact, there's one going out tomorrow at noon, and then after that she's going up to Maine and back several times."

Inching to the edge of her seat, Zoey tidied her posture for the monologue she knew she had to nail. "Boone, may I ask a favor?"

"Of course."

"You know I have relatives in South Carolina."

"You did say that but—"

"I know you think I'm crazy because of my ramblings but it's true. I really do have relatives there. They're the Winslows and Mase Winslow is my cousin. He owns a large plantation in Beaufort, South Carolina, which is just outside Charleston."

"And you want me to take you there on one of my ships?" he said flatly.

Not expecting him to pick up on her ploy so quickly, a reply failed her. All she could do was nod. Her expression spoke what she could not.

Time stood still as her request hung in the air. The sounds of the gulls accented the silence as she watched him turning her plea over in his mind.

"And this would make you happy?" he said.

She clasped her hands together. "Oh yes! More than anything!"

"And then what?" he said.

"What do you mean?"

"What would you do then?"

The lie she knew she had to tell came harder than expected. She swallowed. "I would come back."

He put his drink down. "Really? You would want to come back to New York?"

The sudden desire to blurt out her true intentions of falling into Mase's protective arms caught in her throat. Her stomach churned. "I-I would come back, grateful for your generosity."

Looking into his eyes, she saw something that had evaded her until now—a longing, the anticipation of something she had reserved only for Mase. Was it lust or something else? She could not tell. She would, however, play it to her advantage. "I would come back."

Slowly, the corners of his mouth crept upward. "Very well then. Tomorrow at noon we'll go to Charleston."

"Oh, thank you! Thank you!"

"But first you have to answer one thing. How did you know about the bronze statue of Tweed? The idea only came up two days ago in private. Nothing has been released to the public."

"For heaven's sake. Think about where we were and all the loose lips flapping about that pompous garden party. One couldn't help but overhear it being passed about amongst all those gossipy politicians."

His face suddenly lit up as he exploded into laughter. "Of course, and there I was thinking you could tell the future." He paused then slowly leaned forward, following her pink strands of hair across her cheeks and next to her lips. He continued to draw closer. Zoey's heart raced at the scent of his cologne. Inches from her lips he tilted his head and lightly pressed his lips to her cheek.

"Time to head back," he said, smiling.

"Uh, yes, of course," she stammered.

He stood and walked toward the mast. Following him, she noted how the sun had dried his slicked black hair into full, wavy locks. Sipping her wine, she watched him bring the sail taut, the muscles in his forearms flexing with each pull of the rigging. Watching him move about the boat was a fascinating study in grace. While most men stumbled their way around their boats, he moved as if dancing with a lover. A moment later he was standing proudly behind the wheel, his hair waving freely in the wind.

He turned to her. "When we get back, I'll have to go out for the evening again, I'm sorry to say. More business, I'm afraid. But then tomorrow," he paused, his eyes glistening with the sun's reflection off the waves, "we sail for Charleston."

With an unexpected rush of gratitude, she watched him steer them back to shore. Pleased with accomplishing the first part of her plan, she smiled as the vision of Mase slowly took his place.

Chapter 15

The next morning Zoey awoke to the sound of curtains flapping violently as a grey mist blew through the room. Jumping up to close the window, she could barely hear Boone downstairs directing Gibson on the affairs of the day as shutters beat against the side of the house.

"I'll go tell her," she heard the little man say, followed by footsteps ascending to her room. "Miss Antonelli, are you up yet?"

She grabbed the doorknob and turned it, surprised to discover it unlocked. She opened the door just as Gibson was about to knock.

"Good morning, Miss Antonelli, Mr. Vanderson said to take your time. Breakfast is downstairs for you whenever you're ready, and he said you may wear whatever you wish but to bring your day dress."

"Not the one I wore to the garden party? The plain one?"

"I would hardly call it plain but yes, that one."

After a quick change she bounded downstairs in anticipation of the day's journey. Under her arm were her jeans and T-shirt.

"That was fast," Gibson said, ushering her into the dining room where another bountiful breakfast awaited. "I see you opted for the plain dress."

"I figured I should at least appear somewhat respectable, given the size vessel we're sailing on today."

Just then Boone entered. "Unfortunately, it doesn't appear we'll be sailing today."

"Why?" she said, slapping her hand against her leg.

He walked up to a set of plantation shutters and parted them. "This is why," he said, flinging open the window behind them. As a huge gust of wind whipped through the room, doilies flew off cabinets, the curtains into the hall thrashed against the walls, and a stack of napkins exploded into the air. He slammed it shut then turned around, his face dripping from the rain that had accompanied the wind. A crack of thunder provided the accent to the storm that was raging through the city.

"Unless this beast of a weather front decides to move along, the *Lady Anne* stays put."

"But—"

"I'm sorry. It's just not safe."

"Well, what if the storm passes by the end of the day or tomorrow? We can leave after that, can't we?"

"I'm sorry, but that would be altering the schedule too much. I'll lose out on this short run, but I have to fulfill what's scheduled after."

"Which is what?"

"Six junkets to Maine and back. The *Lady Anne* won't be going to Charleston for another two months."

She groaned. "Two months?"

"I'm sorry, there's nothing I can do. Trust me, I'm as upset as you." He turned and headed down the hall. As he opened the front door, the wind wailed through the house.

"I'm headed to the docks," he yelled. "I have to check the fleet." The door slammed shut.

Zoey sat with her head down as thunder clapped and sheets of rain pounded the roof.

"Aren't you going to eat, Miss Antonelli?" Gibson asked.

"I'm not hungry," she muttered.

"I understand. If you would like to eat later, just call me." Noticing the sudden change in her mood, he put his hand on her shoulder. "Don't worry, Miss Antonelli. There will be other days for sailing."

"That's it," she said. "I'll just call him." She turned to Gibson. "Where's your phone?"

"Phone?"

"Yes, yes, your phone. You've got a phone, don't you?"

"I'm afraid not, ma'am." He began to laugh. "I've heard of the invention, but having one… well, that would be impossible."

Zoey sighed, realizing phones would not be widely used for another decade. *Besides*, she thought, *who would I even call?* "What about the telegraph office? I could send a telegraph, couldn't I?"

"I assume you could, but why don't you tell me what you would like to do? Maybe I can help."

"Yes, of course. I need to get someone a message but I'm not sure what their address is. I just know the name of their plantation, the city and state."

"Why, that's easy. Just write your letter and I'll take it to the post office and have them deliver it. Now granted, it may take a few days longer because you don't have the exact address, but I am sure the name of the plantation will help them narrow it down and it should get there just fine."

"They won't send it back for not having the exact address?"

"Don't worry about that, Miss Antonelli. I'll be using Mr. Vanderson's connections to make sure the postmaster pushes it through. Being part of Boss Tweed's political circle comes with perks."

"Oh, Gibson, that would be perfect!" She wrapped her arms around him. "I think I'll give you that kiss," she said, planting her lips on his cheek.

The little man blushed a deep crimson.

"Can this be just between us though?" she asked.

"I would have to tell him, Miss Antonelli, considering I'll be using his contacts to push it through."

"I understand, but this is different. You see, he's taking me there, and in appreciation of his kindness, I want to surprise him with a party once we're there. The people on this plantation where we're going, they need to know we're coming. It has to be a surprise for Mr. Vanderson. Please, Gibson, pleeeease!"

"I-I really don't know."

"Trust me, he'll love you for it. He'll be making some very powerful connections through this, and you know how he loves connections." She stood awaiting his answer, amazed by and ashamed of the way her ability to lie had improved so much.

"Oh, alright." He angled his cheek up to her again. "Another kiss then?"

"Of course." To seal the deal this time, she delivered a prolonged, wet one on his left cheek followed by another on his right.

The little man stood fast with his head raised, eyes twinkling.

Breaking his trance, she tapped him on the shoulder. "Paper and pen, please."

"Oh, yes, you'll find both in the side table next to your bed."

"Wonderful!" she said, racing toward the steps.

"Don't you want breakfast?"

"No, thank you. I have a letter to write."

When she got upstairs, she opened the nightstand and found two pencils along with a small stack of paper under a beautiful leather-bound copy of *Pride and Prejudice.* As the torrential rain continued, she propped herself up on the bed and began crafting her message. A half hour later she scribbled out her name, kissed the paper, then placed it in the back of the book and pressed down for a proper crease. With her task complete, she opened the book to the first chapter and began reading. By the time she reached chapter three, her head was bobbing. Halfway into chapter four, she was fast asleep.

"Wake up!"

Zoey's eyes popped opened and flashed to the door.

"Wake up, Antonelli! We have to go."

"Wait—what?" she said, not yet fully roused.

"Are you asleep?" Boone's voice suddenly registered with her.

"I-I guess I was," she said, shaking her head.

"Come on. We have to go!"

"Go?" She suddenly realized the dull grey room she had fallen asleep in was now warm and full of light.

"The storm passed sooner than I thought. We can—"

She flew open the door. "What about the rest of your schedule? Won't it be messed up?"

"No, I also had some buffer time figured in that I forgot about, so we're okay to sail to Charleston."

"Well, what're we waiting for? Let's go!"

"We have to hurry," he said, taking her by the hand. "The Lady Anne leaves in a half hour. Grab your extra clothes. The carriage is outside waiting."

After grabbing her jeans and T-shirt, she held up the copy of *Pride and Prejudice*. "Can I bring this?"

"Of course."

A minute later they were in the carriage, clopping down the rain-soaked streets, the city temporarily cleansed of its dirt and filth, its corruption and vices still lingering in the gutters for the poor souls who remained. She turned ahead in anticipation of seeing the seaport and the vessel that would take them to her new future.

"Ahoy, Mr. Vanderson!" shouted a sturdy man in a long dark trench coat positioned at the top of the ramp going up to the *Lady Anne*. As he waved them aboard, smoke from a long, thin pipe circled his head, partly hiding a bulbous red nose set between a pair of squinty baby blues. "Didn't think you were going ta make it, sir."

Boone heaved a large duffle bag from inside the carriage out onto the street. A second later a man in a sailor's cap whisked it off the dock and carried it up the ramp.

"I'll be on deck in just a minute, Mr. Pettigrew." He turned to the great ship. "Hello, gorgeous."

Zoey scanned the object of his admiration from bow to stern. Overnight the ship had come alive. Sixteen sails of varying sizes now occupied the three masts that had been barren the day before. Colorful flags waved to the seagulls as they swooped in and out of the hundreds of taut ropes attaching sails to riggings. The air was full of chaotic chatter as men rushed about, tossing cargo to one another and occasionally commenting on the adventure ahead, seasoning it with the salty language of hardened sailors.

Boone turned to her. "What do you think of my ship now?"

She tilted her head back, climbing the main mast with her eyes. "She's incredible," she said, leaving her mouth hanging open.

"Let's get a closer look, shall we?" He took her under the arm and guided her up the gangplank where they met Mr. Pettigrew.

"Zoey, I would like to introduce you to Captain William H. Pettigrew. Captain, this is Zoey Antonelli."

"Pleasure to meet you, ma'am."

"Pleasure to meet you, Captain," she said with an abbreviated curtsy. "May we have permission to board this magnificent vessel?"

The captain slid the pipe to the corner of his mouth. From the other corner he said, "I like this one here, Mr. V." He threw up a stiff hand to the bridge of his nose and clicked his heels. "Permission granted, m'lady."

Boone tipped his head to the captain, acknowledging his playful token of formality. "Come, I'll show you to your quarters."

She trailed him across the deck, navigating through the myriad of ropes, pullies, kegs of rum and other provisions while weaving in and out of the frenzied swarm of crew members as they finalized the stowing of their gear and remaining cargo. Boone, wrapped up in the excitement of being aboard his beloved ship, failed to hear the guarded catcalls from the testosterone-rich sailors. Making sure neither he nor the captain could see them, several of the bolder men puckered their lips and blew kisses at her. Except for the officers, they were a mangy lot. Years of salt and sun had transformed their skin into thickly wrinkled, dark hides. Years of drinking, poor eating, and little oral hygiene had also stolen their smiles. She cringed as they flaunted their yellow gaggle of gapped teeth at her.

Boone raised his head toward the elevated platform at the rear of the ship. "It's a handsome bridge, don't you think? That's where the—"

"Captain commands from," she announced proudly.

"Oh, I forgot about your love of sailing." Taking her by the hand, he led her to a large dark hole a few yards in front of the bridge. "Now watch your step," he said, placing one foot into the darkness. With his other arm, he wrapped it around her waist and led her down a steep set of stairs to the ship's second deck. Small patches of light spilled out the doorways through the portholes from the cabins lining a long corridor.

"Here we are," he said, zeroing in on his duffle bag lying on top of a narrow cot suspended above another one by a set of ropes.

Zoey ducked her head inside. "And I thought my dorm room was tiny." She squeezed past him. Standing between a miniature dresser and the cots, she held her arms straight out, both hands coming close to touching the walls. "Wow! One could get lost in here," she said wryly. "Where's your cabin? Are you in the luxury suite under the bridge?"

"My dear, that would be the captain's quarters and therefore where the captain resides." He looked to his bag on the cot then back to her. "Hello, bunk mate."

"What? Don't you have your own cabin?"

"I'm afraid not. To my good fortune, in addition to being cargo heavy, we're also fully booked with passengers."

"But this isn't right!"

"We could always wait a couple months, when I would have the time to arrange for separate accommodations. The decision's yours."

"I guess it's fine."

"Relax, Miss Antonelli. It's only a day and half trip. You can put up with me for that long, can't you?" His right eyebrow arched upward. "Do you want to be on top?" he said with a sinister side glance.

"No, no, it's fine. I'd rather you be on top."

His left eyebrow sprang up to match the right one.

"Dad blame it, Mr. Vanderson, you take the top bunk." She shoved her way past him out into the hall, "And get your mind out of the gutter," she said before pounding her way back up to the main deck.

For the next hour she stood at the tip of the bow, as far from her cabin as possible. Gazing out over the harbor, her temper simmered as she admired how blue the storm had painted the October sky. In a few hours the temperature would drop, and she would have to go back downstairs and confront her temporary living conditions. Given her lack of options, she would have to be on her guard for the entire duration of the trip as Boone Vanderson's unpredictable nature continued to befuddle her.

Chapter 16

The ship's gentle rocking along with the sounds of the gulls proved to be the perfect combination to reduce Zoey's anxieties.

"I'm sorry," came a voice from behind her.

She turned to find Boone holding a blanket. "I thought you might need this."

"I'm fine," she said, resisting eye contact.

"I honestly didn't mean to imply anything. Well, actually I did. You see, I was just trying to make light of the situation and it just didn't come out as such and, well—I'm sorry is what I am."

She spun around with her head drawn back. "What an odd man you are."

Her words were direct, with a tone of certainty that stripped him of his bravado. He stared down at his feet and shook his head. "Yes, I-I suppose I am."

She stood contemplating his remark, once again taken aback by his unnerving duality of character. "Thank you," she said, taking the blanket with a side glance of suspicion.

He took a few paces toward the cabin then turned back. "The captain has invited us to dine with him tonight. That is, if you'd like."

"Yes, that would be nice," she said softly.

"Good, I'll be sure to vacate the cabin whenever you'd like to prepare."

She held her hands out by her sides. "Given my extensive wardrobe, lack of makeup, and no hairbrush, consider me ready."

"Untrue on all accounts."

"What do you mean?"

"We'll be heading out to sea in an hour. During that time, I need to be in the cabin with some work. Once we set sail, I'll be on deck. You'll have an hour after that to get ready in private." He turned and walked away.

As soon as the *Lady Anne* pulled away from the dock, Zoey headed for the cabin, passing Boone on the way with only a nod to acknowledge him.

Upon opening the door, the answer to his riddle was laid out on her cot. Next to her copy of *Pride and Prejudice* was the dress she had worn to the garden party. Beside it a small hand mirror and ivory-handled brush lay next to a delicately carved wooden box containing a small tin of rouge and other makeup essentials.

An hour later a knock came. "Miss Antonelli, I'm here to escort you to the captain's quarters."

She pushed the door open into the hall where a young sailor stood rigidly waiting. He smiled broadly at her, revealing a full set of teeth.

Pleased to see the first crew member with decent hygiene, she said, "You must be an officer."

"No, ma'am, but one day I will be."

"Well, keep brushing and you will be."

"Excuse me, ma'am?"

"Nothing. I'm ready. Lead away."

After passing through a dark alcove located directly under the bridge, the young sailor waved her up to a large teak door, grabbed the door knocker, and rapped it twice.

Before she could thank him for the escort, the door swung open. With his pipe cocked out the corner of his mouth, Captain Pettigrew said, "My heavens." Stepping back, he added, "I do believe we have an angel on board. Please come in, fair lady."

From the other side of the room, Boone appeared. The closer he approached, the farther his jaw fell. A lump formed in his throat. "Why, you-you look—you look… nice this evening."

"Come now, Mr. V, you can do better than that," said the captain before turning to Zoey. "My dear, you are indeed the most exquisite creature to grace these quarters, and on behalf of the tongue-tied Mr. Vanderson, we are charmed to have you dine with us tonight. Won't you please be seated." Just then a sailor appeared at one end of the table and pulled out a chair for her. "Shall we?" the captain said.

For the next two hours the conversation was jovial, filled with tales of the sea and how Boone and the captain had come to meet at a mutual friend's wedding. To her delight it was free of any incriminating or in-depth questioning that might jeopardize her plan or her sanity. Only on two occasions did the captain ask about her past and what she was doing in New York. Surprisingly, Boone interjected by deflecting the conversation to another topic. With a belly full of wine and the captain's personal cuts of prime rib, Boone thanked his ship's commander and bid him a good night. "Come, Zoey, let us leave the good captain to his task of getting us to your beloved Charleston."

"That I will, Mr. V.," he said as they walked to the door. "If my almanac proves correct, as she always does, there should be a full moon tonight." He nudged Boone's shoulder. "You wouldn't want to let Miss Antonelli miss that now, would you?" Stuffing his pipe, the captain lifted his head to the eastern sky. "The almanac never lies." He exhaled a large puff of smoke.

"Oh my gosh! You were right, Captain," she said as Boone led her on deck." Off the ship's port side hovering above the vast Atlantic was the biggest moon she had ever seen. Like an endless shimmering silver path, its light stretched across the glassy black water up and onto the *Lady Anne*'s bow. "It's so beautiful. It's like we could just walk out onto it and across the sea.

"You should join us," she added, turning to find the captain had disappeared back into his cabin. Except for two sailors stationed at the farthest ends of the ship, they were alone, accompanied only by the soothing rush of water cutting alongside the hull as they headed south. For several minutes they stood entranced by the most perfect backdrop nature had to offer.

Zoey folded her arms around her chest, rubbing her hands up and down her shoulders.

"You're cold, aren't you?" he said.

"I'm fine."

"No, you're not. I can see you shivering. Here," he said, wrapping his jacket around her shoulders. "The last thing we want is for you to catch a cold before you see your relatives."

"Thank you," she said. "I guess I was a little cold."

Silence permeated the air.

"That was a nice meal, wasn't it?" he finally said.

"Yes," she replied.

A minute later. "The captain's a fine fellow, don't you think?"

"Yes, he is."

He shifted his weight from one foot to the other. "Did you enjoy yourself?"

"It was nice."

Another moment passed as he turned back to the moon. "I really am sorry."

"I know," she said. "And I'm sorry for not being able to take a joke." She began fidgeting with his jacket's collar.

"Here, let me," he said, pulling it up around her neck.

"Thank you. I guess I was colder than I thought." She ran a nervous finger across the ship's railing, "I want to thank you for steering the conversation this evening. When the captain started to ask those questions about my past, you jumped in. I just want you to know I appreciate it. My past is… well, not exactly ideal."

"I just recalled that it didn't go well when I began my own interrogation."

"Yes, I can be rather—"

"Please don't apologize. I would've been the same way. I don't care for it when people try and pry into my past either."

"Yes, I recall how that went when I had my little rant about the meaning of happiness."

They both laughed and returned to gazing at the moon. A minute passed before Boone turned his gaze downward. "I don't think you hold me in high regard."

She hesitated. "I just don't know you is all. You don't like anyone to pry so I can't get to know you. I can respect that. I mean I just told you I don't like it either."

"Hmm," he said, angling his head toward her. "You know, we never finished our question-and-answer game, did we?"

"What game?"

"When we were in the carriage, you started this game. You asked a question, then I asked one, then you did. That game."

"Oh, yes. And as I recall that didn't end well either."

"I know but I guess I'm more open to it now. Maybe it's the wine—"

"Maybe it's the moon."

"Maybe it is," he said, slowly moving toward her. For a second, he held back then slowly leaned in.

"So should we play?" she said, quickly turning a cheek to him.

"Uh, yes, why not," he said, averting his eyes back to the moon. "You can go first."

She cleared her throat. "Let's see. Okay, where were you born?"

"Atlanta, Georgia," he replied immediately. "And where were you born?"

"Asheville, North Carolina." Then immediately she blurted, "Have you ever been in jail?"

"Oh, we're on to the hard stuff already, are we? The answer—no. My turn. Where did you learn to fight? Prison maybe?"

"No, silly. I learned in a dojo."

"What's a dojo?"

"It's a place to learn martial art."

"But where?" he asked.

"Did you forget the rules? No two questions in a row."

"Darn rules," he said, shaking his head.

"My turn again. Did you ever kill anyone in the war?"

"Yes." He cleared his throat. "Where did you get all your tattoos?"

"At a tattoo parlor," she smirked.

"Confound it, Zoey, you know what I mean."

"You've got to learn to play by the rules, Mr. V. And no, I don't know what you mean."

He feigned a sullen expression. "Go on, ask another one."

"Do you enjoy working for Mr. Tweed? And be honest."

"I did at first but…"

"But what?"

"No, not really—that's my answer. That's all you get. Remember the rules."

"Darn rules," she said, mimicking him. "Okay, go ahead."

"Have you ever been in love?"

The image of Mase next to the pond suddenly appeared to her. She bit her lip. "Yes. What about you?"

"No."

"Really?" she said.

"Really. Now it's my turn again." His focus fell to her right arm. "Why did you get all those tattoos?"

"Ohhh, we're back to the tattoos," she said, grinning. "You really want to know?"

"That's the purpose of the game, is it not?"

"I got them to mark milestones in my life. Each one represents a special occasion. If you want to ask about them, then each one will cost you a question."

"This game gets more complicated by the minute. I'll pass on the tattoos. Go ahead, your turn."

"Why did you name your ships as you did?"

"Aha! That would be four questions, Miss Antonelli. I'm catching on, aren't I?"

"Very impressive. Okay, I'll go with the little one named *Tess*. Why that name?"

"Tess is my little sister's name," he replied flatly. His eyes suddenly darkened as his thoughts went elsewhere.

"Boone—are you okay?"

"Yes, yes, I'm fine. Where were we?"

"Do you want to stop?" she asked.

"No, I'm fine. I'm just thinking of my next question." He skewed his lips. "Now no trickery on this one, okay?"

"Okay."

"When we first met, do you recall what you said?"

"Yes! That's a question that—"

"No trickery, I'm just qualifying that you remember is all. Is that fair?"

"Oh, I suppose."

"When we first met you said some things that were rather strange. You said you were in New York then South Carolina, that you were stabbed and died and that a stone brought you back and then you didn't know what year it was. Can you tell me what that was all about?"

As calmly as she could, she placed her hands in her lap and began her prepared answer. "I mentioned my past was not ideal. Unfortunately, when I was six years old, I fell off a stool and cracked my head open, causing my brain to swell. As a result, I've gone my whole life with constant headaches that are accompanied by wild lucid dreams that follow for several days. In this case I had a doozy, which resulted in the ramblings that followed." She studied him. "Why are you smiling?"

"Because I truly thought you were crazy."

"And now?"

His lips parted, his teeth shining brightly. "Maybe a wee bit."

"Are you getting tired yet?" she asked.

"I'm okay."

"Are you sure? They could get harder."

"It's not exactly the Spanish Inquisition. I think I can manage a few more."

"Okay then, here goes," she said, taking a quick breath. "You started to say something about working for Tweed. Why'd you stop?"

"Because—there you have it. *Because* is my answer."

"That's not fair and you know it. I promise to answer your next question in full detail if you'll tell me about working for Tweed. I promise."

He took a deep breath. "After the war I was bitter, as you can imagine. I had fought and lost with the Confederacy, and I lost everything—everything! It was…" He grimaced through a long, slow exhale. "It was the worst time of my life…" His breathing grew heavy, and he closed his eyes, pausing to collect his thoughts. After another long breath, he began again. "When Cody came to me about the job with Tweed, I didn't hesitate. I took it because it gave me the chance to come north, to where I could take from those who had taken from me. And there I've been ever since, smiling and charming them with my sweet Southern ways while covertly wreaking havoc on those I considered my enemies."

"What do you mean by 'wreaking havoc'?"

"If you didn't hold me in high regard before, I guarantee you won't after I tell you." He turned away, grabbing the ship's railing, his fingers curling around it like eagle talons. "I'm not proud of these years, but I have had to do what I've had to." His voice rose. "Cody was doing some of the same things, but he got out. They took his arm from him, but me…" His chin fell to his chest. "From me… they took everything!"

"What did they do to you?"

"No, I'm sorry. No more, okay?"

"Yes, of course. I'm sorry. I-I shouldn't have pressed."

For the next few minutes, they watched in silence as several small clouds drifted in front of the moon. "Look at them," he said. "There they are—the same size as the moon from here, but so tiny and insignificant in reality."

In a faraway voice she said, "I told you I got my tattoos to mark special occasions. Well, that's true but those special occasions, they weren't so special."

He was quiet for a moment then softly replied, "You really don't have to—"

"No, you shared with me. Now I'm sharing with you." She slowly pulled up her sleeve then ran her finger to just above her elbow. "You see this horse? He rode in to cover the scar from the cigarette burn my father gave me after he spent a night on the town with a hooker. These stars above it? They circle another scar he left in the same way after tearing my mother's arm out of its socket during a fight because she didn't put lettuce on his ham sandwich." She began to lower her head as she spoke. "And this little gemstone that I got to match the color of my eyes is really there to hide the stab wound I received from the kitchen knife he threw at me when I tried running away." Her voice quivered. "And this little peach here is—"

"That's enough." He placed his hand on hers. "I understand."

She peered up at him to find a sympathetic smile. His eyes were warm and caring, glistening with the emergence of tears she had thought him incapable of shedding.

Just then two new crew members popped up on deck, energetic and ready to replace their counterparts at their respective ends of the ship.

Boone and Zoey waited as the temporary hubbub of the switch calmed back to the serenity from before.

"I wonder what it's like to be a crew member on one of my ships," he said, indiscreetly wiping away a tear.

She laughed. "You know you have a great skill at deflecting at just the right times."

"Part of my bag of tricks. One doesn't do well in my line of work without a special set of skills."

"What are those skills?"

He put his hand to his head and started rubbing it. "I'm sorry, I think we should consider our game over for now. Maybe we should retire."

She started to realize how right his friend Cody was. The man in front of her was indeed teetering over the edge of an abyss. She would not press any further. "Yes, I believe you're right. Besides, it's gone from chilly to cold."

As they made their way downstairs, he stopped short of the cabin. "I want to thank you for the wonderful evening."

"You mean, you're not staying here tonight?"

"No, I've arranged to bunk elsewhere. I was afraid I might slip with another poor bit of humor and… well, you understand."

She leaned into him and kissed his cheek. "Thank you."

Boone's dimples deepened. "Good night, Miss Antonelli." He turned and vanished down the hall.

That evening Zoey dozed off with visions of Mase once again on the banks of the pond. But something was different. The faintest outline of someone or something standing behind him against the black backdrop of the pond slowly emerged. Whether it was on land or floating on the water, she could not tell.

Slowly it faded back into the darkness.

Chapter 17

Zoey awakened the next morning, the ship's gentle swaying trying to rock her back to sleep, when the sounds of heavy boots outside her door accompanied by murmurings about a mistaken stowaway caused her to sit up. She tiptoed to the door and pressed her ear to it.

"So there I am with me grain scoop in hand. I open the lid to the bin and lo and behold, there be a corpse—but weren't no corpse a'tall."

"Who was it, Danny?" came an eager second voice.

A snicker followed. "Laid out, stiff as three-day dried tuna with his hands crossed just like they be before dropping ya six feet under, was the man himself."

She pressed her ear closer.

"I liked to jump out of me knickers, I did."

"Who was it?"

"And get this…" A high-pitched giggle accented the pause in the storyteller's narrative. "The bloke had him an empty grain sack wrapped 'round him. Cuddling wid it like it was his blanky."

"Come on, who was it, for Pete's sake?"

"Then, all of a sudden his eyes flied open."

"Come on, Danny. Who was it?"

"Twas none udder than the money man himself." A hushed moment followed. "Twas Tweed's boy!"

Zoey threw her hand over her mouth.

"Now listen to me, Danny, don't go spreading this about. You know the tales."

"What tales might that be?"

"And whatever you do, don't be making light of it. I'm telling you, that man will—"

At the sound of boots coming down the steps from the main deck, the unknown gossipers scurried off.

"Miss Antonelli, breakfast is in the captain's quarters," came the voice of the young sailor who had escorted her to dinner the night before.

"Thank you. I'll be there shortly," she said, pulling on her dress. After squeezing the last button through its tiny hole, she interlocked her cramping fingers, flexed them outward, then headed to breakfast. Just as she was about to enter the captain's quarters, Boone emerged. His hair was a wild fluff of wavy locks, his eyes puffy and red from a night of restless slumber. Absent his regal air, he presented the tousled version of himself to her in a manner reserved for children who had been caught with their hand in the cookie jar. Still able to manage his customary bow, he said, "Good morning, you appear well rested."

"As do you," she said through a taut grin. "You know—I think I like your hair that way."

He rolled his head to his right shoulder, releasing an audible pop. "What way would that be?"

"Not so flat. Dry and full, like it is now," she said, avoiding commenting on his obvious discomfort.

"Hmm. Things to consider." He strained his head to the other shoulder. "Would you mind if I occupy the cabin for a few hours? I'm afraid I didn't rest well last night."

"By all means. If you'll let me go grab my book, I'll spend the morning on deck, reveling in Mr. Darcy and Lizzy's love affair."

"Of course."

Noting the tiny grains of wheat matted into his jacket, visions of him crammed into a coffin-sized storage bin conjured images of Dracula in a stove pipe hat. "Have a good rest," she said backing away.

After finding a secluded spot near the ship's bow, she eased into the center of a wound-up pile of two-inch-thick rope and leaned back against the inside of the hull, the constant rocking of the ship creating the perfect spot for her literary retreat. Rather than diving into her book, she laid it in her lap and daydreamed about her and Mase gazing upon each other after over a century apart.

She glowed as she envisioned them sitting next to the pond holding one another, kissing and laughing. Just as Mr. Darcy had professed his love to Lizzie in *Pride and Prejudice*, Mase would do the same with her. How perfect they would be together, both writers with an extraordinary story to tell. Together they would use their literary skills to craft the perfect masterpiece. No greater romance would ever be written. The preface would begin with the letter she had tucked away in the last chapter of the very book that lay in her lap. Eager to reread it, she flipped to the back, only to find it empty. Clutching her chest, she ripped through the pages in search of the missing sheet.

"Ma'am, do you need anything?"

Her gaze fell from her pages onto a pair of scuffed-up boots which she followed upward until her eyes came to rest on the leathery face of an old sailor.

"You seem like you needed something," he said.

"I do. I mean I lost something."

"Want me to help you find it? It can't be far. We're on a ship, after all."

"I'm sure it will turn up. Thank you though."

"Here, use this," he said, pulling out a two-foot-square piece of fur from behind his back.

"What is it?"

"It's a piece of a grizzly's pelt." He pointed across the deck toward two bashful young sailors fidgeting with a length of rope. "Some of the young fellas thought it'd make things a little cozier for you."

She nodded her appreciation to the sailors who promptly turned their blushing faces out to sea.

"Let me know if you need help looking for whatever it is you lost." He tipped his cap. "Good day to you."

"Thank you," she said, wedging the fur between her neck and one of the hull's large, curved beams.

As he walked away, her thoughts returned to her missing letter. If she lost it, so be it. She had plenty of material to work with anyway. She closed her eyes and began replaying everything that had led up to where she was now. Nestled into the side of the hull with a gentle breeze and the undulating rhythms of the ship to comfort her, she soon fell asleep.

Off in the distance, amid cawing sea gulls and chatting sailors, came the sound of a bell. One ring sounded followed by a rapid succession of clanging notes. Zoey jerked upright. The sun that was just over the horizon when she fell asleep was now directly overhead.

"Have a nice nap?" asked a sailor hobbling past her toward the stern.

"If you want lunch, you might want to get crack'n, missy," said another one coming up from behind.

She rolled her shoulders and squinted up at the sun, confirming her little siesta had spanned at least three hours. With the rumblings in her stomach verifying she had missed breakfast, she headed toward the stern where a lunch line had formed on deck and flowed down into the ship's galley. Realizing she had left her book, she ran back to retrieve it. From over her shoulder a voice rang out, as jarring as the bell that had awakened her.

"Antonelli!"

Shoving his way through the line of hungry sailors, Boone came toward her, his head down, his strides long and purposeful. Clenched in his fist was a piece of parchment flapping against the back of his hand. The closer he got, the faster his pace and the dourer his expression. Suddenly he was a foot in front of her. Gone were the soft, caring eyes of concern from the night before. In their place was a penetrating glare that caused her to step back. She instinctively knew that look to be part of his skills of which he would not speak. His chest rose and fell like a bull ready to charge.

"What's wrong?" she said.

"This," he said, dangling the paper in front of her face.

"My letter? You found my letter?"

"What a witch you are—a deceitful, maniacal, conniving witch."

"What?"

"Or maybe you're just insane. Just like I thought you were."

"I-I don't understand."

Taking the paper in both hands, he began to read. "My dear Mase, I am sure this letter will be a shock to you, given it is coming from me. More than ten years in the form of a century have passed between us. I never thought I would have to use it—or that it would work—but thanks to the stone, here I am in New York and on my way to you. I will be in Charleston on the sixth of October on a clipper ship owned by a man named Boone Vanderson. Can you please be there for me? So much to tell you but too little time. I long to be with you again. Love, Zoey." He released the paper, letting if flitter to the deck, stomping his boot heel into it, putting her words out of their misery.

She gulped, staring wide-eyed at him, waiting for the volcanic eruptions she saw growing in his face.

A crevice deepened between his brows as he began his interrogation. "'More than ten years in the form of a century have passed between us? You never thought you would have to use the stone'? What kind of gibberish is this?"

"It-it's just too hard to explain," she stammered.

"Is this the result of one of your made-up headaches again?"

"No! It's-it's…" Her mouth locked up. Trying to explain the miracle of the stones was beyond comprehension, even to her. All she could do was stand with her arms hanging by her sides, her palms opened to him, hoping for mercy.

He snatched the letter from under his boot, boring into it then up at her.

The wind, the gulls, the murmur of the crew from around the deck, even the flapping of the sails fell away as she stood waiting.

In a low, gravel-filled voice, accenting each syllable with more anger than the one before, he reread the line she had toiled over. "I long to be with you again." He grimaced with such intensity she grabbed the railing for fear of being tossed overboard. Then stretching out each word through clenched teeth he read, "Love—Zoey." Holding the page in front of her, he crumpled it into his fist then flung it into the sea. Turning on his heel, he began to walk away then suddenly spun back toward her. "So when exactly do you think your Mr. Winslow will be in Charleston?"

"He won't be," she said, her voice quivering. "The letter, as you can see, was never sent."

"So how will you get to his plantation? Is that something you expected of me? Is that just another way of using me? What would you have me do—put a bow on you and deliver you like a present to your lover?"

Suddenly all the pent-up anger and frustration of having to be bound and subservient to him surfaced. Her cheeks flushed red as she stared daggers into him. "Hold on just a minute, you two-bit shyster. You're the one who bought me off a pig farmer, dressed me up like a doll, and paraded me around in front of a bunch of your low-life political cronies." Her chin jutted out, exposing the bottom row of teeth. "And how dare you lock me in that gilded cage until you got up the nerve to do God knows what with me?"

Boone stepped toward her, his lips drawn tight. "Why, you little—"

"What? You think I don't know what you want? You-you…"

He moved to within inches of her face, the dimples in his cheeks flattening as he gnashed his teeth.

She arched her head back, looking down her nose at him in defiance. "Go on, I dare you!"

He licked his lips as he slowly leaned forward. His breath whispered across her cheeks as his lavender cologne filled her nostrils. Her heart pounded.

Suddenly his eyes softened. His lips parted. He leaned closer then stopped. A moment passed. "The ship docks in four hours. Have your items ready and be prepared to depart one hour later." He turned and began walking away.

"Go ahead—just-just leave!" she yelled after him. Unable to complete her thought, she stomped her foot and groaned in frustration. Grinding her teeth, she watched him disappear into the line of sailors. Exasperated, she fell back into the pile of rope, bewildered by her feelings and more troubled by the uncertainty of what now lie ahead.

Chapter 18

As soon as the Port of Charleston was sighted, the ship became a buzz of activity. Ropes were pulled and wound up, winches turned, and sails loosened. By the time it drifted up against the dock, it had become an exercise in choreographed chaos. Sailors rushed back and forth, tying and loosening huge ropes, sails came furling down from their masts in huge waves of white canvas. Officers' bellowed orders filled the air as beleaguered crew members humped their way up from the bowels of the ship carrying cargo, which they dumped at the foot of a massive, barrel-chested man who picked up the items and passed them to another large man behind him. So the process went among another ten men until the items finally reached land where another group of men stacked them onto growing heaps.

Zoey almost tripped as she dodged in and out of the organized madness, trying to find a place she would not be trampled or knocked overboard.

"Stand over here, ma'am," a young crew member said, ushering her to a vacant three-foot space behind a large keg of rum rolled against the ship's hull. "When we come for that there keg, we'll be done." He winked at her. "It's where we head to celebrate."

"Thank you, you boys deserve it," she said, preoccupied with her attempt to locate Boone. Although she had purposefully avoided him for the last four hours, she knew she would need to find him. Tapping her fingers on the top of the keg, she thought, *But then again, why wait? Why even try to find him?* She was in Charleston, and he was nowhere to be found. She could just leave. She had been planning to ask him to help her with the rest of the journey, but that was certainly not going to happen now. Besides, waiting on him meant being at his mercy yet again. Leaving now made perfect sense. She would hitch rides on wagons, hop train cars, or walk. Even if she had to walk the entire way, she figured she could do it in a week's time. Whatever it took, she would make it to Willow Creek.

Emboldened by her decision, she rushed to her cabin, grabbing a burlap sack along the way. In one fell swoop she swiped her two sets of clothes into the bag, along with the makeup box that was hidden underneath. Back on deck she wove through the frantic cargo transfer. Confident Boone was not on deck, she worked her way down the gangplank, holding her breath as she ducked behind two crew members carrying a large crate on their shoulders. The second her foot touched the dock, she exhaled. The men and their crate continued on, leaving her standing suspiciously alone in the middle of the horde of burly sailors. She turned in a circle. Still no Boone.

Just forty yards ahead was a small newspaper stand with a half-dozen men huddled over a table in a heated conversation. Next to the stand was her escape route, a small alley. Once she made that turn, she would be out of sight and free at last. Tucking her bag under her arm, she began walking toward it at a pace teetering on a run.

Her eyes flew back and forth, checking her perimeters for Boone or anyone else who might impede her way. As she got closer, she could hear the men's argument escalating. Within twenty yards her senses heightened as she noticed their voices tapering off with each step she took. She swung to the far side of the street. With an indiscreet turn of the head, she noticed one man's head rise from the huddle in her direction, just as a predator would, catching wind of its prey. Quickening her pace, she continued to monitor him. Just as she was about to make the turn, his mouth fell open and he extended his arm toward her. Seeing him direct his index finger at her, she dropped her bag and sprinted toward the alley, running smack-dab into the chest of a leather-vested cowboy. Back she stumbled over the bag she had just abandoned.

"Excuse me, ma'am?" A voice rolled down on her in a slow raspy drawl.

She looked up at an aging frontiersman, the kind she had only read about or seen in movies. In addition to his spurred boots, chaps, and gloves, he wore a red bandana around his weathered neck. His face was broad, with high bony cheeks hovering above a white mustache that fell two inches below the corners of his mouth then curled up into twisted points. His upper lip was nowhere to be found underneath it. The trail was still with him—he was covered in dirt and dust. Through the narrowed slits of deep-set eyes, a twinkle appeared as he suddenly produced a show-stopping, yet shaky bow, which he accentuated by pulling off his dirty brown Stetson and swinging it behind him in an exaggerated swoosh. With his head bent to his waist, he held an unsteady pose. "May I have this dance?"

She stepped back from the curious proposition. "Wha—"

"Allow me to introduce you," came a voice from behind the man still struggling to maintain his balance as he awaited her reply.

Her chest tightened as Boone walked from behind him. "Logan Crenshaw, I would like you to meet Zoey Antonelli."

"Phewwww… I thought I was gonna be down there forever." The cowboy straightened up with a groan, pulled off his glove, and offered a callused hand to her. "Pleased to meet ya, Miss Antonelli."

"Uh, yes, pleased to meet you as well."

"So, Miss Antonelli," Boone said, "it appears you already have plans for making your way to your plantation. Excuse me—your Mr. Winslow's plantation."

"Well, no, not exactly."

His jaw tightened. "Then I assume you were venturing out for a sightseeing trip of Charleston."

"No, I-I was just—"

"Mr. Crenshaw, would you pardon us? I need to speak with Miss Antonelli in private."

"Why sure. I need to attend to my wagon anyway. I'll be at the livery. A reminder though—a half hour, if ya please." He turned to Zoey, took her hand, and kissed it. "Ma'am, I'll be seeing ya soon."

As soon as he turned the corner, Boone wheeled back to her with a look in his eyes that was surprisingly vacant of the anger she knew raged inside him. He pursed his lips. "I'm sorry I found the letter. I suppose it was for the best. More than anything I'm sorry you feel as you do. You think me a monster, but you don't know me. And I certainly don't know you."

"No, you don't, but—"

"It doesn't matter now."

"I wish I could tell you the whole story, but you wouldn't believe me. You would think I truly was mad."

"Again, it doesn't matter."

"But—"

"Enough," he said, holding up his hand. "When I said I wanted to help you, I meant it. I've arranged for Mr. Crenshaw to take you to your Willow Creek destination."

"What?"

With an outstretched finger, he led her down the alley that was to be her escape route. "You see the sign that says Cagon's Livery? That's where you need to go. He has a wagon boarded there. In thirty minutes, he's heading to Georgia, but I've paid him to make a detour that will take you to Beaufort first. You should arrive there on the eighth, two days from now."

"I know you think I'm crazy, but if there was anything I could do or say to make you believe my story, I would. It's just not possible. It's too much."

"Yes, that and the fact that you and Mr. Winslow are in—" He abruptly stopped. "I have to go now." He started to walk away then stopped. "I'll miss you, Zoey." Placing his top hat on his head, he turned and headed to the *Lady Anne*.

A tinge of unexpected sadness fell over her as she watched him disappear into the crowd. As quickly as it had come, however, it vanished. In only two days, she realized, she would be with Mase. From out of nowhere, a muddy thought, distant and blurry, suddenly cleared, rushing to her with the clarity of a crystal-blue stream.

"The eighth of October," she muttered. "Yes, it *was* the eighth." Should she tell him? He wouldn't believe her anyway, plus there was no point in it. He was simply a means to an end. She had put up with his fluctuating moods and the uncertainty of his motives, and in turn, she had been granted a ticket to happiness. She shook her head, trying to dispel the idea she had an obligation to tell him, only to be overcome with a sudden desire to tell him. Tossing her bag at the alley's entrance, she ran toward the *Lady Anne*. "Wait!" she shouted. "Wait!"

Boone retreated a step as she came barreling toward him.

"You said I would arrive on the eighth," she said, panting and holding her side. "The eighth of October, correct?"

He inhaled slowly then exhaled one short, frustrated breath. "Yes, the eighth of October."

"And it's 1871. You said that, right? It's 1871?"

He rolled his eyes. "Yes, it's 1871."

"Okay then," she said, bouncing on her toes. "I know how you can trust me. I can tell you what's going to happen two days from now. Something big and there's only one way I could have known it."

He turned his head from her as if being presented with a piece of spoiled fruit.

"I know that sounds crazier than all the gibberish you think I've been telling you, but you have to hear me out!"

"Go on then," he groaned.

"In two days, something's going to happen, something huge—"

"Might I remind you that you have less than thirty minutes until your escort leaves."

"In two days, on October eighth, there will be a fire in Chicago. It'll be the largest the country has ever experienced."

"And *how* exactly will this fire start?"

"A cow!" she squealed in delight.

"A what?"

"A cow, an everyday barnyard cow will start it!"

Boone stood slack-jawed.

"A cow owned by a woman named O'Leary will knock over a lantern and that's how it starts." She ran her hand through her hair, recalling all the trivia she had picked up while researching Boss Tweed. "Hundreds of people will be killed, over a hundred thousand will be homeless, tens of thousands of structures will be destroyed, millions of—"

"I get it. A big fire will happen in two days." His lips tightened over his teeth.

"I know you don't believe me. And I totally understand. But in two days' time, I'm telling you—this—will happen."

He hung his head, releasing a tempered sigh before turning back to his ship. "I have to—"

"Time travel," she blurted.

"What?"

"That's how I know."

"I don't understand."

"I know you don't. I wouldn't either, but it's true." She glanced to the alley then back to him. "I may never have the opportunity to explain it, but just know when the fire burns down half of Chicago, you'll know I had to have some way of predicting it. I'm not a psychic either. It's because of where I'm from and the things I've been through. All those things I said, those *ramblings* as you call them, will all make sense in two days."

He was speechless, astonished at the degree of lunacy her tales had dipped to. "You mean to tell me…" He placed his hands to his head, massaging his temples. "I'm sorry, I have a ship to attend to and you have a wagon to catch." He started to turn away until she grabbed him by the sleeve.

"You'll see. I swear—you'll see!"

His eyes fell on the wadded piece of his sleeve in her fist. "Please release me."

Her palm flew open. "I'm sorry, I didn't…" She took a step backwards. "You'll see—I swear, you'll see."

He began inching backwards, examining her as one would a rabid dog. With no hint of emotion, he took one step then stopped. "I really am sorry." Without further hesitation he turned and walked away.

"You'll see!" she screamed. "Two days. You'll see!"

Not wanting to chance being left, Zoey ran all the way to the livery stable where Logan sat holding the reins to a canvas-covered wagon with a two-horse team. Behind him were another two horses hitched to a dark wooden, rectangular box on wheels that resembled a mobile jail cell—complete with a barred window in a small rear door bolted shut with a long iron bar and fist-sized padlock. Manning the jail cell was a man in a natty, dark-grey tweed jacket and a large-brimmed hat tilted downward, hiding his face.

Logan smiled warmly as she bounded up to him.

"Nice to see ya, Miss Antonelli. Let me help ya up?" he said, reaching down to take her hand.

She placed her hand in his leather glove. With a hefty pull she was climbing on board next to him.

A sliver of teeth was visible below his substantial mustache. "I'm pleased that you'll be my riding partner today. Are ya excited?"

"You can't even imagine," she said, searching for a place to store her bag.

"Just toss that in the back with the rest of our treasures."

"Wow, that's a lot of supplies," she said, gawking at what appeared to be a month of provisions.

He laughed. "Sure is."

As she finished placing her bag behind her, she caught a glimpse through the opening in the back of the man on the wagon behind them. His head still hung low as if he were nursing a hangover or tired from some ordeal. In his lap he held the reins with two colorless hands.

"Giddyup!" Logan yelped, snapping the reins.

The wagon lurched, and she pitched backwards.

As they started down the street, she looked over her shoulder. "What type of wagon is that behind us?"

"I believe they call it a *Black Maria.* I hear they use 'em to tote prisoners around then sell 'em as cargo wagons 'cause they keep the weather out so good."

"Is it yours?"

"No, it belongs to the fella driving it. He's coming along for protection."

"Protection?"

"Yes, ma'am. He came up to me just a bit ago wanting to know if he could tag along. It's always good to travel in groups—especially along the lonesome trail we're tak'n. Besides, he seemed to be the type who knows how to use a gun. And me being a little advanced in years, it's always good to have a young buck by your side."

"How come it's falling behind?"

"I'm sure he'll be along shortly."

Zoey watched as the *Maria*'s driver started to raise his head then dropped it again. He tugged at the brim of his hat, his chalky white hands pulling it down, securing his anonymity. Slowly, he and the repurposed jail cell faded back into the distance.

Chapter 19

By the time they were out of the city, the *Black Maria* was nowhere in sight. The sounds of sea gulls and sailors were slowly replaced with the harmonious swishing of leaves as a tender wind wisped through the evergreens, Charleston's sandy soil slowly changing to red clay as the wagon ambled along.

"Mr. Crenshaw, how do you know Boone?"

"If you'll call me Logan, I just might tell ya," he said with a wink.

"Sorry, Logan," she said cheerfully. "How do you know Boone?"

"I've done a few jobs for him in the past. Basically, haulin' cargo from his ships inland. Stuff like that."

"So you know his boss?"

"Tweed? Yeh, I know him. Can't say I cotton to him, but yeh, I know him."

"So you've worked for him too."

"Only once and that's the way it's going to stay. In fact, this is the last job I'm gonna do for Mr. Vanderson too."

"Do you not like Boone or what he does?"

Logan raised his chin and appeared to gaze into his future. "It's my last job, missy. I'm retir'n."

"Well, congratulations," Zoey said.

"Yep. I'm push'n toward seventy years on this earth and it's time this old crow went home to roost. Me and the wife are settl'n down on a parcel of land down in Texas. A little ranch where my daughter can also raise her baby girl." The tips of his mustache rocketed up, revealing the smile of a man whose world revolved around his family. "Oh, ya should see that little nugget, Miss Zoey, the most precious baby girl God could ever grace us with."

"What's her name?"

"Tabitha Jane. She just turned three. We call her Tabby."

"I'll bet Tabby's got you wrapped around her finger."

"Wound tight with a hook, line and sinker attached," he laughed. "She'll melt yer heart, she will." He slowly swung his head side to side. "You know she can already count to ten. And soooo happy. If she ain't giggl'n about someth'n, she's outright cackl'n loud as her mama. I truly don't think I've heard that sweet child cry more than a dozen times." He stopped and sighed. "Oh, how I can't wait to be sitt'n on my front porch rock'n that little gal to sleep."

Zoey smiled. "Now that's a picture of happiness everyone should have."

"Yep. It's a pure shame everybody can't have it."

"What do you mean?"

"I mean that some folks don't seem to want it. Ya know the type. The ones who got it handed to 'em and all they do is complain or ruin what they been given. Rich folks mainly. Then there's those who got it ripped from 'em—like Mr. Vanderson—and there's those who're only happy when they're unhappy. You know the type, they're always—"

"Wait! What do you mean?"

"Just that some folks seem to be born unhappy and—"

"No—you said Mr. Vanderson. What'd you mean when you said he had it ripped away?"

"You don't know?"

"No."

"Oh. Well then, I-I don't know if I should be say'n anything."

"No, tell me. Please, Logan. I need to know."

He took a slow breath. "It's the dang war's fault is what it is."

"How?"

"Saddest thing I ever heard. You see, Mr. Vanderson got run over pretty good during the war—like a lot of us—but then there's him and his story."

"And…"

"Lost everything. Renegade Yankees burnt his farm and killed his family."

"Oh no!" she said, placing her hand to her chest.

"Killed 'em all, I hear—his pa, big sister, even her baby girl. Lucky for him he was somewhere else. I think he was off on his uncle's farm help'n with a harvest." He shook his head. "Damn shame."

Zoey bounced hard in her seat as the road transitioned into little more than a rutted path. As the sun waned over the western horizon, she stared blankly into a melancholy sunset of deep purples and burnt oranges, Logan's words lingering with her. The falling leaves and crisp autumn air combined with the knowledge of Boone's loss made her heart ache. He had not been lying. He truly had lost it all.

"Ya okay, missy?"

"Yes," she said in a somber tone.

"I know ya gotta be tired."

"A little."

"We'll be stoppin' for the night soon. We got a smidgeon of travel light left, then we'll be makin' camp and ya can get some rest."

"Whoa, ladies," Logan called out an hour later as he reined his horses to an abrupt halt, almost sending Zoey flying over the buckboard.

"Sorry about that. Didn't mean for ya to disembark just yet. Hang on a minute and I'll help ya down…" He turned to find her already on the ground, bent over and touching her toes, trying to stretch away the miles of road. She turned side to side then rolled her shoulders and neck with a groan. "Never been this stiff and achy. Would you happen to have any aspirin? I've got a terrible crick in my neck."

"Any what?"

"Aspirin? You know, it's for—oh, never mind. Say, where's the other wagon?"

"Don't worry, missy, I'm sure he'll be along shortly. Right now, we need to get ya some vittles, and if yer up for a little snort, I got some of my dearly departed granny's corn liquor in the back. It'll take care of those aches of yers. Lord knows these old bones need it too."

"Thank you, but I'll pass. Nothing but bad experiences with that stuff."

"Suit yerself. I'll start us a fire and get some grub goin'. I don't know about ya but I'm starvin'"

Forty-five minutes later they were sitting around a campfire watching a slab of pork roast over a fire.

"Logan, how come you haven't asked anything about me?"

"None of my business." He paused. "I mean the hair, them tats and the funny shirt seem like they got a story for sure but hey, I ain't one to be a nosy Gus."

She laughed. "Well, I've got one left for you. Do I sleep under the wagon or next to a tree or what? I'm new to this camping-out thing."

"Best place for ya is in the wagon, and I'll be under it so that…" He cupped his hand around his ear as if listening for something off in the distance. "If these ears don't deceive me, I do believe our molasses-paced friend is just over the ridge."

A moment later the *Maria* appeared from out of the darkness. Instead of pulling up close to them, it stopped under a large oak tree forty yards away. The anonymous driver motioned for Logan to come to him.

"Dad blame it. What's he think we got—a plague or somethin'?" He started toward where he had been summoned. "I'll be back in a minute."

Zoey watched the elderly cowboy's image fade into a shadow next to the *Maria*. Even in the dark she could see the other man's white hands waving about as he engaged in a muted conversation that for some reason had Logan pacing in circles. Unable to hear much above the crickets and croaking toads of the forest, the word *no* broke through the muffled exchange several times followed by more of Logan's pacing. Twenty minutes later he reappeared into the firelight, shoulders hunched, both hands stuffed into his pockets.

"Is everything alright with… Excuse me, what's his name?"

"Dag."

"Dag? That's his name?"

"Yeh, just Dag."

"Is he okay?"

"Yeh, yeh, everything's fine." His voice went flat. "Just iron'n out the rest of the trip is all."

"Are you okay? You look a little shaky."

"I'm fine. Just tired and hungry. Why don't ya cut us off a slab of meat and I'll get some water from the wagon."

"Want me to fix some for your friend?"

"He ain't my…" His voice trailed off with a sigh. "Sure, yeh, cut him off some. I'll be back with the water."

"Are you sure you're okay?"

"Yeh missy, I'm fine. Like I said, I'm just tired and hungry. Go on now, carve me up a piece."

Zoey watched Logan move toward the wagon, his head appearing lower, his gait slower. He was old but seemed older after his conversation with the socially averse Dag. She looked back at the *Maria,* anticipating the driver's approach, but there was only darkness.

Meanwhile, on the opposite side of the wagon, Logan was filling two tin cups with water from a large barrel strapped to the side. After filling the second one, he reached into his pocket and pulled out a glass flask of amber liquid. Holding it above the mug, he tilted it down, then jerked it back as a line of sweat formed across his forehead. He stood glaring at the tin vessel, his hand shaking. He squeezed his eyes shut but opened them a moment later as a tear rolled down his cheek and disappeared into the bristly hairs of his mustache. Slowly he lifted the flask above the cup, hesitated, then turned it upside down. "Furgive me, God," he muttered as the liquid spilled into the water.

By the time he returned to the campfire, Zoey had three wooden plates piled high with pork along with a small helping of pinto beans.

"Wow, this pork is some kind of salty," she said, rocking contentedly on a log she had fashioned into a chair.

"Yep."

"Do you want me to give Dag his plate?"

"No, no… uh… I'll take it to him in a minute. He'll be okay if we go on without him."

Zoey glanced toward the *Maria.* "Definitely an introvert."

"What's that?"

"Oh, nothing," she said, lifting her mug. "A toast, Mr. Crenshaw—I mean, Logan. Here's to you for taking me to Charleston. Thank you for your kindness and hospitality. And here's to your sweet Tabby. May your retirement be filled with nothing but love and happiness."

Within seconds Zoey had downed her cup and was wiping her mouth. "A little bitter but good enough to quench a thirst. All that salt was making me so dehydrated."

Logan sat with his head down, eyeing his plate.

"Aren't you going to eat?"

"Lost my appetite," he said, placing his plate on the ground.

"But I thought you were…" She blinked, then began rolling her head from side to side. "Wow, that's amazing. I don't feel achy anymore. The crick in my neck is gone completely. In fact—I feel great!"

Logan poked the fire with a stick, sending sparks floating into the sky.

"Ohhhh wow! Lightning bugs. They're everywhere," she said, peering up at the sparks flittering about. "They're so beauteeeefulll. Everything is so beauteeeefulll. I didn't know the outdoors could make you feel so good." She put her hands to her cheeks. "Oh my, I feel absolutely wonderful." She turned to him, her eyelids starting to droop along with her speech. "Duzz you feelz as goooood az me?"

Logan said nothing.

When she placed an unsteady hand on the log to push herself up, it slipped, sending her flopping back onto the ground. "Whoopsy daisy," she said, climbing to her knees. After a minute of bumbling around on all fours, she finally made it to her feet.

With her hands out to her sides, she slowly began to twirl around. "Whhheeeeeeee," she said, arching her head back.

The sparks from the fire mingled with the stars, swirling above her. Faster they went until they'd morphed into streaks of neon circles. Faster and faster, they revolved as she spun. Growing bigger and faster, they suddenly filled the sky until it was a whirling kaleidoscope of orange and red streaks.

In an instant, darkness stole back the night, erasing all trace of floating embers. No sound or color, only a black void.

Chapter 20

Three shadowy lines fell across Zoey's face. As if on a swivel, her head wobbled side to side as random jolts caused her head to bop up and down. The lines grew darker, separated by equally growing bands of light. Occasionally the lines and light disappeared completely then sputtered back, followed by longer periods of growing intensity. For an hour the light came and went, with her only movement produced by the constant jarring from some unknown force. Slowly her slumbering serenity gave way to a jittering heart, a forehead beaded with sweat, and an image of a campfire with Logan staring into his plate.

Another jolt and her head banged against the side of something hard. Her eyes sprang open only to be met with the full force of the light coming from above. Squinting her lids into thin lines, she looked up into a small window with three bars spaced vertically within its frame. Through it she could see tree branches, blue sky, and clouds passing by. Halfway down and to the right was a door handle. She rolled her head to the right into a wall of thick dark boards that ran five feet up into a ceiling made of the same. She rolled her head left and found the same wall of boards just out of arm's reach.

Struggling to her feet, she took one step to the door when suddenly her body careened forward, her right leg suspended in place by a leather ankle strap affixed to a chain that ran to the back of the wagon. With the full weight of her upper body moving forward and the blunt restraint of the chain, she slammed elbows down onto the floor. Gasping for air, she slowly pushed herself up while groping for the door handle. The two inches between her outstretched fingers and the curved handle felt like miles.

"Crenshawwww," she roared, straining for the door, hoping some hidden slack in the chain would allow her to grasp the handle. "Crenshaw—let—me—out!" She waited. "For God's sake, somebody open this door!"

"Can you stop doing that?" came a tiny voice from behind her.

Zoey turned to find a dirty beige linen dress with a pair of bare feet sticking out from underneath.

"Who're you?" Zoey said, her own voice suddenly sounding unreal to her. Like a wave undulating back and forth, it echoed in her head, each syllable a mushy, soft audible soup. She swiped her palm over her forehead, attempting to stop the sloshy reverberation.

From deep in the corner, a mangy head of brown hair rose. The fair angles of the face below ragged bangs revealed a young girl, probably in her mid-teens. "Please stop screaming," she said.

"Who are you?" Zoey repeated with more intensity.

"I'm Birdie. Who are you?"

"I'm Zoey. What is this place? Where are we?"

"Can't you see? It's a wagon," the girl replied in a lazy, toneless voice.

"Where's it going? Why are we in here?"

"Don't know where it's going," she replied with a slurred giggle.

"What do you mean you don't know?" Zoey said, a second later banging the wall with her fist and yelling, "Logan—please—open the door."

The girl cringed at the high-pitched wail, tucking her head back into the corner. "Please stop."

"Why are we in here?" Zoey demanded.

There was no answer.

"I said—whyyyyy are weeee in here?"

The girl remained wedged into the corner, offering nothing.

Zoey struggled for a breath then rolled onto her side and slowly pushed herself onto all fours. Her body felt waterlogged—her arms, legs, even her fingers were ten times heavier. She groaned and fell back down.

"Best you don't move," the girl said in a distant voice.

"Why?"

"Wait until it wears off. And stop screaming. It won't help."

Zoey lay on her back across a stained patchwork quilt that covered the floor of the six-by-eight-foot box. Under it was a thin layer of hay with a tiny, mildewed pillow in the corner next to it. She stared at the ceiling, waiting for her mind to right itself and for the cobwebs to clear. Whatever it was, she could not shake the stupor she was experiencing. She started to yell for Logan again but suddenly lost the energy to do so. A minute later she couldn't stop yawning. Just as the girl in the corner had faded off, so did she.

When she woke again, the window was a black rectangle framing a full moon, its filtered light giving the inside of the wagon a creamy, soft glow. She lifted her hand in front of her face. Gone was the weight and the fuzzy sluggishness from before. Gone too was the wagon's cruel threshing. The moon hung fixed in its spot. The *Maria* had come to rest for the night.

Zoey leaned her head back, filled her lungs with air, and released another ear-piercing demand to be released from the wagon.

The girl in the corner stirred. The top of her head slowly rose. "Why do you keep doing that?"

Zoey rolled onto her knees. "Because I want out of here, that's why."

"I told you, screaming won't help. Nobody will come."

Zoey's shoulders came up as rage engulfed her. Her arms hung tense at her sides. "What do you mean nobody will come?" she fumed.

"Just won't."

Zoey arched backwards and began to yell.

"Please don't. I told you, nobody will come."

"But this doesn't make sense."

The girl shrugged.

Zoey grabbed the leather strap around her ankle, twisting and turning the thick piece of cowhide in every direction. She followed its chain to the wall where it was affixed to a steel ring coming out of the floor. Unable to yank it out, she clawed at it until her fingers bled, then finally collapsed onto her knees.

"Where does your chain go?" she said, scanning the girl for her shackles. "Maybe we can loosen yours."

"I don't have one."

She studied the girl's chainless feet. "Then *why* don't you go?" She swung her head toward the rear of the wagon. "For heaven's sake—go!"

The girl hiked her dress up and shuffled to the door.

"Go on," Zoey prodded.

Birdie grabbed the handle and twisted it unsuccessfully. "There's your reason. It's always locked."

Zoey leaned her head back, clasping her hands behind her head. "Logan—open—this—door! Why am I in here? Let—me—out!" After several more minutes of unanswered pleas, she fell back against the wall exhausted.

Another ten minutes passed in silence before Birdie spoke. "How were you got?"

"Nobody *got* me. I was told I was being taken to a friend's home."

The girl twirled her hair with her finger. "I was got when I was down on the waterfront in New York watching the sunset. A nice lady came and sat beside me. We started talking. She offered me some strange-tasting tea then the next thing I knew, I woke up in here."

"How long ago was that?"

"I don't know. A couple of weeks maybe. I can't really tell because I've slept so much."

"How can you sleep in this god-awful thing?"

"I don't really know. I'll get this strange tingling then I start to feel good. The next thing I know, I'm out. Sometimes it's for half the day, other times it's all day. In the beginning it was longer when we weren't moving. Anyway, I've lost track." She peeked up at Zoey. "I got to where I like it."

"Who's feeding you? Is it the cowboy or the other man?"

She looked around as if someone were listening. "It's not a man."

"A woman's here?"

Bending down on her hands and knees, the girl crawled toward her then cupped her hand to the side of her mouth and whispered, "It's a ghost."

Zoey reared her head back from her.

"Whenever I'm hungry or thirsty, I'll bang on the walls and before long a hand paler than the moon will stick food and either a wine skin or flask of water through the little door at the bottom there." She pointed to a ten-inch-square metal plate with hinges. She shuddered. "You think we've died and gone to hell?"

Zoey leered at the tiny metal door, trying to figure out who, besides Logan and the man named Dag, was holding them hostage. The other question was why they were taken. Turning to Birdie, she saw what every man wanted. A thought came to her, but she forced it aside, refusing to acknowledge it. Instead, she continued to focus on the door and the men outside while her new cellmate fell back asleep.

An hour later she rustled Birdie awake. "I've got to use the bathroom."

"Just bang on the wall and yell it out," she said before rolling herself deeper into the corner.

"Hey, out there. I've got to use the bathroom." She pounded her fist against the side of the *Maria*. "I said I have to use the bathroom!"

A minute later, she heard a metal latch being opened. The tiny door swung out and a tin pot, about the same size as the little door, slid through the opening. Inside it was a dirty square piece of cloth. "I don't know why you're doing this," she screamed at the opening, "but—"

The door slammed shut.

Grabbing the pot, she slung it against the door. "I swear you're going to regret this, Crenshaw!"

A few minutes later she banged on the wall again. "I'm finished!"

The sound of the latch being unhooked came again, and the door slowly opened. With the length of chain restricting her from handing the pot through the opening, she could only shove it to the edge. Her foot, however, could almost reach the wall. As soon as a finger appeared through the door, she kicked the pot through it. The door slammed shut, followed by a string of obscenities that faded into the night.

The next morning the sound of a gun barrel clacking manically around the inside of the food door woke them. The end of the gun disappeared back outside then seconds later a bowl of mashed-up biscuits and gravy passed inside, but no flask or wine skin of water, only food. Birdie snatched the bowl, dove her fingers in, and began stuffing her mouth. A minutes later another bowl slid far enough inside so that Zoey did not have to stretch for it. Rather than pouncing on it, she sat frozen.

"Aren't you going to eat?" Birdie said through puffed cheeks.

"I will."

When finished, the girl wiped her hands across her dress. "Are you still not hungry?" she said, eyeing Zoey's untouched bowl.

"I'm just waiting," she replied.

"For what?"

"Just waiting. How're you feeling right now?"

"Fine."

"You're not sleepy, tingly, or anything like that?"

"Not at all, why?"

"Just curious." Satisfied with her response, Zoey plunged into the bowl and scooped out a handful of the gravy-soaked biscuits, devouring them twice as fast as Birdie. Just then the *Maria* jerked forward, sending the bowls rolling to the back.

"You'd think they could give us a little warning," Zoey grumbled.

"You said *they*. How come?"

"Because there're two of them."

"Two?" Birdie said.

"Yes. There's an old cowboy and…" she yawned, "and then there's another one who…" she yawned again. "I don't know who or *what* he is." Leaning toward Birdie, her head bobbed as the girl's form started to fade in and out. She rubbed her eyes and began again. "You know, you could be right about the guy with those bleached out hands." She held her fingers to her lips and giggled. "Maybe *he is* a ghost." She began rocking back and forth then side to side. Before long, her body was swaying in a slow circle. "I feel gooooood. How 'bout you? You having a grooooovvvvvy trip too?"

The girl's lip jutted out. "I don't feel anything—rats!"

"Sooorrrry, Tweety bird," Zoey teased. "I feel just—wonderful." She staggered to her feet, swaying one way then the other. "Absolutely wonderful." Just as she had done the night before, she began twirling in circles, colliding from one wall to the next until finally tripping over her chain and falling on her backside where she belted out a series of belly laughs.

Birdie, frustrated that her daily dose of the drug had been given to Zoey, sat in her corner, stewing, as she watched her new friend enjoy the high she had come to rely on.

Chapter 21

Birdie nudged her elbow. "Can you hear me? You gotta get up. There's food and a flask of water this time."

"What happened?" Zoey said, scrutinizing a dark-purple sky through the window.

"You had a—what'd you call it? —a groovy trip."

"How long have I been out?"

"All day."

Zoey's hand fell limp to the floor. "Oh no, they did it again." Her head slowly fell.

"Come on now, you've got to eat." Birdie said, shoving a bowl of biscuits and gravy toward her.

In a moment of clarity, she snapped to. "I can't," she said, pushing it away. "And you can't either because they're putting—"

Birdie tipped her head to an empty bowl. "Too late," she said, her torso swinging in a lazy circle as her pupils rolled up under their lids. She tilted her head back. "Ohhhh yeah, grooovy."

As Zoey watched her fellow hostage ease into a semi-coma, her stomach rumbled. Ten minutes passed as she contemplated the bowl's contents until she could no longer resist. Taking the bowl, she slowly dipped two fingers in, then stuck them in her mouth. After ten minutes with no side effects, she took two more, then waited another ten. With no fuzziness, tingling, or groovy trip on the way, she rationalized the contents to be drug-free and ate it all. As parched as she was from a day without water, she left the flask unopened. She had rolled the dice and won on the food, but she wouldn't chance it with the water. Knowing water to be more important than food, she would have to figure out some way to obtain it or do without as long as she could.

With nothing but time, she sat contemplating the quarter-inch-thick leather strap around her ankle and counted the links in the chain to the wall and back. Exactly fifty-two links in the seven-foot chain. Just ten more links and she would have been able to reach the window. She continued to count. In place of sheep, she counted the links. Back and forth she counted, dozing off somewhere between 120 and 130.

A gunshot rattled Zoey and Birdie into the next morning followed by a brief angry exchange between Logan and the other man Zoey continued to assume was Dag. A moment later the *Maria* was back in action. Back and forth the wagon swayed and bounced, occasionally pitching violently in whatever direction the rutted trail veered.

Zoey mused on how peaceful Birdie appeared through it all. For whatever negative powers the drug now had on her, at least she didn't have to deal with the constant torture of being hammered about in the belly of the *Maria*. Observing Birdie's petite frame, she realized the reason for her lack of physical restraints was the chain of addiction. Birdie couldn't run because even if she did escape, she could not fend for herself—she was too frail. If freed, she would only hunt for the drug they used to control her.

On the other hand, Zoey was strong, but having experienced several stints in rehab as a teenager trying to escape the ordeals of her childhood, she knew drugs could be more powerful. What scared her most was the memory of how easily she had fallen under their control. Her fate with any drug could put her in the same position as Birdie. Her martial arts skills would amount to nothing. She would be defenseless. The only answer was to escape. Until that opportunity came, she had to figure out how to sustain herself and her strength.

By noon Birdie had mostly returned to her normal self, including her appetite. When a bloated wine skin and two bowls of mutton stew appeared through the tiny metal door, she lunged for them.

"Wait!" Zoey grabbed her hand. "Let me go first."

"Why do I have to wait for you to go first?" she replied with a huff.

"I want to make sure it isn't going to make us sick."

"It never makes me sick. It makes me feel good!"

"Trust me. I just need to check it okay?"

"Oh, alright, but can you hurry?"

Zoey provided a reassuring smile then put the bowl to her lips and took two small sips. She sat back and waited.

"That's all you're going to have?" Birdie said.

"Patience, young lady."

"You sound like Mama. When me or any of my brothers or sisters would get fidgety, she'd always say that."

"You come from a big family?"

"Yes, ma'am. Six of us all told. Was seven but we lost Haley to the typhoid."

"I'm sorry," Zoey said.

Birdie's eyes warmed as they moved toward the left side of Zoey's face. "I like your hair."

"Thank you."

"Do you think when we get to wherever we're going that you could put a pink stripe in mine?"

"Absolutely. And I'll even show you how to do make-up. How's that sound?"

Birdie's lips formed a timid curve. With remnants of the drug lingering in her, she said with a slight slur, "I'm glad you're here."

Zoey studied her gaunt body, all angles and bones. A sadness filled her as she thought about the torture her family had to be enduring.

Just then she felt a shallow ground swell of calm come over her. Her shoulders loosened and the stress of her confines dissipated—subtle but certain signs of a drug-tainted stew. She pushed her bowl to the side.

"It's no good," she said, shaking her head. "Don't eat it and don't drink the water…" She suddenly needed sleep, and within a minute she was out. Thirty minutes later she awoke to find Birdie balled up in the corner, two empty bowls at her feet along with a half-empty wine skin.

"Wake up," Zoey grunted.

The young girl rolled over

"Why'd you eat all the stew? And you drank half the water!"

Her eyes rolled around behind half-opened lids. Her head rose slightly then abruptly dropped. Barely audible, her tiny voice filtered out from the corner. "Grooooovy…"

Zoey smashed a bowl against the wall. "Done!"

A minute later the metal door swung open. Zoey jumped to her feet kicking the other bowl through the opening with deadly accuracy into the shins of the man outside. The door slammed shut with a bang as loud as the gunshot that had wakened her that morning.

In retaliation, the recipient of the bowl hopped onto the driver's seat and whipped the reins hard, causing the horses to bolt forward. She flew to the back of the wagon, coming to a jarring halt as her ankle chain clanked into a taut line. Pop! The sound of her knee ligaments tearing preceded the fiery pain that shot through her joint up into her thigh. She fell to the floor, pulling her leg into her chest while rolling back and forth, writhing in agony. The *Maria* bounced and twisted on its axles in a deadly sprint designed to inflict more suffering upon the prisoners within.

After twenty minutes of the relentless ordeal, the wagon came to a sobering stop as the two kidnappers engaged in a heated argument. Meanwhile, she lay on her back still clutching her leg, grimacing from the pain of a dislocated knee and the vengeful ride she had just endured. Birdie, meanwhile, remained silently tucked into the corner.

She feverishly ran her hands up and down the sides of her knee. The skin around it, already gorged with fluid, molded between her fingers like dough. She had heard the same pop and experienced a similar pain during a match when she had attempted a leg sweep on an opponent, but her foot failed to pivot. This, however, was ten times worse. Slamming her fist against the wall, she cursed the *Maria* and its driver. Through gritted teeth she also cursed the memory stone for where it had taken her.

By nightfall, the *Maria* had logged another countless number of miles toward its unknown destination. With the wagon stationed for the night, the food door opened again, and another two bowls of the same mutton stew were passed through without water.

Zoey looked at the bowls with contempt as the pain in her knee continued to radiate up and down her leg. Despicable as it was to think, the effects of eating the drug-infused dish suddenly became an appropriate alternative as she rationalized it to be the only solution to her pain.

With a groan she slithered toward the door. After taking a long drink from the first bowl, she moved it to the side, waiting for the comforting effects of the drug to kick in. In less than five minutes her head was swimming as the pain in her knee began to fade away. Relief was on its way.

While still lucid she poured out the bowl meant for Birdie. She patted the girl's frail body and lay down next to her. With her head hanging, she slurred her way through half the Lord's Prayer before falling into a deep, pain free sleep.

The next morning her eyes fluttered open when the first rays of light beat past the bars in the window and across her face. Turning to Birdie, she found her in the exact same position as the night before, the only difference being a thin string of saliva dribbling from the corners of her mouth.

Reaching down, she felt the cantaloupe-sized bulge wrapped around her knee. Too tired to test its flexibility and still under the drug's effects, her head dropped back onto the floor with a thud.

Several hours later she wakened to a horrific hammering coming from the *Maria*'s underbelly as its wheels clanged and banged over a rock-infested terrain. Her body vibrated with such force that it sent her bouncing into Birdie. "How can you stand this?" she said, clambering back to the other side of the wagon.

Suddenly the wagon stopped, the horses neighing in protest the only sound to be heard.

Zoey turned to Birdie. "Seriously, how can you even catnap through a horror show like this?"

The girl did not reply.

Crawling next to her, Zoey gave her a nudge. "Come on, Birdie, wake up now."

The saliva from the young girl's mouth had dried, forming white triangular crusts at the corners.

"Birdie! Come on. You've slept enough." She nudged her harder. "Come on! Get—up!"

The girl's arm fell to the floor.

"Oh no—no!" Zoey stretched two fingers onto her neck, just below her ear, she held her breath, waiting, hoping. "Noooo!" She buried her face in Birdie's chest and began to sob.

A minute later a small click of metal against metal came from the other side of the door. The shrill screeching of an iron rod being pulled from one position to another followed, then a thud of metal against wood. She lifted her head and peered into the crack of sunlight sneaking through the parting of the *Maria*'s rear door. Slowly it swung out into the daylight. Zoey shielded her face from a sun she hadn't fully seen in days. Through the glare, two silhouettes emerged.

"What's wrong, Miss Antonelli?" Logan said.

She narrowed in on his fuzzy image. "You killed her!"

He walked closer, stopping short of entering.

"Careful," came a voice from the side of the wagon.

"You killed her!" she screamed again.

Logan jerked his head to the side of the wagon from where the other voice had come. "I warned ya about givin' her too much of that stuff." He turned back to her. "I'm sorry, Miss Antonelli, really I am."

"I'm not," came the other voice again. Out from beside the *Maria* walked the cowboy's accomplice.

She squinted, training her eyes on a silver pistol and the hand that held it, a hand that belonged to the ghost Birdie had feared. With his large, floppy hat pulled down to cover his face, he walked in front of Logan, then slowly grabbed the brim and pulled it off, releasing a full head of platinum-blonde hair that fell down around his shoulders.

Her jaw dropped as she scanned the specter in front of her. The hair… the white, near translucent skin… the faint brows and lashes… "Why, you were in New York. I remember you from the street fight. You're the one with the bat."

He walked to the edge of the wagon. "And you're the tart that ruined me and my boys' day." The corners of his mouth angled up into a wicked grin. "And now you're here to make amends."

Suddenly the door slammed shut, and the metal rod screeched again as it slid back into place, locking her in. She stared up through the bars of the small window, out into the sun-filled day, then back to the dark cell of the *Maria* and the corpse of yet another young girl she could not save. She curled up into the corner and wept uncontrollably.

Chapter 22

At approximately the same time that morning, Mase Winslow sat in his office preparing for his day while Boone Vanderson did the same from his in New York City. Both were men of routine, early to rise and always eager to be about their work, the first order of business being taking in the news of the previous day. On this particular autumn day, Mase received his information through the telegraph machine located in the corner of his office while Boone received his through the paper dropped off on his doorstep.

Mase pulled off a three-foot length of paper tape from his telegraph, grabbed a cup of coffee off a credenza, and proceeded to his desk where he began deciphering the headlines for October 8, 1871. The headline to a story that he had seen more than a century before anyone else now scrolled out before him.

"Still hard to believe," he muttered, recollecting the time his history teacher presented the horrific event to him and his classmates. At that time, it was just another mundane event in US history. Except for the cause of it, it was just another piece of trivia he would never use again. It wasn't until today that it became real.

In New York, Boone stood inside his doorway staring at the floor, transfixed by the headline on the page that had just slipped from his fingertips. Off in the distance a young newspaper boy cried out, "Read all about it! Chicago ablaze! Whole city on fire! Cow kicks over lantern and the city burns! Read all about it. Chicago ablaze…"

Setting aside the ticker tape, Mase picked up two letters that had arrived that morning. The first he opened with little interest—another letter informing him of his holdings in one of the many companies he was now invested in. The second one's return address, however, brought his hand to his chin. Instead of the thin, low-grade paper of the day, this was a fine piece of parchment accented by a wax seal of the elite. With his nickel-plated letter opener, he slit an opening across the top then pulled out a single piece of matching paper. His eyes raced across the page, growing larger with each word. A moment passed, his concentration holding fast to the last word. He swallowed hard then reread it again, his mouth moving silently with each syllable.

"Benjamin!" he shouted.

"Yes, sir," said a black man, entering the room.

"Go fetch Maudie and Sissy. Go tell them…" he paused, beaming, "just tell them to come."

"You gonna tell 'em about that fire in Chicago we been hearing about?"

"Something bigger! Now go on."

"Yes, sir, Mr. Mase. But I hear Sissy's feeling a little poorly this morning."

"How poorly?"

"Don't know, sir. Just poorly is all I heard."

"Okay, I'll go to them," he said, stuffing the letter into his pocket. "Oh, happy day," he exclaimed as he bounded out the door. "Oh, happy day!"

Chapter 23

For the remainder of the day, Zoey sat in the corner of the *Maria* lost in thought, oblivious to its relentless jerking and swaying, her head occasionally whipping left and right after a wheel encountered a large rock or tree root. Although the swelling in her knee had stopped, the throbbing raged on. Along with the stiffness in her leg, a body-wide ache stemmed from her spine outward. Her inability to stand, along with the rigors of being jostled about for hours on end, was taking its toll. Along with the emotional strain her state of health had plummeted.

As the powder-blue sky outside the *Maria*'s window darkened into deep shades of purple, the caravan came to a stop. She tried standing but fell back with a groan as her knee collapsed on her, a searing pain shooting through her joint. She hiked her dress and began rubbing it feverishly.

Just then the door swung open. "Are ya okay?" Logan said, leaning inside and waving a torch.

"I'm fine," she said defiantly.

"Well, get up then," barked Dag from behind him.

She looked up, her brow knit tightly in hatred. "I would if I could," she growled.

Logan held the torch higher. "I can see from here ya got a lot of swell'n in that knee. What happened?"

She continued rubbing.

Dag grabbed the torch and brushed him to the side. "I do believe you've broken something." He giggled. "That thing's the size of a melon. Bet you can't walk on it." He leaned forward. "And I bet you can't do any of that fancy kicking either." He turned to Logan, zeroing in on his waist. "Pull your smoke wagon."

"Why?"

"Aren't you the one who said we should let her out for a spell? Well, put the gun on her and if she moves one hair, you splatter her guts." He turned and held the torch toward him. "And hold this."

Dag jumped into the wagon as Logan stood holding the flame while pointing his revolver at her. "Don't move, Miss Antonelli. I'm tell'n ya, please don't move."

Dag shuffled toward her as if approaching a hornet's nest. "One move," he said, "and the cowboy shoots."

Following his approach, she analyzed the mechanics of his gait. His weight was shifted forward, one leg trailed the other, and he was hunched over and off-balance. With one simple roll to her right, she could swing her good leg around the back of his hamstrings and pull him into a death grip.

"Hold out your hands," he said.

From the corner of her eye, the glint of light against Logan's pistol convinced her to abort her idea.

"I said, hold out your hands!"

As she raised her open palms toward him, he pulled a pair of rusty shackles from his coat pocket. Her hands drooped as the weight of the iron cuffs wrapped around her wrists.

"There, that'll keep you," he said, turning the key in the padlock centered between the two metal clamps that now rendered any remains of her martial arts skills useless. He turned his head a fraction toward Logan while still keeping a bead on her. "Now hand me that rope off the side of the wagon."

In less than a minute Dag affixed the shackles to one end of a ten-foot length of knotted plow line. Backing his way out of the *Maria*, he grabbed the other end of the rope and jerked it tight, wrenching her arms out in front of her. She winced as the metal edges dug into her skin.

"Don't pull her dang arms out of socket, for heaven's sake," Logan said.

"Listen, old man, I've seen what this wild cat can do. I'll treat her like I please."

"If ya go damagin' her, your madam's gonna crawfish yer deal."

Zoey's chest tightened as the reason for her kidnapping crystalized.

"Come on, little kitty," Dag said, backing away from the wagon with the last knot of the rope firmly in hand.

Zoey drug herself to the edge of the wagon, turned sideways, then shimmied her legs over the side.

"Go on now, scoot on down like a good girl."

With only one good leg, the four-foot drop might as well have been ten yards. Eager to continue his revenge, Dag waited until just before she was about to lower herself then used all his weight to yank her out. Instead of landing on her healthy leg, she planted with the injured one, screaming as the full force of her body collapsed onto it. Immediately her leg swelled to twice the size as the first injury.

"Ya idiot!" Logan roared. "Ya done killed the other girl. Ya wanna kill her too?"

Dag threw the end of the rope into Logan's chest. "Take care of her then. I've got to go take a leak," he said, disappearing around the side of the *Maria*.

Logan knelt beside her as she lay twisting in the dirt, clutching her leg. "I'm sorry, Miss Antonelli."

Through clenched teeth she responded in painful starts and stops. "Sorry? You have—a strange way—of showing it." She pinched the bridge of her nose. "You got any more of that drug? The drug you've been putting in our food and water."

"Ya sure ya want it? That's a monkey ya don't want climbin' yer back."

"I didn't want my knee to be dislocated twice either. Just give me the medicine," she moaned. "I'll handle the monkey. And I'll take it straight. I don't need the stew."

A short time later he was back with a shot glass topped off with an amber liquid. "Here ya go. I think this is half of what he's been givin' ya."

"I guess I should thank you," she said, snatching it from him, "but I'm not." With a quick tilt of her head, she swallowed the liquid.

"Miss Antonelli, I-I'm not a bad man. I promise I'm not but—"

"But you're kidnapping me. How's that not bad?"

"Ya don't understand. This Dag's a monster. He works for that man named Tweed and Tweed knows about my plans to retire. He knows where. He even knows my daughter and granddaughter are gonna live with us." He angled his head toward the wagon, listening for Dag's footsteps. "He said if I didn't help him, he'd kill all of 'em. I-I'm so sorry. I know these types of men. I know he'll do it." He hung his head. "I'm so sorry. I never wanted to hurt ya, I swear."

He raised his head to find her slumped forward, the narcotic having already taken effect. "Come on, missy, let's get ya to bed," he said, carrying her into the *Maria* and laying her next to Birdie's lifeless body. He pulled the quilt back and with several sweeps of his hand pushed all the hay into a big heap. Then, spreading the quilt back over it, he gently laid her on top of it. After unlocking her shackles, he tossed them into the corner, then he carried Birdie's body to a nearby elm tree where he spent the next two hours digging her grave.

The following morning, she woke to her empty jail cell. The frail girl with the large family was gone. Fighting back tears, Zoey tried to ignore the pain that had reentered her knee. Just as she began to rub it, the tiny metal door opened. A bowl of gravy and mashed-up biscuits slid through, a wine skin tumbling in moments later. For twenty minutes she stared at them, not wanting to indulge, knowing that every time she ingested the narcotic-laced food, the closer she came to becoming Birdie.

What drove her to finally take the risk was not only the pain in her knee, but the dehydration brought on by going a day and a half without water. She simply had to have water to survive, and the effects of whatever they were lacing it with would again relieve her pain. As lines of sweat formed around her mouth, and her hands became clammy, she grabbed the wine skin and began to guzzle. Leaning her head back against the wall, she rolled it side to side, smiling as the drug gradually began to ease her suffering.

For the next week, Zoey remained confined inside the *Maria*. Knowing her food and water were tainted with the narcotic, she still had to eat and drink. On the few days she tried to refuse to do so, the pain in her leg made it a necessity. Slowly she came under the drug's control.

At the beginning of the third week, early in the morning, Logan opened the door to the *Maria*. "Miss Antonelli, time to get up."

Zoey knew to open her eyes but couldn't.

"Ya need to get up, Miss Antonelli."

She tucked her chin to her chest, then with a trembling finger, she pried her left lid open while the other hesitated to follow.

"Time to get up," he persisted.

As her vision adjusted, the image of a lush green knoll appeared in front of her. Beyond it, tiny ripples twinkled in one direction then the other as the wind blew them across a pond surrounded by trees with thin, weepy branches flowing down. A pair of snow geese glided across the water and into a perfect landing. There she blissfully waited for Mase to appear as he had in her dreams.

"Oh my God!" Logan's voice blared, shattering the picturesque scene.

"Hi," she squeaked out in a stupefied haze.

He turned to Dag. "Look at her."

"What?"

"She's a mess. Just look at the poor girl's dress."

"Ooo wheeee, it appears somebody's gone and lost control," he cackled.

She ran a slow hand below her waist, discovering the moist results of being in and out of a near comatose state for the last few weeks. "Oops," she said as her head fell back.

"Oh no ya don't," Logan said, rushing up into the wagon. "We can't have ya goin' the way of Birdie." He glared down at Dag. "Go to my wagon and get her bag and bring it to me. I'm takin' her down to the pond."

After several feeble attempts to heft her over his shoulder, he grabbed her under the arms and dragged her to the water's edge.

"Where're—we—going?" she stammered, her head bouncing off his thighs.

In one fluid motion he grabbed her around the waist and flung her into the water, as if casting a fishing net. "This'll get ya going," he said.

The instant she hit the water she was jolted awake. For several minutes she flailed about, sending the geese flying off, squawking angrily at having their serenity disturbed.

"Are you trying to drown me?" she said, standing dripping wet in the waist-high water.

He laughed. "Hard to drown half a person."

She splashed the water with both hands, screaming at it—screaming at him, Dag, the *Maria*, the world, and her misplaced position in it.

"Somebody's a might peeved," Dag said, dropping the bag at Logan's feet.

Logan began pulling her clothes from the bag. "Yer comin' close to killin' her. Ya know that, don't ya?"

"Listen, old man. Don't tell me how to do my job. The madam wants her doves already hooked by the time they get to her. And don't give me any lip about the other girl. She was just weak. This lovely's different—she can take it. Besides, she's just about there anyway." He turned to within a few inches of Logan's face. "So you'd be obliged to keep your trap shut and do as I say. Remember, that dream ranch of yours all depends on you doing what I say. And don't get any ideas of taking me out in my sleep or anything. If I go missing, that sweet little family of yours goes missing too. They'll all—"

Suddenly Dag raised his brow in a lustful arch as he stopped and gawked at Zoey standing in the pond in her thin cotton dress, soaking wet, the material clinging tightly to the curves of her body.

"What's on yer mind?" Logan asked.

"Shut up." Dag glanced back to her then spun on his heel and headed back to the wagons.

Back from the brink of a potential narcotic free fall, she emerged from the pond more lucid than she had been in days. With her arms wrapped around her shoulders, she hobbled up the bank.

Logan sheepishly turned his head to the ground where he had neatly placed her clothes. "I found those in yer bag. Soon as ya change, we'll be on our way again."

"Are you ever going to tell me what's going on?" she said, rubbing her quivering arms.

"Just get dressed before ya catch yer death." He headed toward the caravan. "Yer riding up front with me in the supply wagon."

Dag leaned out from behind the large oak just enough to allow a covert line of sight across the grassy embankment and through the thin cover of a dying bush behind which Zoey had chosen to undress. His pink lips stretched wider as he watched her bend over to slide her dress down to her ankles, small windows of her naked body appearing between the branches. The beating of his heart accelerated with each glimpse of her bare skin.

"Dag! Where are ya?" Logan called out. "We need to hitch up the teams."

Recoiling back against the oak, a lump formed in his throat. He slowly tilted his head back out to find her dressed in her jeans and T-shirt. He watched as she took two steps forward then fell to the ground.

"Ouch. That must have hurt," he said, walking nonchalantly out from behind the tree. "You okay?"

"I'm fine."

"Need any help?"

"No," she said flatly.

"You're not going to get far on that gimpy leg." One side of his mouth angled sharply upward. "Why don't I just pick you up and carry you?" he said, sounding more demanding than solicitous.

"I said I don't—"

Suddenly the thought of getting him in arm's reach wasn't such a bad idea. She was physically weaker than she had ever been in her life, and without the use of her leg, her martial arts skills were virtually nonexistent. But if she could just get her arms around his neck, she could exact a choking hold on him and, if strong enough, snap his neck with one quick twist. It probably would not work but she'd enjoy trying.

"Why sure," she said.

Chapter 24

Dag swaggered toward Zoey, his grin growing with each step. She lay on the ground, smiling up at him as she visualized the deadly sequence of moves to be triggered at the first touch of his hand.

"Come dance, kitten," he said, holding out his hand to her.

"Dag, we gotta get goin'," Logan said, coming up from behind.

"Can't you see the lady needs my help?"

Logan looked daggers at him. "I know the help ya wanna offer."

"I swear, Crenshaw, if I didn't need your help, I'd…" His eyes dropped to Logan's shaking hand heading for his revolver. "You don't have the guts—or the strength—to jerk that thing," he smirked.

Sweat poured from under the cowboy's Stetson as he retracted his hand away from his weapon.

Dag's shoulders rose while his fingers curled into a claw. "Get out of my way," he said, storming by him.

Logan closed his eyes and drew a long deep breath.

Zoey pushed up to her knees. "Thank you."

"I brought ya this." From behind his back, Logan produced a rudimentary crutch fashioned from a tree limb, an ax handle wrapped up on top of it inside a small rabbit pelt for cushion.

"Come on, we need to get out of here as quick as we can."

She pulled herself up onto the crutch. "Why?"

"See that there mound up ahead, just past the supply wagon? That's an Indian burial mound."

"The little hill of stones next to that drop-off?"

"Yep, this here's sacred territory. We didn't see it last night com'n in. Most likely Cherokee."

"You mean there're Indians here?"

"Nah, they've been gone out of these parts pert near twenty years. But I don't cotton to disrupting their ancestors."

"How's that?"

"Ya go mess'n with their ground, like movin' stuff or takin' one of them rocks, then it's disrespect'n 'em and their kin. Ya disrespect 'em, then all their livin' relatives suffer. That's why they protect 'em like they do."

"But they're all gone now, right?"

"I reckon. At least for the most part—I think. Anyhow, we don't wanna chance it. Never can tell when Junior might be check'n up on Grandma and Grandpa."

Zoey's attention to the landscape perked up as she frantically inspected the thicket of nearby brush, the line of trees across the pond, and, up ahead, the mound at the edge of the ravine that lay beyond it. Suddenly she was seeing dark figures behind every bush, rock, and tree.

"Ya okay?" he asked.

"Yeah, I-I guess," she said. With a third of her weight shifted onto the crutch, she managed to drag along behind him.

As they approached the *Maria*, Dag walked out from in front of the horses. "Getting acquainted with the goods, are you?" he said, tossing a rock from hand to hand.

Logan nodded her forward. "Why don't ya go on up to the supply wagon. I'll be there to help ya up in just a minute." As soon as she was out of earshot, Logan turned to Dag. "Where'd ya get that stone?" His voice was flat with no nonsense.

"Indians gave it to me."

"Don't tell me ya took it off that mound."

"I told you. Indians gave it to me."

"Dang it, boy! This here's sacred ground. Ya try'n to bring hell down on us?"

"You're not superstitious, are you?"

"Ya gotta put that thing back."

"There's no harm in taking a souvenir. Besides, these things have magic."

"It ain't no souvenir. Ya know these parts and ya know they come back sometimes. We can't chance nothin' on this trip. Besides, that's *bad magic* yer talk'n about. Ya gotta put it back."

"You're serious?"

"I'm ask'n nice. Would ya please put it back?"

Dag's lips drew to a thin line. "I swear, old man. You're really starting to annoy me. Alright. I'll put your precious pebble back on its little pile. Now get on about your own business."

As Logan headed to the supply wagon, Dag squeezed the stone, beating it against his thigh. "Enough with this," he muttered. With his left hand held straight out, he leaned back and cocked the arm with the stone. Targeting the back of the cowboy's Stetson, he wound his body tight for a split second, then, thrusting all his weight forward, he hurled it.

"Watch out!" Zoey yelled.

The stone whizzed by Logan's ear, past the wagon, and slammed into the hindquarters of one of the horses hitched to the wagon. The stunned animal reared up, kicking his hooves while screeching high-pitched cries. Startled, the other horse jolted away from him, and the wagon lurched ahead. Logan grabbed Zoey, pulling her out of harm's way as the panicked team bolted forward.

The wagon skewed violently left and right. Biting at their bits, slinging their heads and trying to free themselves, the horses bounded over the burial mound, bouncing the wagon into the air, then sending it crashing back down, hurling boxes, crates, and barrels in every direction. With only a few yards between the mound and the drop-off, the momentum of two tons of horseflesh and a wagon behind them was too much to stop. The horrible whinnying of the frightened beasts as they plunged over the edge, the wagon hurtling into them, was too much for Zoey. She covered her ears, her screams combining with those of the doomed horses as they plummeted to the bottom of the ravine.

Logan ran to where the wagon and team had vanished. A covey of quail flushed from their roost as remnants of the wagon rained out into the forest below. For several minutes he stood, his chest heaving as he scanned the debris field. Zoey lay on the ground, shaking, while Dag disappeared behind the *Maria*.

Crushing the brim of his hat into his fist, Logan yanked it off and flung it to the ground. He turned and marched toward the *Maria*.

Dag reappeared from the back of the wagon holding a revolver. "Don't come any closer."

"Ya idiot!" Logan threw his arm back toward the drop-off as he continued toward him. "Look what ya done!"

"I said don't come any closer. I swear I'll blow you away."

Logan stopped ten paces from him. "Ya done gone and killed us. That's all our provisions—and two good horses. Everything's gone!" He turned in a circle, his hands in the air. "I should've known better. Heaven help me, I should've never signed on for this." He walked two steps closer to Dag.

"I'm warning you, old man. Any closer and I'll shoot."

Swinging his head from side the side, Logan stopped and turned back toward the site of the wagon's demise. He ground the heel of his boot in the dirt.

Dag stood holding the gun at him.

Logan started walking back to the ravine, then stopped, his voice suddenly calm. "Well, nothin' to do but round up as much as we can." He turned to Zoey. "I'm sorry, Miss Antonelli. I think it's best you lay down in the back of the *Maria*. It may be a spell while we gather up as much as we can."

After helping her into the back, he turned and said, in a hushed voice, "Listen, I need this fool to help me get as much of our supplies back as possible. After that—"

"Logan, I've been thinking. What if I just escape somehow? If you can help me do that, then he won't blame you."

The old cowboy smiled. "I thought about that too, missy, but I'm afraid ya wouldn't get thirty yards on that leg. Besides, after we pull everything together and the time's right, I'm gonna turn this wagon around and we're headin' back."

"But your family—you'll be putting them in jeopardy."

"Don't worry, missy. I'll figure it out." He looked at her with eyes full of regret—and shame—for not acting sooner. "I'm just sorry it's taken me this long to do the right thing. I hope one day you'll be able to forgive me."

She clasped her hands together and began to sob. "Thank you—thank you—thank you."

As he turned to leave, she asked, "Where are we anyway?"

"Best I can tell we're close to the Alabama-Mississippi line."

"Where were we going? You can tell me now, can't you?"

Craning his head around the side of the wagon, he spotted Dag standing just beyond the burial mound, his revolver held tight against his chest. Bending back toward her, he whispered, "We was headin' out west to a new mining camp, to a place called The Lucky Spaniard."

"Is that a saloon?"

He hesitated. "No, ma'am. It's a brothel."

A shot suddenly rang out.

Logan flinched. "What the—"

Two more shots followed. He ran around the side of the wagon to find Dag holding his pistol out toward the woods, smoke drifting from the barrel.

"What're ya shoot'n at?"

"Dinner."

Logan turned to the woods where a downed buck lay splayed out. "Good," he replied flatly. "We're gonna need the meat, considering our supplies done got scattered all over creation." Recognizing their current dire situation, Logan suppressed his desire to rant, deciding instead to maintain the peace until he could exact a plan to get them home. "If ya wouldn't mind, I could use a hand gatherin' up our supplies and putt'n 'em into the *Maria*."

"No, sir. I'm going to carve up this buck while you do the gathering." Dag turned and walked into the woods.

Logan glared into his back. He raised his revolver, aiming it between Dag's shoulder blades, when suddenly the image of his granddaughter crying on the front porch of a burning ranch house popped into his head. Minutes later he was groaning as he hoisted a crate into the back of the wagon. "This is gonna take longer than I thought." He grabbed his back. "Just pray I don't have a heart attack before it's all done."

A moment later Dag dropped a bag of potatoes at his feet.

"I thought you were workin' on the deer."

"If we have to rely on your decrepit body to reload us, we'll be here a month. I'll do the deer later." Heading back down the hill, Dag yelled over his shoulder, "Now quit your yapping and let's get this over."

Logan leaned into the wagon. "How ya doin', missy?"

"O-Okay," Zoey said from the corner where she sat rocking back and forth. Across her face her hair drooped with sweat.

"Ya alright?"

She looked up through red, swollen eyes. "I've been better."

"I'll try and find the drug—I mean, the medicine."

She replied with a barely audible, "Thank you."

"Try to hang on, Miss Antonelli. I promise, I'm gonna make this right."

After three hours of combing the forest and trudging up and down the ravine, they were able to find half their original provisions. On his last trip down to the crumpled wagon, something drew Logan's attention to the middle of a tiny stream running parallel to the wreckage. His thick whiskers turned upwards as he grew closer to its golden shimmer. Kneeling beside the water, he dove his hand in and pried the object from between two rocks.

"Yes!" He held it up in front of him for a moment then stuffed it in his pocket.

A few minutes later he was bent over, panting outside the rear of the *Maria*. The wagon was now crammed with supplies from floor to ceiling. The only free space was a three-foot-wide path leading to the back where Zoey sat on a pile of hay, her knees drawn up to her chest. She rocked side to side, her shoulders bouncing between the side of the wagon and a stack of broken crates.

After catching his breath, he climbed inside and bent down in front of her. "I found gold, Miss Antonelli," he said, holding up a small, corked bottle of amber liquid. "It was just layin' there in the creek, pretty as you please."

She licked her lips as she held up a shaking palm, then suddenly swiped at it, knocking it out of his hands.

"Wait just a minute, missy." Logan picked up the bottle, holding it away from her. "We gotta use this more like real medicine now. No more doses like that moron's been givin' ya. We're gonna taper you down and only give ya enough for the pain in that knee. That monkey's climbed far enough. Time we start pull'n him down."

"For goodness' sake, just give it to me please," she said, reaching for it again.

"Would ya please just wait? There're only four doses in here, so we gotta be careful and spread 'em out." He pulled a small shot glass from his pocket and filled it a quarter of the way. "Here ya go. That'll calm the pain and help ya saw some logs."

She snatched the glass from him and downed the liquid in one swallow.

From behind him he pulled out a blanket and pillow. "I found these too." He put the back of his hand to her forehead. "Thank goodness, no fever." His lips turned into a fine line. "As soon as that knee gets better, we're quittin' ya on this stuff altogether." He pulled her chin up with his fingers. "Is that understood, young lady?"

"Yes, sir," she said.

"I'm afraid yer gonna need to stay back here for now since there's no room up front."

She nodded.

"Alright then," he said, jumping back out of the wagon. "We're gonna ride 'til dark and then make camp. Anything happens back here, ya bang on the wall, okay?"

Her head moved up and down slowly as the drug began to make her drowsy. Her eyelids fell as the *Maria*'s door slowly shut.

In the front of the wagon, Dag sat patiently waiting to continue their journey, his hands planted in his pockets, one firmly wrapped around his revolver. The other held another stone from the burial mound.

Several hours later the wagon stopped.

"How ya doing back there, missy?" Logan said, holding a torch inside the *Maria*.

Warm ripples of light rolled through the door's tiny window, illuminating Zoey's raised hand. Without any words she waved her response.

"We're packin' in for the night. How's yer leg?"

A lazy thumbs-up replaced the wave.

"Good. If ya need anything, I'll be out back here. I'll leave the door cracked open."

"Does he…" came her voice, thin and weak, "…does he know yet?"

"Never ya mind him. Just rest now. I'll see ya tomorrow."

Chapter 25

A grey mist chilled Logan awake the next morning. Rolling his head side to side, he surveyed the camp. Dag lay snoring on the opposite side of the smoldering campfire, his blonde hair shrouding his face and contrasting harshly against the black bear fur under which he lay. Lugging himself to the back of the *Maria*, Logan could see through the crack in the door that Zoey was in the exact same position as he had left her the night before.

"How're ya feeling, Miss Antonelli?" He pushed the door back, freeing a tower of boxes and crates to topple down on him. He cursed under his breath. "Ain't room enough for a family of fleas back here." He began restacking the tower in the same random way, pushing it back to the same unsteady spot as before.

"Are ya hungry, Miss Antonelli?"

No answer.

"You need to eat somethin'. Maybe ya can ride up front today."

Still nothing.

"Miss Anto…" He leaned in, anticipating the stirring of the blanket, but there was no movement. He jumped in, squeezing his way through the narrow pathway, scraping his shoulders between the wall and the jagged edges of the busted crates and boxes. Unable to position himself next to her, he stretched out as far as he could. Able to reach her only with his fingertips, he slid them under her wrist, raising her hand only to have it slip off and fall by her side.

"Oh no, ya ain't," he said, shaking her by the ankle. "Miss Antonelli, wake up!"

Her head wobbled to the side. "I'm up already—okay?"

"Pheewww, I thought ya were… well, I—I'm glad yer awake. Do ya want some breakfast?"

"Noooo," she said, trying unsuccessfully to push her hair behind her ear. "I'm not hungry."

"What about some coffee then?"

"No, thank you."

He examined the limp silhouette of her T-shirt. In less than three weeks the drug and her injury had robbed her of her former self. Her curves were now angular. Her arms, once firm and muscular, were splotchy and bruised. Her vibrant pink strip of hair was now only a few muted strands, and her cheeks were slowly sinking into a dull, quivering jawline.

He pulled out a canteen of water. "Here, ya at least have to drink somethin'."

Cupping it to her mouth, she began to drink. "Do you have more medicine for me?" she panted between gulps.

"Ya don't need any more of that stuff."

"But I do." Her head bobbed. "Please, Logan." A long, weary breath left her body as her head fell forward.

He pulled the bottle of elixir from his pocket, holding it up to confirm the remaining contents. "I only got three doses left. I'm goin' to keep 'em, but only in case of a real emergency, not just to feed the monkey."

"Give her a swig, old man."

Logan turned to find Dag holding out a flask to him. "Go on, give it to her."

"She's done tak'n that mess. Can't ya see she's already hooked?"

"What did I tell you about doing what I said? Now give her the bottle."

"Yes, pleeeease, just one taste for a few hours of relief," she begged.

Logan sighed as he stuffed his bottle into his pocket, at the same time taking Dag's from him. "Just one taste, missy, that's it." He leaned forward. "And then no more," he whispered.

With both hands she took a slow drink from Dag's bottle, handing it back to Logan with a nod. "Thank you."

"Alright, let's get this wagon rolling!" Dag barked. "We've got to make up time. We'll eat later."

With Logan manning the reins, Dag snuggled up against the seat's railing with his bearskin tucked around him. After taking a long swallow from his drugged flask, he smiled. "Wake me in a few hours." Ten minutes later, he was snoring, buried beneath the mound of fur.

After nudging the bearskin several times and getting no response from underneath, Logan began looking for a wide enough area to make the move he had promised Zoey.

A few hours later, without having to be awakened, Dag began to stir. As he did, Logan slowly reached down and pulled his revolver from his holster. Just as he began to point it toward the furry heap, Zoey screamed.

"Snake! Logan, help! There's a snake in here!"

Logan yanked on the reins, slamming Dag into the front railing. Within seconds he was flinging open the back door. The light entering the wagon landed across her cowering in the back corner.

"Get it before it bites!" she pleaded.

"Where? I don't see anything."

"Th-there!" she said, kicking her feet toward two small kegs.

He stymied a laugh as he watched all eight inches of the harmless reptile slither into the chaotic safety of the supplies. He shoved his gun into his holster as he started to climb up. "Why, ain't nothin' but a little ole black snake, Miss Antonelli. He cain't hurt ya, In fact—"

"But *I can*." came a voice from behind.

Logan slowly turned to find the barrel of Dag's pistol clutched between his pasty white palms, his head tilted in the curious pose of a man mulling over some delectable decision.

"Tell me, Mr. Crenshaw, why are we facing east? And those ruts in the road. Those are our ruts. Are those the tracks we made coming from that direction yesterday?" He glanced upward. "And the sun's in the east. It's past noon, Mr. Crenshaw. Shouldn't it be in front of us? Shouldn't it? So I'm asking you," he continued, his voice rising with each word, "why—are—we—moving—east?"

Logan moved his hand toward his gun.

"I wouldn't do that."

Logan's eyes narrowed.

"Like I said before, you don't have the guts or the strength to pull that—"

By the time Logan cleared his revolver from its holster, Dag had pulled his trigger, sending the lead projectile blowing through Logan's left cheek and into his brain, splattering the back of his head into the *Maria*. Like a puppet with its strings cut, his lifeless body plunked to the ground.

Zoey screamed.

Dag wielded the gun back at her. "Shut up or you're next." Then rolling his head from shoulder to shoulder, he knelt beside Logan and lightly patted the dead man's cheek. "Sorry, old man, it was just a matter of time."

Zoey remained crumpled up in the corner, small red dots of Logan's blood spattered across her face and shirt. "What are you going to—"

The door slammed shut, and the iron latch screeched back into place. A few seconds later the wagon catapulted forward, then tipped hard sideways, causing the unstable mountains of supplies to come crashing down, burying her under broken crates, boxes, and sacks of flour, her cries for help lost in the horrid sounds of the wagon's violent turn back westward.

Chapter 26

With the small window in the *Maria*'s back door now covered with boxes, the only source of light was a tiny half-inch gap in the floorboards beside her head. For the next five hours she stared through it, watching as the dirty road below faded from hues of brown and grey to solid black. Where her pink strip of hair used to be was now a thin line of crimson that extended across her forehead into her right eye.

Unable to move, she lay trapped in the same position, absorbing the impact of every rock, root, and pebble the *Maria* traversed. Twinges of new pain accompanied those of the road. From head to toe, her skin was on fire, thanks to the scrapes and bruises inflicted by the avalanche of crates and other provisions that had in an instant been transformed into lethal weapons. She tried to sleep but found it physically impossible. Another dose of the elixir was the only remedy.

Finally, the wagon slowed, and she groaned a sorrowful plea for help.

From outside the wagon, Dag respond by banging on the wall and yelling, "Shut up!"

A few minutes later, after the wagon had come to a complete stop, the back door swung open, sending a dozen loose items tumbling out onto the ground at his feet. He angled his torch toward the back of the *Maria*.

"What the..." he said, examining the disastrous arrangement of supplies.

As if miles away, Zoey's voice filtered through the layers of provisions crushing down on her. "Please help me."

Kicking several boxes out of his way, he jammed his torch between the door hinges and began pulling more items out of the wagon until he had finally cleared enough room to climb up.

"Where are you?"

"Left corner," she squeaked out.

Accompanied by a string of obscenities, he began excavating her from the rubble. Pulling away the last broken crate from her chest, he gasped. "What happened to you?"

She struggled to her knees. "You really are that dumb."

His face tightened. "You look horrible." He jumped out of the wagon and began pacing.

Hoping to regain some strength, she waited on her knees, watching him walk back and forth as an occasional cuss word echoed through the woods. After several minutes the pacing stopped. He sprinted back to the front of the wagon.

With a second torch in hand, he demanded, "Get out!"

"I'm trying," she said, crawling toward the entrance.

"There's a creek out there. Get your bony hide down there, wash all that blood out of your hair and clean up all those scrapes on your arms. Take this with you," he said, placing a torch in her hand. "You'll not fetch a fraction of the deal price in that kind of shape. Now go!"

She slinked over the edge of the *Maria*. "Where's the creek?" she said, hunched over and favoring her bad leg.

"Past those bushes," he said, rocking his head toward two large magnolias. "And don't think about running off."

She shuffled toward him. "Really?"

"Well, don't try anything."

A half hour later she hobbled her way out of the darkness toward a burgeoning fire he was building. Her T-shirt and jeans were dripping, and her hair was a rat's nest of tangled knots.

"Oh, for God's sake," he exploded. "You look worse! How can such a honey pie go from here to there like you have?"

She threw the torch onto the ground, took one step, and collapsed beside it.

"Wake up!" he said, ramming his boot into her ribs, jarring her the next morning.

"Hey, don't damage the merchandise," she said, rolling on to her back.

With one leg on either side of her, Dag loomed over her. "I've got the answer." He held a brown cotton bag down in front of her face.

"Is that my bag?"

He dove his hand inside and pulled out the makeup tin she had mistakenly put inside. "Yep, and this face powder and red paint is going to spruce you up."

"I-I don't understand."

He pulled her up by the shoulders. "We've got another week before meeting Madam Cortessa. We'll fatten you up again, dust on these lady powders, and prime you back up for full price."

Unable to make a solid fist, she released her fingers with a frustrated huff. "I need some more medicine."

"Not yet. We've got to prime you up again. You're going to eat first." He dropped the bag, reached behind her, and produced a plate piled with eggs and biscuits. "Now eat!"

"What if I don't?"

"You'll starve and you won't get any more medicine," he replied flatly.

"So if I eat I can have the medicine?"

"Yes," he said, pushing the plate to her.

Within a few minutes the plate was clean. "Now where's my medicine?"

He held out the bottle, took a tiny sip, then dangled it in front of her. She unsuccessfully lunged for it. Drawing it back, he kissed the cork. "I didn't say *when* you could have it."

"But you said—"

"What I say and do don't mean the same thing."

She pounded the ground. "I swear, if I ever see Boone Vanderson again, I'll-I'll…"

He leaned forward. "You'll what?"

"I'll tell him how you kidnapped me and killed two innocent people. You'll be sorry. He'll send somebody after you. Mark my words, you'll pay dearly."

He placed his hand over his mouth, muffling a haughty laugh.

"What's so funny?"

"Boone Vanderson, you say? That's who's going to get revenge for you?"

"Yes. And he's going to make you pay."

"Why, kitten, it's because of Boone Vanderson you're here."

"What do you mean?"

"It was Vanderson who sold you to me, to sell to Cortessa." He chortled. "You're nothing more than a transaction."

He walked to the back of the wagon and began tossing out supplies. "We won't be needing all this now that it's just us." Twenty minutes later he was wiping his hands across his chest, admiring the new space he had created for his prisoner. "Come on back, kitten."

Only the sound of the distant creek and the wind between the leaves answered.

"Oh no you didn't!" He leaped from the wagon. "I swear if you're trying to run, I'll—" He almost tripped over her.

Tucked against the back wagon wheel, she sat staring blankly into the woods, trying to resolve the revelation of Boone's betrayal. Slowly she began to rock.

"Get up. And stop that rocking. It gives me the willies."

Her hollow eyes crept up his body, stopping at his chest before returning to the woods.

"Dad blame it." He pulled her arm. "I said get up! We've got to use the daylight."

Wrapping her arms tightly around her shoulders, she shuffled to the back of the *Maria*. Climbing inside, she silently moved to the far corner. Seconds later the door slammed shut and the bolt clanged home.

With her back against the wall, she eased to the floor and buried her face in her palms.

Chapter 27

For the rest of the day, Zoey sat fixated on the three bars splitting the tiny window in the back of the *Maria*. Clouds rolled across them, tree branches passed, and birds flittered by, but all she could see was Boone Vanderson standing behind them, incarcerated for all his offenses. At the same time, the monkey Logan had warned her about poured sweat down the shivering strands of hair across her forehead, occasionally she wiped them back with her equally shaky hand. The unrelenting torment of the wagon continued to beat her up, but she felt none of it. All she felt was the burning desire for revenge on the man who had sold her.

When night fell, the expectation of the door opening came and went. Only twice did the small metal one at the bottom open—once for Dag to slide in a bowl of drugged stew and once for him to retrieve it.

The following day came and went the same as before, the only exception being a quick bathroom break that involved him instructing her on how to shackle her own wrists together while he held his revolver to her head. Besides that, he had given up on communicating with her and only spoke when directing her at gunpoint to throw certain provisions down from the wagon for meals.

That evening, when she was sorting potatoes for the stew, she said from a place of unnatural calm, "You know I don't blame you."

"For what?"

"For what you're doing."

He cast her a dubious glare. "I'm only doing what I have to."

"But you *don't* have to."

"You don't know anything, rich girl. You don't know why I have to do anything because you've never had *to do anything*."

She dropped a small sack of flour at his feet. "First of all, I'm not rich, and second of all, you don't know what I've been through in my lives."

"Lives? You really are a kitten? How many *lives* are you on, kitten?"

The sadistic irony of it prompted a crooked smile. "Two," she replied.

"That's all? A cat with only two lives used up—that's not much living."

"You wouldn't be able to comprehend my…" A surge of hope suddenly rushed over her. "Two have been used," she muttered to herself, "there's more—I have more." She began vigorously rubbing her shoulders. "I'm so cold. Can I wear Crenshaw's coat?"

"Just grab that blanket over there."

"It's not very warm. I'm sure his coat will be."

"You want to wear a dead man's coat?"

"He was a good person. I don't think he'd mind."

"He was a worn-out curmudgeon is what he was? Besides, he shouldn't have tried to trick me by turning back like he did."

"I'll make you a deal. If you'll let me wear it, I'll make dinner tonight. I'll make you a different kind of stew my mother used to make. I promise you'll like it."

He leaned back, glaring at her suspiciously. "Why're you being so nice?"

"Because I'm freezing!"

"Well, I'm tired of the same old stew so go ahead, grab the pintos in the back and whatever else you need I'll get the coat." He waved his pistol at her. "And don't try anything funny."

A minute later he returned, the coat in one hand, a box of kindling and his pistol balanced on top of it. "Here," he said, dropping the jacket then backing up. "Now go on. Get to it. I'll have a fire burning directly."

Logan's tent-sized coat was so heavy on her small, weak frame, her shoulders drooped under it. Sticking her hands into the pockets, she contemplated the recipe she had promised her captor.

"Well, what're you waiting on?" he yelped from across a tiny fire he had just started in front of the wagon.

"Coming," she said, ducking behind the wagon. From out of the pocket, she pulled the elixir she remembered seeing Logan place there. Plucking out the cork, she leaned her head back, opened her mouth… then stopped. The bottle hung in the air, shaking between her fingers, taunting her, calling her to indulge. *Just one sip*, she thought. Her leg was healing, but she needed everything else it brought. She needed it to soften her nerves, to take her to a place where there was no anxiety or despair. She could handle it. She was strong, she was a champion. Licking her lips, she bit hard into her own flesh as she re-corked the bottle. After the meal. She would wait and celebrate then.

Thirty minutes later she was dropping handfuls of vegetables along with a shredded strip of venison into a pot of boiling water while Dag sat on a log, watching her from across the fire. His gun rested on his knee, pointed in her direction.

"Can you get me some salt? I left it on the edge of the wagon, near the door hinge."

"Whose cooking for who? You go get it."

"Please. I need to watch these vegetables to make sure they don't get too soft."

"Oh, alright then," he said, picking up a lantern hanging from a nearby branch. "This better be good."

As soon as his light disappeared into the wagon, she whipped out the bottle of elixir and poured in one of the three remaining doses, saving the other two for herself.

"Salt," he said, dropping a small box next to the fire, "that's your secret ingredient?"

"Among other things," she said, sprinkling in a few teaspoons of the white substance.

After a few swirls of her wooden spoon, she tipped the pot over a bowl, letting her drug-infused delicacy fill it to the top.

He grabbed the bowl with one hand while still holding his revolver. "Go on, eat," he said.

"I already had some from the pot while you were getting the salt. I only wanted a little bit anyway."

Sitting on his log, he stuffed his nose into the bowl. "Smells good enough." He took a sip then licked his lips. "Dang, that ain't half-bad." He placed his gun beside him.

She watched as he turned the bowl up, obscuring his face as he wolfed it down, not bothering to take a breath. If her reactions were keener and her leg completely healthy, she could have easily taken advantage of his defensive gaff. A quick leap over the fire with a straight right hand into the bottom of the bowl would send hot stew into his face, blinding him the second before the clay vessel slammed into his forehead, knocking him cold. Alas, she would wait for her recipe to do her dirty work.

"Wow," he said, running his sleeve across his face. "You weren't joking. That's some kind of tasty. I know who's going to be doing meals from here on out."

"It'll be my pleasure," she said with a grin.

He began digging through his pockets. "Not a smoker, are you?" he said, producing a small ivory pipe.

"No." She examined the dexterity of his fingers as he packed tobacco into the tiny ivory bowl. He was quick and exact, showing no signs of an immediate reaction to the elixir.

After a long drag, he exhaled a lengthy plume of smoke into the star-filled sky. "You ever wonder what it's like out there?"

She followed his gaze upward. "Sure. Lots of times."

"Wish I could be up there sometimes. Way out where nobody could ever…" Failing to complete his thought, several minutes passed as an uneasy silence shrouded the campfire.

Across the fire, dappled in the flickering firelight, she saw, for the first time, a boy who had gone his entire life ridiculed for his physical imperfections. He suddenly turned to her, a glint of a tear sneaking down his cheek. Like a child caught in an awkward adolescent moment, he jerked his head away.

Speaking into the blankness of the forest, he said, "Why did you say you forgave me?"

"I just do."

"No." He turned back to her. "That's not enough. I want to know *why*."

"Because it's Boone Vanderson I blame," she said flatly.

"You blame Boooooone?" He rolled out the name in a slow wave.

She smiled at the first sign of the elixir's effects. "Yes. That's who I blame."

His sullen demeanor suddenly vanished. "Hey, guess what I have?"

"What?"

"Go on, guezzz?" he slurred.

"I don't know," she said, patting her fingertips together.

He leaned toward her, almost toppling into the fire. Giggling, he rocked back on his log, cleared his throat, and whispered, "I've got something special."

Pleased with the drug's progression, she played along. "What kind of something special?" she asked, feigning excitement.

He put his finger to his lips. "Shhhh, you can't tell anybody." He searched the darkness for imaginary eavesdroppers then reached inside his coat pocket and pulled out a handkerchief with something wrapped inside. "Isn't it pretty?" he said, pulling back one corner.

She sat rigidly in place as he cradled the object of his affection.

"You know what this is?"

She held her hand above her eyes. "I can't see it."

He pulled the handkerchief away with the dramatic flair of a magician producing a rabbit from a hat.

"It's—it's a stone."

"It's no ordinary stone," he said, cradling it. "See this marking?" He touched his fingertip to the bottom of a small cross-shaped indention. "This is a—"

"Memory stone!" she blurted. "You—you have a memory stone, don't you?" She jumped up with the enthusiasm of a child spying her present on Christmas morning. "That's what it is, isn't it? That's exactly what that is!"

He stood holding it above his head, gradually beginning to turn in a circle. "This stone has the power," he howled. Then faster he turned, repeating, "The stone has the power, the stone has the power…" With his arms stretched straight above his head, he leaned back, his voice echoing through the woods as the smoke from the fire carried his manic mantra into the heavens.

Zoey watched from across the fire, oblivious to how much control the drug now had on him. Instead, her attention was riveted to the object within his grasp.

Suddenly his circling began to waver into a sloppy combination of rubbery dance steps, each leg moving out of sync with the other. As the drug's effects amplified, the more unstable he became, his chants rapidly degrading into inaudible slurs. Then, with one foot tripping the other, he went flying back over the log he had been sitting on.

She gasped at the harsh thud. Running around the fire, she dropped to his side just in time to see him lose consciousness. Lying next to him were both the stone and his revolver. Snatching them up, she sprang to her feet then slowly backed away. With the weapon twitching in her hand, she trained its sights on his forehead.

"Dag!" She waited. "Dag!" Satisfied with his non-responsiveness, she circled the campfire back to her stump and sat down, her heart pounding. In her possession was more than she had envisioned her plan would yield. With the revolver, her kidnapper was now in her control. With the stone, she had so much more—she had her way home.

As the forest fell silent again and her adrenaline leveled out, the monkey Logan had warned her about pulled her hand to the bottle in her pocket. She had denied herself long enough. With all things as perfect as they were, she would reward herself and take just enough to calm her nerves. Pulling the elixir from her pocket, she swilled down the second-to-last dose, relishing her victory.

Chapter 28

From the base of his hairline, the tiny droplet formed, growing larger until finally, succumbing to its own weight, it rolled down his forehead, pausing for a second at the bridge of his nose then slowly creeping downward, gathering speed until it became wedged between a flared nostril and cheek. A sudden twitch of snarling lips jarred it loose. It dropped the length of his body and landed squarely between her eyes, lost within the hundreds of tiny water beads from the morning's rain.

"Get up!"

Zoey wiped her face, unmindful of the danger looming above.

"I said—get up!"

The side effects of her swig of elixir from the night before made her sluggish. "Whoever you are, go away," she groaned.

A boot full of lightning struck her temple, slamming her face into a mud puddle. She began hacking and spitting out the dirty water. Standing over her, Dag held the stone in one hand, his revolver in the other, the barrel centered on her chest.

"You think you're so smart. Didn't think to tie me up, did you?" He lifted the stone over his head while pushing his gun at her. "I don't know what I want to do more—crush your skull or blow your guts out."

Her addiction had cost her the only chance she had to regain her life. Now, lying flat on her back with no other alternative but to plead for mercy, she contemplated why she even wanted to be spared. Letting her hands fall out beside her, she closed her eyes and waited for him to make his choice.

When she opened them again, she was back inside the *Maria* in the black hole of the far corner at the end of the narrow tunnel of boxes and crates. Running from the wall down to the shackle on her ankle was the chain that helped wrench her knee out of joint. Through the tiny window all she could see was a blanket of grey while the steady drumming of rain rumbled through the wagon's interior. She folded into a fetal position, wanting to cry but unable, wanting to bang her head against the wall but too weak. What she wanted most was to wake up from her nightmare. As the drug's effect lingered, she once again drifted off.

When she woke this time, the wagon was at rest, its window a black rectangle with a three-quarter moon hanging in the lower-right corner. The rain was gone, its steady beat replaced by the rhythmic hum of chickadees and belching bullfrogs.

Anticipating Dag would feed her, as was their routine, she scooted to the rear of the wagon as far as her chain would allow. Before long she heard the meal door's metal latch flipping up. As soon as it swung open, she threw her arm out to it.

"Don't go yet. There's something I have to tell you."

The bowl flew in.

"Please don't go. I have to tell you what you have. You're right about the stone. There is something special about it." Her statement faded within the confines of the *Maria*. "Did you hear me? You're right about the stone. It's special. I know."

"How?"

"If you'll let me out, I'll tell you."

"You were going to kill me!" he yelled.

"I wasn't going to kill you. I-I was just—I was just trying to get away."

"Tell me from in there, witch!"

"Please let me out. I have to use the bathroom anyway. You want me clean, don't you?" The sound of the metal lock being released drew her to the door.

Four ghostly fingers folded around its edge, pulling it back and allowing the moon's light to fill it with an eerie haze. A set of keys clanked to the floorboards at her feet. "It's the biggest one," he said, brandishing his pistol at her.

"I can't—get—it—in," she said, jabbing the key over and over at the hole in the lock.

"Hurry up," he barked.

After another unsuccessful attempt, she wiped at her forehead and asked, "Do you have the medicine? Just a sip? I can do it then. Just one sip."

"For heaven's sake," he grumbled, climbing into the wagon. "Lay on your stomach."

She slowly rolled over. A second later he was pulling the shackle from her ankle.

Still fearful of her fighting skills, he scurried back out of the wagon. "Let's get this over with," he said, vanishing into the night as clouds drifted across the moon.

"I want to talk about your stone," she said, shimmying out of the wagon on her belly. "It's got powers." She turned. "Where'd you go?"

"I know it does." His voice came out of the darkness. "Now go to the bathroom and let's be done with this."

"But—"

"Just use the dang bathroom!"

"Where? I can't see…" Suddenly the clouds passed, revealing a rutted length of dirt road hemmed in by walls of towering hemlocks, their under branches sticking out in sharp, treacherous points.

Taking advantage of the light, she hurried into the woods, reappearing several minutes later just as another large cloud bank floated overhead, cloaking the forest in darkness again.

With the caution of someone who had been dog bit before, he inched his way toward her while keeping his gun barrel fixed on her.

"You don't have a limp anymore. But those shakes are still with you," he said, nodding to her hands.

In an attempt to quiet her tremors, she wrapped both hands under her T-shirt. "If I had some medicine, I could calm them. You've got some, don't you? Please, just a little. Just enough to calm my nerves"

"Keep walking. When we get to—" He stopped. "You hear that?"

"Hear what?"

He angled his head. "There's no chirping or croaking going on."

"What do you mean?"

"It's too quiet. A minute ago, every toad and chipmunk was chatting it up like they were—"

Her eyes flashed past him.

"What?" he said.

Her throat tightened. "Be-behind you."

"Oh no, you don't. You're not besting me again. You just keep—" A branch breaking cut his thought short. "Is there something back there?" he whispered.

The concern on her face provided the answer.

He slowly turned around, following the road into a black void where the silhouettes of two figures stood, the moonlight reflecting off their outstretched muskets. They began moving toward them.

Raising his pistol, he waved it from one to the other. "Who are you?" he demanded.

The figures continued toward them, both gun barrels now aimed at him.

"I-I said, who are you?"

A gentle breeze whispered through the tension, thinning the clouds, allowing the moon to expose the vague images of two men clad in leather, one completely bald, the other with long, dark hair. "*Nihu uha gohusdi udotsali itsulayayy*," the bald one said in his tribal tongue.

"Wha-what'd you say?" Dag replied.

"*Nihu uha gohusdi udotsali itsulayayy*."

"Speak English!"

From out in the darkness came a mild voice. "He say, you have something that belongs to us."

"Who said that?" He twisted his torso, searching for the person delivering the accusation.

Out of the blackness appeared the diminutive figure of an old man dressed in the same leather as the others, the only exception being the tall stovepipe hat upon his head. Waves of silvery grey hair flowed from under it down past his shoulders.

The little man shuffled silently in between the two others.

Suddenly the remaining clouds broke apart, giving way to the moonlit standoff below. Less than twenty yards in front of them were three Indians. The young ones' faces were stern while the smaller one was stoic, emotionless.

"What do we have that belongs to you?" He grabbed Zoey by the arm, thrusting her out in front of him. "You want the girl?"

"The stone," the old man said.

"The stone from the burial mound?"

"Yes."

"I-I lost it."

The little man extended a wrinkled hand. "The stone. You must give it back."

"I already told you. I lost it. I swear I lost it."

The man continued toward them, his hand still reaching. "You must give it back."

Dag pulled Zoey into him while backing toward the *Maria*. Too weak to resist, she sagged against his chest. He wrapped his arm around her neck, dragging her to the corner of the wagon and using her as his shield while waving his gun at them.

"Give the stone back now," the old man continued.

"Take her," Dag hollered, shoving her out in front of him.

She fell forward at the Indians' feet. "Don't leave me," she said, turning her head back to the vacant wagon. Off in the distance, she could hear his frantic escape as he tore through the woods, stumbling and ripping through underbrush to get away.

The long-haired Indian lowered his gun and began to run after him.

The old man threw up his hand, stopping him. He grunted two unfamiliar syllables then limped up to her while signaling the two younger Indians to his side. In his native tongue he spoke to them in a serene yet direct manner.

Zoey clung to the ground, avoiding eye contact, occasionally catching glimpses of the two younger Indians as they listened reverently to their elder. They were lean, their sharp features wrapped tightly in honey-toned skin. The frames of their rough-cut leather shirts denoted solid torsos beneath. In her condition, she would be no match for these braves.

When he had finished speaking, the older Indian clapped his hands, sending the two in different directions. The bald one disappeared into the woods while the other dove into the wagon and began rummaging through the supplies.

"Come," the older Indian said, walking to a large fallen tree. "I am old and must sit often." He pointed to a mossy patch running along the bark. "Rest with me."

She started to sit then stopped, waiting for his approval to continue.

He replied with a shallow nod accompanied by a slow blink from soft eyes surrounded by the craggy trappings of a weathered face that had seen many years of blazing suns and frostbitten winters. His movements were serene and measured in a manner not brought on by his advanced years but through a lifetime of understanding ways of conserving energy in the wild. He was a study in nature's mystics in the form of a chief or medicine man. Whichever it was, she felt the aura endowed upon him from a sacred position he held in his tribe.

"This man you are with," he said calmly, "he is a bad man."

She swallowed. "How do you know?"

"For three days, we have watched him. We watched him kill the other white man and take what was not his." He removed his hat and gingerly laid it on the log next to him. "And he treats you like the dog in camp who howls too often." He placed his hand on his knee, touched it, then looked to her left hand.

"I-I don't know what you want."

He turned his palm up, signaling for her hand. "I cannot take it. You must give freely so that I may know your heart."

Her mouth fell slightly open. She moved her hand toward his open palm reluctantly, holding it back, then in a moment of conviction dropped it onto his.

As his lids shut, he said, "Now you close."

Her chest tightened. The idea of willingly blinding herself at the hands of one of the savages she had read about in history class caused her whole body to quiver. With no other recourse, she complied. A second later she felt his other hand rest on top of hers. In an instant she forgot how much she was shaking as all tactile senses transferred to a tingling in her fingertips that ran up her arm, into her chest, and then to her head. A cleansing calmness rolled along behind. For whatever length of time it lasted, she didn't want it to end. When it did, she found him sitting with his hands folded across his lap, a shadow of a smile on his face. Her first instinct was to thank him but all she could muster was, "Who are you?"

Just then the faint sounds of twigs and leaves crunching beneath stomping feet came from the forest. The bald Indian appeared from the trees, hoofing his way toward them. In one hand was his musket, in the other what appeared to be a white cloth. The elderly Indian stood and walked out to meet him while pressing his hand back at her to stay seated.

From behind, all she could see was him placing his hands on the young Indian's shoulders. With the brave's head bowed, he arched backwards while raising his hands in the air, chanting in a manner she assumed a Cherokee medicine man would. When finished, the bald Indian ran to the wagon, leaving him alone with the white cloth laid across his palms. For a short time, he stood motionless, observing her. Seemingly satisfied with what he saw, he slowly walked her way, his hands held out in front. Her heart gained a beat as each step brought his hands more into focus. She clutched her chest as he lowered in front of her a six-inch swath of bloody flesh attached to greasy strands of platinum-blonde hair.

"Wh-what is that?" She tried banishing the image by wiping her eyes. "What do you—"

"The man who beat the dog is no more. His fate is yours to decide." He pressed the bloody offering closer. "It is yours to decide."

"But I—"

"You must take it for you to control. If not, the spirit lives on."

Her gut churned as a bloody glob oozed through his fingers. Dry heaves followed as he continued to push the gruesome article upon her.

"I-I-can't," she said, holding up her hand. Turning to the woods for emotional refuge, she tried to wash the image from her mind. When she finally turned back, he was placing his hat on his head.

"I have seen your heart. It is good and pure," he said in a solemn tone. His head tilted down ever so slightly, his voice lowering with it. "But it is your warrior spirit that will fulfill your destiny. Go now in peace."

Taking one of the horses, the braves hoisted the old man onto it. Walking alongside him, they vanished into the night.

For a minute she sat staring into the darkness as the sounds of the forest with its chattering inhabitants slowly came back to life. Her mind was a whirlwind of contradictions and feelings, unable to grasp enough of any of it to form a coherent thought. *Was any of it even real?* she wondered. Her sanity wavered through the wee hours of the morning.

As the sun peeked timidly through the sharp branches of the hemlocks, the only thought that rose to the surface was of sleep. She had been sitting in the same spot all night, a chilling dew clung to her feet, and she was shivering. With the wagon less than ten yards away, she staggered to it and climbed in, leaving the medicine man's gift of Dag's scalp on the log.

Chapter 29

It was midafternoon by the time Zoey woke the next day, and a cool breeze whisked through the *Maria*. Rays of sunshine weaved through the forest canopy, dappling spots of light and shadow across the debris field left by the Indian assigned to search the wagon for the stone Dag had taken from their tribe's burial mound.

Her stomach hanging painfully hollow, she rubbed trembling hands over it. Her need for food would have to wait.

Like a ravenous dog rooting a garbage heap, she clawed and scratched through the stacks of boxes and crates in a desperate hunt for the elusive bottle of elixir. Twenty minutes later she sat exhausted, her whole body now a quaking scaffold of skin and bones. Her smiley face T-shirt frowned a dirty mud-stained expression across drooping shoulders.

Unable to find her drug, she began hunting for the strip of venison she had seen Logan stash in a small burlap sack. Unsuccessful in her search and craving anything to fill her belly, she dove into a crate of potatoes. With both hands she pulled one out, knocked off the dirt, and began gnawing. Several bites in she began gagging. With her head bent over the wooden box, her body heaved in empty waves. She spat while pounding her fist against the floorboards.

"I hate you!" she screamed, followed by a string of obscenities—all directed at Boone Vanderson. She grabbed another potato, flung it against the wall, and swore some more. Again and again, she pulled them out, cussing him as she smashed them against the wall. "As God as my witness," she said, pulling the last one out, "I will have my revenge!"

Unlike the others this one produced a denser thud, dropping into the shadows on the floorboards with an equally weighty thump. She pushed back her sweaty locks and dug through the scattered objects of her frustration. There, nestled between three potatoes, was the stolen stone. She grabbed it with both hands, raising it into the light and rotating it until she found the crude indentation of a cross. Caressing it as if it were a newborn, she lowered her head and held it against her cheek. Slowly rocking her head, she began repeating a prayer of thanks, one for every time she had cursed the name Vanderson.

With the stone in her possession, she had a sudden surge of energy, enough to hitch the one remaining horse to the *Maria* and repack some of the supplies thrown out by the Indian. Unable to start a fire, she resorted to eating a handful of raw beans and a wafer-thin slice of dust-covered jerky. In less than an hour she was sitting on the front seat, reins in hand, heading east. Beside her was Logan's coat. In its left pocket was the stone, in the right, the forgotten bottle of elixir.

For the rest of the day, the overburdened horse pulled the wagon at a snail's pace. As easily as she could have whipped him into a faster gait, she could not bring herself to strike him. They shared the same pains—no food and no compassion. Every hour she would stop to let him rest and console him with a hug meant as much for her as him. Meanwhile, her tremors continued to grow along with her hunger pangs.

During her journey, she had counted on meeting other travelers. The road, as heavily rutted as it was, must have been traveled by more than just them. As far as she could remember, she had heard only one other wagon pass by during the whole time she had been held captive. But then again, she had been drugged most of the time and was either comatose or without enough wits to realize the presence of anyone other than Birdie or the black snake who had been calling the stack of supplies home. Refusing to spend another night in the back of the *Maria*, she put on Logan's coat, wrapped her blanket around her, and curled up on the bench seat.

Just before dawn, a crack of thunder jolted her up. Tiny water droplets tap-danced on the overhanging roof in a random pattern, preventing her from dozing off again. Rumblings off in the distance confirmed she needed to be on her way. Her stomach, in knots from the night before, would once again have to wait. Water, though, could not. With the water barrel completely dry and only a few ladles remaining in a small bucket she downed one and gave the remaining two to the horse.

"We'll find more, boy," she said, stroking his mane. "You know, I used to have a horse just like you. His name was Copper." She wrapped her arms around the beleaguered animal's neck. "You're my Copper now." She pulled back, holding his long face in her hands. "Don't worry, boy. I've got enough oats for you. We're going to make it. You just have to keep pulling."

After replacing his bit and securing the back of the wagon, they were off again. Slow and steady, they plodded up the road that had gradually begun to ascend into a little more than a windy foot path. A light drizzle began to fall.

With a pounding head, a hole in her stomach, and hands that would not quit shaking, she suffered through the morning, growing more worried for Copper as he slowly worked himself into a sweaty lather. Just before noon, as he was about to make it to the top of a steep switchback, he stopped.

"Come on, boy, ten more yards and we're on flat ground." Off in the distance thunder rolled. "Come on, Copper, we've got to go." She snapped the reins. Instead of moving forward, he reared up, almost backing the *Maria* off the road into a deep gorge. "Okay, okay, we're done for the day," she said, rushing to unhitch him.

After coaxing him into the shelter of some thick oak trees at the top of the hill, she stopped to look out over the smoky layer of clouds that had rolled in, muddying the gold, crimson, and orange canvas that stretched over the mountainous terrain.

"You'll be okay up here," she said, freeing him of his harness. "I'm going back to the wagon. Soon as the rain passes, we'll try again."

By the time she made it to the wagon, the drizzle had become a cold, steady rain. Shivering, she threw on Logan's coat then pulled out the empty bucket and placed it behind the wagon under a nice stream of water coming off the edge of the roof. "At least we won't die of thirst," she muttered before jumping back inside the *Maria*.

A prickling wave of anxiety followed her inside. With her spirit as grey as the sky, she faded into the dank recesses of the jail cell she had now become reliant upon. Only her adrenaline and a scant helping of dry beans from the night before had fueled her to this point. She sat monitoring the bucket, her body begging for sleep yet too frazzled to receive it. As it slowly filled, her thoughts receded into blurred images of home—her tiny New York apartment, warm and cozy, a fireplace, a bowl of hot soup in her lap.

A crack of thunder refocused her to the bucket. Rainwater had started to overflow the rim, thanks to a sudden downpour from the tumultuous Appalachian skies. A tiny river carved its way around it, eroding the soil, causing it to wobble. Just as a chunk of earth washed out from underneath it, she sprang out and grabbed it before it tumbled over. A heavy, slithering sound cut through the wind and rain. A wave of angst washed over her as she watched the *Maria* slowly snaking toward her as a river of mud pushed it begrudgingly down the hill.

She threw her hands out in front of her, demanding the beast to stop. "No! No!"

The rain came harder—and with it, more mud. "Please stop!" she cried as she dropped down and wedged the bucket under a rear wheel. Arching back, she wiped a mud-caked hand across her forehead. The wagon sat motionless as her heart continued to beat in time with the pounding rain. Glaring into the muck, she cussed the wagon and the rain for their cruelty while giving thanks for the bucket's strength.

At the same time the *Maria* awoke. Inching around the bucket, it pivoted sideways, groaning as it twisted against its will. Instead of moving straight down the hill where it would end up safely at the bottom, it was now angled toward the gorge. With only ten feet to spare, it stopped again. In this position a branch under the other wheel would be all she'd need to keep it in place for good.

As she searched, the wagon suddenly decided to spit the bucket out and shift its weight, giving it enough momentum to continue its slow-motion death slide toward the gorge. All she could do was stand and watch as the wagon slunk closer to the drop-off. In a matter of seconds, the back wheels rolled over the edge, the door swinging wildly as crates, bags, boxes, and cannisters spilled out into the forest below. Teetering on top of a rotting log, its wheels spun as if trying to climb back to safety. The log broke as thunder clapped, and the *Maria* plunged into the abyss.

Standing in the middle of the road, water pouring down her face as a chilling river of silt and rock washed over her feet, she held her hands to the heavens. "Why me?" she cried, falling to her knees and beating her fist against her chest. "Why? Why? Why?" Her sobs were lost in the downpour, her tears washed clean before they crossed her cheeks.

For the next half hour, she sat sinking slowly into the sludge, falling further into despair. She stared blindly across the gloomy landscape, rocking gently, saying nothing, thinking nothing. It was only Copper's whinnying that brought her back.

"It's okay, boy," she called up to him. She climbed to her feet, took one misplaced slippery step, and flopped back into the same puddle. Copper neighed. "I'm coming," she said, rising again. This time each step was calculated and steady.

Sheltering the horse in the oak trees as protection against the rain had been wise. Although wet, Copper had fared better than she had. When she finally reached the top of the hill, she threw her arms around his massive neck, holding her shivering body against the warmth of his.

Gradually the rain stopped, leaving in its place a stubborn grey sky. "I'll be back," she said, running her hand along his mane.

With short, measured steps she walked to a small grassy overhang at the corner of the switchback they had been trying to reach. A tiny surge of hope rose within her as she followed its winding path downward. From the road's apex, she could see through sporadic holes in the forest's canopy the way that would lead them home. As soon as the road was dry enough, she would mount Copper and they would begin again, praying they would meet someone along the way that could help them.

For the rest of the day, she slouched on top of a large rocky outcrop, shaking uncontrollably while looking down at the road. Unable to piece her thoughts together, she battled a pounding headache and fever, accompanied by the searing pain of a red-hot poker shoved down her throat every time she coughed.

As dusk fell so did the temperature, leaving the road still muddy and her still shivering. Sweat trickled down the sides of her face as she watched the horizon grow darker and more sinister. A pale quarter moon rose between spotty patches of dense clouds that rendered the forest pitch-black. When the clouds passed, the treetops shimmered like whitecaps across a mountainous ocean while the rays of light passing through the foliage onto the road created a moving river of quicksilver.

Lacking the energy to keep her arms wrapped around her shoulders any longer, she slipped her hands into the bulky jacket. Embracing the cold, smooth surface of the stone in her left pocket brought a moment of relief, knowing it to be her true way home. In the right pocket her fingers played curiously around the top of the elixir bottle she had forgotten.

In an instant the stone's importance paled in comparison to the amber liquid she now held in front of her. A smirk rippled across her face as she yanked the cork, sucking out the last dose. At that moment, the forest lit up again as the moon peeked through a hole in the clouds. Several minutes later her lips slowly turned upward as the first euphoric wave rolled over her. Swaying in harmony with the leaves, she became one with all she could see. Her senses, with a surreal awareness, picked up every movement along the road below—an opossum scurrying between bushes, a field mouse burrowing out of harm's way from the hawk circling above, a fox sniffing out roots. Whether imagined or not, she saw it all, including the ghostly figure of a man fading in and out of the shadows. Her heart pounded as she watched the apparition retreat into a group of trees just as the moon fell back behind its own cover.

Summoning all her strength, she yelled out, "Up here—Help—I need help…" Her words trailed off into a pitiful moan. She stood, begging for a reply. "Heeellllllp!"

Her plea unanswered, the clouds melted away, allowing the moon to concentrate all its nocturnal powers on the figure of a man in the middle of the road. Bathed in a ghastly white glow, he gazed up at her, his washed out skin fading into the background. She threw her hands over her mouth as he angled his head down, revealing a jagged streak of crimson running across the top of his head. Tracks of the same ran down an unrecognizable face.

She grabbed the stone from her pocket. "Please, dear Lord—please, please—Please don't let…"

She began waving her other hand behind her, searching blindly for something—anything—to help keep her balance. As the full effects of the drug surged through her veins, she began to wobble, then she stumbled back against the boulder where she had been sitting. Thinking the ghoulish specter had materialized from behind, she spun away, rushing backwards to escape. Catching her heel on a tiny root, she fell backwards, her head slamming against the rocky outcropping.

Blood trickled from her ear and into the puddle of muddy water where her head had come to rest. With her left hand still clutching the stone, she held the right one up toward a light hovering above. Suddenly a sense of peace enveloped her as her body slowly rose into the air.

"Time to go home," came a voice from far away, soft and sweet. "Time to go…"

All went black.

Chapter 30

A warm light grew from inside her, slowly expanding to outside her body before falling back against her eyelids, a gentle melodic humming growing along with it. Brighter the light became until all she could see was a hazy grey backdrop. The humming continued, rolling over her into syllables, rising into words of praise, phrases and stanzas of thanks. One by one the words came together in a long-forgotten hymn she had heard only when her grandmother had taken her to church.

"Who's that singing?" Zoey said in a thin voice.

"She's awake!" came an unknown voice, followed by the shuffling of someone moving into some distant place. "She's awake, you got to hurry!" the voice echoed from afar.

Suddenly, the air was thick with the sounds of clamoring feet against hardwood floors. Hushed tones and murmurs followed, then the silence of anticipation.

With the same intensity of a newborn drawing its first breath, she inhaled, gathering the energy to gain consciousness.

Warm fingers wrapped around hers. The voice came again. "Come on, deary, you can do it."

One eye slowly opened then fell shut. Darkness began to settle back until…

"Zoey, can you hear me?"

Her chest rose as the words resonated upon her heartstrings, as warm and kind as they were so many years ago. From out of the darkness, she emerged.

"Mase?" she said as the world came back into focus.

He brushed aside a strand of her straggling hair. "You made it."

Raising a feeble hand to his cheek, in a tiny voice she said, "You grew your beard back."

With just a small cropping of grey around his ears and a hint of crow's feet cornered against tender eyes, he was the same handsome journalist she had fallen in love with from the future. Taking her hand, he turned it over and kissed her palm. "It's been ten years. It was about time for a change."

"The stone worked…" she said with a faint smile before she dozed off again.

One by one the room emptied. The only person left was a plump black woman rocking quietly in the corner, an open Bible in her lap, a small pine box at her feet.

The sun tracked low across the fields, casting long shadows from the workers as they harvested the last crops of the season. Their voices calling to one another, mingling with the honks of the geese as they glided onto the pond for a night's rest before heading farther south, the melodies wafted through Zoey's room, scented with jasmine and honeysuckle.

She rolled her head to the side, the fluffy down pillow soft and warm against her cheek. "Are you who I think you are?"

The black lady, still rocking, popped her head up from her scriptures. Placing her Bible aside, she walked to the bed and took Zoey by the hand. “My name’s Maudie,” she said with a slow, widening grin.

“I’ve heard about—I mean I’ve *read* about you,” Zoey said.

“And I’ve *heard* all about you.”

Through her fog, Zoey moved her head side to side, taking in as much as she could—the rich tones of mahogany furnishings, curtains trimmed in white lace and rolling softly in the breeze, a gold sash hanging from the four-post bed waving along with them.

“Am I at—”

“Willow Creek,” Maudie said, her cheeks pushing into shiny mounds of flesh, proud to be the one providing the information. She patted her hand. “Now tell me, how you feel’n?”

“Weak.”

“Rightly so,” she said, disappearing into the hall. A minute later she returned with a tray of fruit, cornbread, molasses, and milk. “Let’s get that strength back. You ain’t nothin’ but skin and bones.”

“Thank you, ma’am.”

“Ain’t no ma’am to it, just Maudie.”

Zoey stuffed her mouth full of grapes. A few minutes later she pushed the tray to the side. “I’ve never tasted better cornbread.”

Maudie smiled. “You know how long you been in this here bed?”

“How long?”

“Two—whole—days… and never once did you stir.” Her face turned grim. “We didn’t think you was gonna make it. Thought Mr. Mase was gonna have a heart attack.”

"If it wasn't for the second memory stone, I wouldn't have."

Maudie cocked her head. "Second stone?" She leaned toward her. "How many stones Mase leave you in that safety deposit box?"

"Just the one, but I found another one—the one that brought me here."

Maudie shook her head. "Child, ain't no—"

Just then Mase came bounding into the room carrying a small flower arrangement, cutting her response short. "Brought you a homecoming gift. Well, more of a welcoming gift."

"Mase!" she said, trying to rise up, only to fall back.

"Now don't you go trying to get up. You've got a way to go yet."

"Oh, Mase," she said between gasps of air, "you wouldn't believe what I've been through. First the Gator Lodge—then the pig farmer—then New York, dirty filthy nasty New York—then the boats—and—and…" Suddenly she couldn't catch her breath, her head spinning as her thoughts jammed against one another.

"Whoa, slow down, Zo. There's plenty of time. Let's just get you healthy and then you can tell us all about it. You're just—"

"Skin and bones. I done told her," Maudie chimed in.

"What I *was* going to say is that you're just going to have to take it easy for a bit."

Zoey put her hand to her heaving chest and managed to squeeze out, "I'm sure I must look a fright."

He leaned his head back and laughed out loud. "Why do I suddenly feel the urge to respond as Rhett Butler? You don't know how much I've missed you." She wanted to throw her arms around his neck but couldn't find the energy. More than anything she wanted to shout out her hidden feelings for him and why she would endure the same gauntlet of suffering to see him again.

"Maudie, would you make sure Miss O'Hara here gets some more rest?"

"Miss who?"

"Sorry, inside joke," he said, winking at Zoey.

"Well, we're inside and I don't get it."

Mase burst out laughing and Zoey joined him, adding a painful bout of wheezing.

"Okay, that's enough for now." He tucked her blanket around her. "Zo, I can't believe this, but I've got to go take care of something very important out of town. I'll be gone four or five days, but Maudie's going to see to it you get back on track." He placed his hand on her shoulder. "If you need anything, she's here for you."

Maudie bobbed her head. "Don't you worry, Mr. Mase. I'll have little missy plump and plenty in no time flat." She turned to a simple cotton dress hanging in the corner above the pathetic jeans and T-shirt Zoey had been rescued in. "And no more funny-face shirts and pants either."

With Maudie continuously loading her up with pancakes, grits, mashed potatoes, and every kind of fatback seasoned cut of meat, she regained her weight with a few pounds to spare. As her energy returned and the aftereffects of the drug subsiding, she progressed from the bed to the dinner table where she would sit, grilling Maudie on every aspect of life on the plantation, always weaving in inquiries about Mase's love life along with subtle queries into Sissy's. With the double talk and verbal two-step of a politician, Maudie evaded both.

On the fifth day, after Maudie decided she was well enough and with only remnants of minor tremors, she took Zoey on a stroll about the plantation, ending up at the pond on a large patchwork quilt placed between two giant willow trees. Zoey fell back, gazing up into the green waterfall of branches cascading down around them.

"I know these trees," she said. "I've seen them in my dreams."

"When?"

"For years. I've thought about them almost every night, even during the day." She sat up, turning to the bank. "And him. He's always there in them. He's always been there, all these years—I just didn't know it."

"Who and what are you talk'n about?"

Blinking away her unconscious ramblings, Zoey realized she had stepped too close to professing what she still could not bring herself to say aloud. "Oh, I'm sorry. I'm just mixing up my dreams, I believe."

"My, my, you sho do have a funny way with words. You and Mr. Mase, he speaks crazy-like sometimes too. Especially after he came back."

"You mean when the memory stone brought him back here?"

"That's right. He came back talk'n like he went and got educated by the president himself. And boy, oh boy, he had ideas about this, that and everything, stuff that didn't even happen yet. All on account of he knew. He knew everything that was gonna happen because he'd been there." She waved her hands across the pond, to the big house, past the fields and tiny cabins that used to be for slaves, now occupied by free men and women still loyal to a man who continued to treat them as equals. "All this is still here because of him and what he learned in the future."

"I know," she said.

"I know you know, because I seen him writing to you in that book he left for you." She leaned toward her. "I was the one who gave him the stone that he put with it," she said proudly. "You know—the one that brung you back."

"Why did I come back though? Mase wrote that you told him the stones take you forward the first time and if you use another one it sends you back."

"That's right. Only I didn't tell him everything." Her doughy face glowed. "You see, there's something about them that's even more special."

Zoey wrapped her hands together under her chin, holding her breath, the hairs on her arms rising.

"Them stones, they know the heart of the one that's hold'n 'em. They see inside your soul. They see your memories. They know where you need to be. For whatever reason, you're here because you're supposed to be."

Zoey spread her hands over her mouth, her smile extending past her palms as thoughts of her and Mase flooded her mind. Of course—the stone knew her destiny, that they were meant to be. "And that's why the second one brought me here too!"

Maudie skewed her lips. "You really think another stone is what got you here?"

"Of course. I was dead and I had my hand wrapped around it just like Mase wrote in the journal. The next thing I knew, I was here. I even remember floating up in the air. It was part of my destiny!"

"Child," Maudie said, resting her hand on her knee, "you got here because Mase and all those men went looking for you. They brung you back. Said they found you lay'n in a mud puddle on top a mountain ridge plumb over in Alabama."

"But—but the stone? It must have been—"

"The stone was still in your hand, honey. Mase brung it back with you. If it was a memory stone, it would've up and disappeared. You didn't see it sitt'n on the dresser in your room?"

"No," she said, turning back toward the house. "But I'm supposed to be here, right?" she asked, her voice rising.

"Of course you are," Maudie said, matching her exuberance with a cheerful pat on the hand.

"Like you said, it's my destiny to be here with Mase—that's my destiny."

For the rest of the day, she was left to meander around the property on her own, her mind wandering off into thoughts of her future and how wonderful life was going to be. But how would she tell him, what would she say? She wouldn't plan it. She would speak from the heart. Everything was different now because she knew her true feelings. When she told him how much she had suffered to be with him, he was bound to fall to his knees and profess his love for her.

Suddenly her heart sank as visions of sunny days, holding hands, and loving embraces were swept away with the autumn leaves. Sissy, the girl she had known only as Elisabeth but had never met, was still in his life. For ten years they had been together. Surely he was in love with her. Or was he? Her thoughts flew from one scenario to the next, from him loving Sissy to him loving her, never landing solidly on either. All she knew was that she had to tell him.

Her eyebrow slowly arched upward. From deep within, from a darkness she had no control over came the same thoughts she had every time she read the passage in Mase's journal about how Sissy was sick and that he feared death was near. Suddenly realizing she had not seen her and neither he nor Maudie had said anything about her, she sprang to the conclusion that threatened to damn her soul. Within the confines of her tormented thoughts, she begged, *Lord, please take these thoughts away.*

Chapter 31

As dusk settled in around Willow Creek, Zoey and Maudie wrapped themselves in flannel blankets and retired to the front porch and the comfort of two wicker rocking chairs. Within the house, servants scurried about, preparing a celebratory dinner in anticipation of their employer's arrival, their voices harmoniously rising and falling amidst the clanking of pots and pans, accented with laughter mixed with the tinkling of silverware against fine china.

"That's a beautiful thing," Zoey said.

"What's that?"

"The workers inside, they're all so happy. You'd never hear that in my office." She looked out across the rolling hills, past the pond and down the winding path leading toward the front gate and fading against the languishing rays of a golden sunset. "And that view… it's so beautiful. It's just all so… What's that coming down the road?"

"That there's a carriage, a Willow Creek carriage." She leaned forward. "That's Mr. Mase!"

Zoey's heart jumped.

"Come on, child. We need to get ready," Maudie said, racing inside the house to rustle up servants to come out and assist in his arrival.

Meanwhile Zoey ran upstairs to her room where she primped as best she could. Pinching her cheeks to the point of drawing blood, she stumbled out of her simple cotton dress into another more elegant, high-neck, white linen one Maudie had laid out for her. Without the aid of a brush, she ran her hands through her hair, fluffing life into it while lamenting the absence of her signature pink strands that Mase not only liked but admired for how they signified her independence.

"Hurry, Zoey, he's round'n the pond!"

"I'm here!" she said, sling-shotting through the front door. The last to join the welcoming party, she stood panting, bouncing in anticipation, then suddenly blurted, "No—this isn't right." Turning abruptly back into the house, she said over her shoulder, "I'll be back."

Inside, she peeked through the window. Being part of a welcoming entourage would lack drama. Being fashionably late with flair and mystique stirred a man's hormones. She would wait to make her entrance, just as Scarlett had done at Twelve Oaks.

A minute later two slick grey mares sauntered to a standstill, bringing to a halt a black carriage accented with subtle touches of gold leafing.

"Welcome home!" said the servant closest to the carriage as he pulled the door open.

"Thank you, Thomas," Mase said, bouncing out. His jubilation over being home was contagious, packed with more than enough charm to cause all the servants to break ranks and crowd in on him for handshakes and even the unthinkable hug, given the normal pomp and circumstance of the time.

"Welcome home," Maudie said, wrapping her arms around him.

"Where's Zoey?" he said, scanning the grounds. "Is she okay?"

Hearing her cue, she pushed open the front door. Head lowered, she walked across the porch, slowly lifting her eyes to meet his at just the right moment, the moment she knew they would remember for the rest of their lives.

"Well done," Mase whispered to Maudie as he followed her step by step toward him.

With pouty lips and the alluring voice of a siren, she curtsied. "Welcome home, Mr. Winslow."

Stunned by her transformation, the proverbial cat latched to his tongue.

She radiated confidence, knowing her timing had hit its mark. "Mase, it's me."

He blinked. "You—you look…" He swallowed. "You look—well! Yes, you look very—uhm—healthy."

"Thank you," she replied, settling for the less-than-exuberant response she had hoped for.

"Where's my baby?" Maudie said, vanquishing the awkwardness.

Mase abandoned his gaze and turned to the carriage, reaching back to its entrance. From out of the darkness an ebony hand appeared. Down onto the cobblestones he led a tall, young black lady draped in a long, heavy shawl of a former slave.

He turned back, beaming. "Zo, I'd like to introduce you to my Sissy, or as you remember her—Elisabeth."

Zoey's mouth parted, unable to release the words caught in her throat as she took in the beauty before her. Tall, with rich brown eyes flecked with hints of gold, Sissy had a sunburst of a smile that belied the drab shawl wrapped around her shoulders.

"Hello, Zoey," she said in a soft, honey-dipped Southern accent. "I've heard so much about you."

Zoey's throat tightened further. "And I—I've heard so much about you," she said, catching a glimpse of Mase basking in the encounter. She hesitated, the words coming harder than she had thought possible, convicted in telling the truth. "You're—you're more beautiful than I had imagined."

"And you're just as beautiful *and* twice as kind as I'd heard." An awkward pause followed only to be dashed a second later as Sissy burst toward her, both arms held wide, ready to engulf her. "Oh shoot—come give me a hug," she said, leaning forward as if bending over a railing. "I'm sorry I can't give you a proper hug, but he's more in the way every day."

Zoey's arms went rigid by her sides as she suddenly saw through the shawl who *he* was.

Coming to her rescue, Maudie wedged her way in for a hug of her own. "Mama needs one too."

"Careful, Mama, he's been kicking up a storm." Pulling back her shawl, she placed both hands on a protruding belly that stretched every fiber of her drab linen dress to its breaking point.

Mase rubbed her stomach. "She thinks it's going to be a boy, but I think it's going to be a girl."

"Doesn't matter, long as it's healthy," Maudie said.

"You know what I think?" he said. "I think I'm starving, and I'll bet little mister or missy probably is too."

"We can remedy that. Dinner's wait'n for us right now. And it's a good one. Even got your favorite chocolate chess pie," Maudie said.

"Tell me, ladies," he said, puffing out his chest, "am I not the most spoiled landowner in the county or what?"

Taking Sissy with one hand and Zoey with the other, they walked to the house, Sissy snuggling up against him as Zoey slowly pulled away, relegated to falling in behind, a mere footnote to his much-anticipated arrival.

In honor of their return, a feast featuring every variety of the plantation's autumn harvest along with heaps of ham, beef, and chicken was laid out on the grand table. Dozens of candles accented the room's ambiance, highlighting how romantic it all could have been if it had been set just for Zoey and Mase.

With him at one end of the table and Maudie at the other, Zoey sat across from Sissy with her hands tightly balled up in her lap, head down, eyes locked on her empty plate.

"Are you still not feeling well, Zo?" he asked.

"I'm fine. Just a little tired, but I'm fine."

"Are you sure? Because I can wait."

"Wait for what?" she said.

"Your journey. You've just experienced something beyond comprehension. You've travelled through time! I want to hear it all and, of course, what the future became during those years."

"And I'm dying to hear how you and that roguish Paul Talbert first met," Sissy said, nudging Mase's arm. "And of course, I have to hear how you convinced the former Mr. Talbert to shave his beard." She started to stroke his whiskered face then suddenly jerked it back. Placing it across her stomach, she winced then relaxed as if nothing had happened.

"Another one," Mase said.

"Only a twinge," she said half-heartedly.

"How bad?"

"About the same."

"That's the third one in the past hour," he said.

"When was the one before?" Maudie asked.

"About fifteen minutes before we got home," she said, bending down with her arms folded across her stomach. "Awwhhh!"

Maudie stood. "That was more than a twinge?"

"Uh huh," Sissy said with a grimace. "A lot more."

Maudie rushed to her side. "That baby's com'n. And he's com'n tonight." With the cool head of a field general, she took charge of the room. "Mase, go get Gerald and have him fetch hot water to her room. Then you go get rags and meet us up there."

"Where do I find—"

"In the closet next to the back door." She turned. "Jackson, get in here!"

A second later a skinny black boy came running in.

"I need you to go get the doc. Tell him Sissy's have'n her baby. And take Big Red, he's the fastest of the bunch. Now get! Zoey, you help me get her upstairs."

"But I—I…"

"Awhhhh!" Sissy doubled over, then fell to one knee, pounding her fist on the floor while clutching her stomach. "Oh, Mama, it hurts!"

"I know, baby. But don't you worry." Her voice was even with brick-hard assurance. "Everything's gonna be alright. Mama's here and so is Zoey." She directed her to Sissy's other side. "You get that arm and I'll get this one."

Zoey bobbed her head.

"Alright, honey, let's get you upstairs. Time for you to become a mama."

Throughout the night they holed up in Sissy's room, working between endless contractions to perform a procedure that an absentee doctor, lost in a drunken stupor, should have been executing.

"I swanny, when I get my hands on that doctor, I'm gonna—"

"She's got to keep pushing," Zoey said, wiping sweat from her forehead. "Come on, you can do it. Push—push hard!"

Every ten minutes it was the same—a failed push starting with a weak moan, igniting into agonizing shrieks that ripped through the house, tearing at the hearts of everyone inside.

Mase paced the hall faster with each moan, stopping only to bang his fist against the wall with every cry.

"The baby's breech," Maudie exclaimed. "It's been almost eleven hours and she's not even crowned yet." For the first time that evening she fell back into a chair, uncharacteristically frazzled and worn. "Oh, dear Lord, please be with my baby girl. Help her in this hour of need. Help her, Lord, please help my baby."

"Mama," she said through feeble gasps. "I—I don't—I don't think I can do it anymore."

"Yes, you can, honey. You have to."

"It's too hard…"

"Sissy, don't you quit, baby."

"I—I don't think I can—make it…"

"Now you listen to your mama." Tears began to well up in Maudie's eyes. "You're gonna make it and so is that little angel of yours. We just gotta give him wings is all."

Laying her hand on her mother's arm, in a fragile breath she said, "Let me go, Mama—but please save my baby." Slowly her eyelids fell shut.

Maudie stumbled back, falling to her knees. "Oh, Lord! No—No!"

Suddenly the door burst open. "Why's there crying? What's wrong? Why are you on the floor? What's—

"Get out!" Zoey commanded.

"But—but I have to—"

"Get out!" She glared at him, pointing a rigid finger to the door. "Now!" Watching him back into the hall, she turned to find Maudie placing a stone into Sissy's limp hand, wrapping hers tightly around it.

"We did it before," she whispered into her ear. "We can do it again."

"No!" Zoey yelled. "Not yet!" She leaned down, grabbed Sissy's wilted jaw and shook it. "You wake up! Wake up! You hear me—I said, wake up!"

A blunt silence filled the room with only a mother's prayers present. Then, with the crack of a whip, the sound of Zoey's palm slapping against Sissy's cheek jolted the ordeal painfully back. Sissy rolled out a long, sorrowful moan.

Maudie bolted to her feet. "Oh, sweet Jesus!"

Sissy licked her lips as if to speak, but no words followed.

"We got to get that baby out now," Maudie said. She looked down at her hands, spreading the fingers wide then curling them back into trembling fists. "They're too big. I—I can't do it." She turned to Zoey, "They're too big. All I can do is push her belly and try to move the baby into…" Her words fell away as she panned Zoey's arms, stopping at her petite fingers.

Zoey turned her palms up. Her eyes flashed down on them, then to Sissy, then back to Maudie. "Get your stone ready. As soon as she passes out again, work her stomach…" She swallowed. "I'll do what I can."

Holding the memory stone in one hand, Maudie brushed back Sissy's hair with the other. Tears streaming down her face, she nodded.

Sissy suddenly lurched forward with a scream then fell back, unconscious. Maudie jammed the stone onto her palm, folding her limp fingers around it, then squeezed her hand around hers, her mouth moving silently in prayer as she feverishly began pushing her daughter's stomach.

Chapter 32

The rooster's crow came, just as it did every morning, resonating throughout the plantation and alerting all who could hear to the new beginning. One by one, master and servants, visitors and friends, would rise and smile at the prospect of a new day at Willow Creek. Servants would scamper back and forth to the outhouse while Maudie, usually awake before anyone, would begin directing them in the chores of the day. Mase would soon arrive in his study, pipe in hand and paper tucked under his arm, prepared to absorb the news from the previous day. Typically bathed in the rays of the warm southern sun, the house was bustling within minutes of the cock's first voice.

Today was different. His caws came and went, yet the house lay silent, the only sound coming from the ticking of the grandfather clock in the downstairs hallway. Upstairs Zoey lay sprawled out, still in her bloodstained dress, staring at the ceiling, her mind continuing to reel.

Just before noon a knock came at her door. "Come in," she muttered.

The door creaked open. "Somebody wants to see you," came the singsong tones of one of the plantation's young female servants.

Zoey sprang to her feet. "Why, hello there, peanut," she said, reaching her arms toward the young girl cradling a small white cotton blanket in her arms. A plump little fist appeared from the cloud of fabric.

"Can I?" Zoey begged.

"Of course," the girl said, slowly lowering the bundle into her arms.

Pulling the warm swaddling against her chest, Zoey kissed the little angel who came so close to not getting his wings. "Isn't he just perfect?

"He sho is."

"Look at those little toes and fingers, and that itty-bitty button nose. He's so cute but so little."

The girl giggled. "They usually is when they come that early."

"I suppose."

"It's past lunch but there's still breakfast fixin's downstairs if you'd like me to bring you up some."

"Thank you, but I'll go down myself," she said, handing the bundle up to her.

Before leaving, the girl turned back, bouncing Mase's newborn in her arms. "We all know what you done, Miss Zoey." She smiled tenderly down into her arms, to the tiny being with the button nose. "He knows too. We all know and we's all grateful to you."

A pleasant breeze followed the girl out the door. The edges of Zoey's mouth turned up as she recalled the events of the past twenty-four hours, replaying the reversal of emotions that began with her own confirmation of Mase's love for Sissy to the point when everything changed, the moment the heir to the Willow Creek Plantation entered the world.

Several minutes later, after shedding her blood-covered dress, she was back in her jeans and T-shirt. As she opened her door, the breeze whisked into a silent hallway. Peering around the corner, her ears perked as she picked up a whimpering coming from Sissy's room at the top of the stairs. Tiptoeing down the hall, fearful of adding to the stress coming from within, she noticed the door was cracked open. Heavy drapes were drawn tight, turning the room a deep, somber grey. All she could make out in passing was Mase kneeling next to the bed, his body flung across the crimson-tainted sheets, sobs coming in waves. Immediately she averted her gaze, quickly passing in a silent rush downstairs.

Through the foyer, across the living room, and into the dining hall she walked, crossing paths with several servants quietly performing their chores, all stopping, lowering their heads, waiting reverently with hands clasped in front of them as she passed.

No sooner had she stepped up to the table than a servant was pulling out a chair for her then retreating to the corner where he waited with military attentiveness. An elderly man dressed in black tie appeared from the kitchen and began buzzing around the table, pushing plates of food toward her. "Try these," he said, shoveling a heap of shrimp and grits onto her plate then breaking open a biscuit and drizzling a huge spoonful of gravy over it. "Best shrimp and grits in the county."

"How'd you know I liked shrimp and grits?"

"Mr. Mase," he replied.

"Well, thank you…?"

"Yancy, ma'am."

"Thank you, Yancy," she said.

A half hour later she sat patting her stomach. "I do believe I just added two inches to my waistline."

"Didn't I tell ya? Best shrimp and grits in the county."

Just then the young servant girl from that morning came in from the kitchen. "Did you want anything else, Miss Zoey?" he said.

"No, thank you, I'm beyond stuffed." She rose and began helping clear the table.

"No, ma'am," said the servant girl, "Yancy and me got this. Besides you should go see—what'd you call him—peanut?"

"Oh no, he's with Mase in Sissy's room."

"That don't matter. You should go on in."

"Oh no. I—I wouldn't dare go in now."

"How come?"

"It just wouldn't be right. It's not my place."

"You really should. I know he'd want you to."

"You think so?"

The girl's smile provided the answer.

Zoey angled her head back to the door as she contemplated the suggestion. Bobbing her head, she finally said, "Thank you," then proceeded back upstairs.

Climbing to the top of the steps, she noticed the sounds of sobbing had been replaced with delicately placed coos amidst a soft, rich lullaby.

For several minutes she waited outside, a voyeur to the tenderness on the other side of the door. Slowly, she pushed it inward, just enough to witness Mase, aglow in the now sun-filled room, cradling his baby boy in his arms, rocking, softly humming. Her heart was a puddle at her feet, joyful tears rolling down her cheeks as she watched the power of the bond being formed between father and son.

She turned back into the hall.

"Where're you going, Zo?" he said.

"I—I was just checking on you and—"

"Come on back. Don't you want to see him?"

"Of course I do!" she said, hurrying up to his side. Bending down, she cupped the sleeping little boy's head in her hands. "He's so adorable."

"He is, isn't he?" Mase crowed.

"I bet he'll grow up to be a writer like his daddy."

"Heaven forbid. As soon as he's able, I'm putting a paintbrush in that little hand. No, wait—" his face suddenly lit up, "let's make that a pair of spoons."

She started to acknowledge his reference to his best friend but abruptly stopped when she noticed the change in the bed. Its linens were no longer a savage shade of red, instead, it was now a vacant down mattress wrapped in pristine white sheets.

He placed his hand on her arm. "How can I ever thank you?"

Pretending not to hear, she stroked the baby's head.

"Zoey, what you did was nothing short of a miracle."

"Maudie was right."

"About what?"

"That I had a purpose. The memory stone brought me back in time, not forward like it did for you and her. She said there was a reason for it."

With a creak of the door, he cast a smile past her.

She turned to find Maudie with both arms stretched out, sunbathed in a white halo of light. Without a word Zoey flung herself into Maudie's arms and began weeping.

"Oh, child, we had some kind of night, didn't we?"

Zoey peered up at her like a child receiving her mother's praise after having experienced something beyond her understanding, something that would forever link them together.

"You done good."

"Is—is she—"

"She's gonna be fine. Just needs some time but she's gonna be alright." She leaned back and took Zoey by the shoulders. "And she wants to see you."

Zoey gulped, wiping away the tears. "Where is she?"

"The end of the hall, where it's not so noisy."

"We're turning this room into a nursery," Mase added cheerfully.

"That's a great idea," she said, sniffing away the remaining tears.

"Come on," Maudie said. "Let's go see the new mama."

Zoey followed her out into the hall. "What'll they name him?"

"Already been done."

"And?"

"Jeziah," she said, beaming.

"That sounds familiar…"

"It should. You already met his namesake here at Willow Creek—in the future, that is."

Zoey's brow slanted. "Your son, the man I met at Belhaven Ranch, the man with the scars on his back. The one they called JC?"

"That's the one!" Maudie said, pausing in front of the last door at the end of the hall. "Let's see how his sister's doing, shall we?"

A half hour later Zoey returned to find Mase still rocking the slumbering Jeziah in his arms, mesmerized with his face, the twitch of his little fingers, the edges of his mouth moving up and down.

"She's incredible," Zoey said, kneeling next to him, resting her head on his shoulder.

"Who, Maudie or Sissy?"

"Well—both actually, but I was really talking about Elisabeth—I mean Sissy."

"She's my everything, Zo. She's remarkable in every way. She's kind, smart, funny, and so creative. You know she's working on her second novel. And her heart… how she cares for others is—"

"I know. She was more concerned about me and how I was doing than about herself. You're so lucky to have found her."

"What about you?" he asked. "Did you ever find anyone?"

Her eyes warmed to his. "I thought I had."

"Someone in the future, back in New York?"

"No—actually yes—I-I mean no and yes. Oh shoot! I don't know how to explain it." Her throat tightened at the thought of blurting out, *It was you. It's always been you!* She took a breath. "Maybe one day I can explain it. The thing is—I know it was never meant to be. And that's okay now."

"Maybe you'll meet someone here?"

"It's funny. I did start to feel something for someone but then it all went south." She laughed.

"What's so funny?"

"The irony of what I said… that it all went south, which is what I did when things started to go so wrong when…" She smacked her forehead. "Oh my gosh, I sound like an idiot!"

Mase laughed. "Time traveling will do that. Speaking of which, Maudie said you thought a memory stone brought you here. Did someone give you one?"

"I thought I had one, but it was just a stone from an Indian burial ground. I got it from some rich guy's henchman."

"So this henchman, he was trying to help you get back here?"

"Absolutely not!" Her body stiffened. "He was trying to sell me as a sex slave."

"What!"

"Some goon," she said, her voice continuing to rise, "hired by a man named Boone Vanderson, kidnapped me and was taking me to a brothel out west where I was going to be used as a prostitute. I was drugged, beaten—"

"Wait, you said Boone Vanderson was at the center of all this?"

Her chest caved, hearing someone else sound his name. "Yes, Boone Vanderson, the most despicable, evil, vile, demented—"

"That can't be."

"What can't be?"

"He wouldn't do that."

"He most certainly would!"

"It couldn't be the same Boone Vanderson. It doesn't make sense."

"What makes sense," she roared, "is a dislocated knee, weeks of being drugged and witnessing murders, and enduring the torment of being chained inside a torture chamber on wheels—that's what makes sense. That's the reality of it all!"

"Zoey, it couldn't be Vanderson."

Her eyes bore into him.

"Vanderson is the reason you're here."

"No! That's impossible."

"But it's true. I have the telegram in my desk that spells it all out. He describes how he hired a guy to bring you here—a guy named Logan."

"That can't be." She began rubbing her temples. "What else did the telegram say?"

He hesitated. "Just that…"

"What?"

"Just that he knew how much…"

"What?"

"He said he knew how much… how much you loved me."

Zoey's mouth fell open as she turned away. Neither of them moved as an uneasy pause hung in the air. In a far-away voice she asked, "Was there anything else?"

"He wanted to see you happy."

She buried her face in her hands, tears flowing through her fingers onto the windowpane. Could it be? Had her thoughts of vengeance been so misguided?

"He really wanted that?"

"I know he did, or he wouldn't have come."

"What do you mean?"

"When you didn't show up that first week, I telegrammed him to let him know. Sensing something was wrong, he immediately sailed down on one of his ships then came here to enlist me and some others to go search for you. Zo, without him knowing the trail that Logan told him you'd be taking, there was no way we would've found you. It's a good thing you were headed back in the same direction, or you would have been lost to us forever."

She stepped back, bracing herself against the edge of the dresser.

"I thought Maudie would've told you all this while I was gone."

"No," she said, staring into the floor. "She-she didn't."

"I'm sorry," said Maudie, suddenly appearing in the doorway. "I don't want to interrupt but Sissy would like to see you and Jeziah."

"You hear that, little fella? Mama wants to see us."

As soon as he was down the hall, Maudie closed the door behind her, walked to the dresser, and pulled out the pine box containing a memory stone.

"I'm sorry, honey, but I couldn't help but overhear you two talking," she said.

"So you know?"

"Of course. I've known from the first time I seen you lay your peepers on Mr. Mase you had feel'ns for him. And I'm sorry I didn't tell you about Mr. Vanderson. I felt that should of come from him. Lord knows you been struggl'n with all kinds of emotions. It's a wonder you're still sane. She raised her arms toward her. "Will you give me your hand."

With her chin tucked to her chest, Zoey walked toward her, pausing then raising her left hand to meet Maudie's.

"Now close your eyes."

Zoey reared back. "You're not part Indian, are you? Last time I did this I received a rather unpleasant gift."

"No, child," she chuckled. "Now go on, close 'em tight."

As soon as her eyelids came together, she felt the smooth, hard surface of the stone being placed in her palm, and Maudie's thick, warm fingers wrapping around hers, sealing it within her grasp. A second later, deep from within her chest, a small vibration emerged—a tickle at first, slowly growing, surging outward through her chest and thighs, out her arms and legs into her fingers and toes. Time passed but did not move forward, a minute, ten minutes, a day, month, years—all within the beat of a hummingbird's heart.

Chapter 33

"Zoey… honey." The voice floated around her, warm, gently tugging. "You can open up now."

Zoey blinked. "Wha—what just happened?"

Maudie removed the stone from her hand and placed it on the dresser. "What I just did, I did with Mase many years ago."

"Did what?"

Maudie took her hand again, patting it with the reassurance of a loving mother. "Never mind, child. What's important is that I've seen somethin', just like I did with him."

"What?"

"That you got a reason to be here."

"I know that. It was to help bring Jeziah into the world."

"That's part of it, but there's more. Like Mase, I couldn't see everything, but what I did see is that your path keeps gett'n narrower. You just have to decide if you're gonna continue down it."

"Is there anything else you can tell me?"

"Wish I could, but I can't make out anymore. What I do know though is that Mase wants you to stay here at Willow Creek."

"He does?"

"Yes. He cares for you more than you might think. When he came back, your name was always com'n up and whenever it did, he seemed to shine. I know he loves my Sissy more than anything but there's a special place in his heart for you too. A different place, but still special."

Her hand over her mouth, Zoey turned to the window, staring past the pond and over the rolling hills, envisioning a couple walking hand in hand through a sun-drenched meadow, her heart soaring as they came closer. From across the field, through tall emerald-green blades of grass, a little brown-skinned boy bounced his way toward them, blowing dandelion thistles into the wind. With open arms, the man scooped him up, whirling him around as the woman danced in circles, her head tossed back, the breeze blowing blissfully through her hair. Slowly the vision faded against the windowpanes.

"You saw something just now, didn't you?"

"Yes," Zoey said, her answer soft, full of longing for something that could never be. "I saw a family."

"Yours?"

She shook her head. Her eyes shimmering, she turned back to Maudie, the glint of tears telling the older woman what she already knew. "I know what I have to do."

"I understand." Maudie took Zoey by the shoulders and kissed her forehead. "I'll go get Mase."

"Please don't. He's with Sissy and Jeziah and shouldn't be disturbed. This can wait. I'd like to be alone right now anyway."

A few hours later a knock came at her door. "Who is it?"

"It's the landlord. I understand you're behind on the rent. I'd like to discuss how this most heinous circumstance has come to pass. I've called for the sheriff and he's—"

"Would you shush it, Mr. Winslow," she said, flinging the door open. "I don't want the entire neighborhood to know what a degenerate I am."

Face-to-face, they burst out laughing.

"May I come in?" he asked with a gentlemanly bow.

"Of course. Pardon the mess though. I haven't spent too much time settling in."

"That's actually what I wanted to talk with you about." He drummed his fingers over the dresser, a crooked grin appearing. "I was thinking you could stay here in Annabelle's old room, at least through the winter, then in the spring we'd build you a cottage next to the creek. You'll love it there. It's got this million-dollar view of the—"

"I can't."

His mouth skewed. "I think traveling through time is affecting your brain again. Of course, you can."

"Mase, I've been so confused and blinded by a misconception of what I thought I wanted that it's blinded me to everything else."

"What else are you talking about?"

"Boone!"

"I don't understand."

"At first, I thought he only wanted one thing from me—what all men want, or at least what less honorable men want. Then it seemed he wanted to help me. Back and forth it went. It was driving me crazy because I couldn't figure him out and with all my thoughts focused on Willow Creek, I didn't really try, I just kept working on a plan to get here. After Dag—that monster who abducted me—told me it was Boone who sold me to him, it all seemed to come together."

"Zo, I don't know anything about what this Dag person told you, but I do know that Mr. Vanderson appeared to be genuinely concerned about you. Trust me, I grilled him from every angle, making sure he was on the up and up. Besides, there's no other reason he would've come here and searched for you the way he did if he didn't truly care."

"Then why'd he leave?"

"Why do any of us men do what we do?" He chuckled. "Sometimes we don't know when were *in love* or when someone's *in love with us*."

"Love?"

"Zoey, I'm still that lowbrow literary Sasquatch you knew in New York, so I have no way to say for sure, but from where I'm standing, I think he was."

"Was?"

"Is—was—I'm only saying I *believe* love has something to do with why that man came here. But the one thing I'm *sure* of is that *he's* the only reason you're alive."

A minute passed as she stood staring out the window, absorbing all Mase had to say. She turned. "I have to go. I-I can't stay here."

"What? Of course, you can stay. I want you to stay! We can be a family."

She walked up to him and placed her hand to his cheek. "Mase—you already *have* a family." She smiled. "Besides, I have to find out if what you said was right. Running her fingers gently through his hair, she leaned forward, her breath drifting lightly over his lips, across his cheeks. "I'll always love Paul Talbert," she whispered.

From down the hall, Jeziah's cries for his father's touch snapped him back, bringing him into the light of what he had, away from what could never be. He gazed into her eyes, waiting for some mystical closure that would allow him to erase feelings that he knew were so wrong. He stepped back. "Are you sure?"

"Yes. With all my heart I know for the first time in my mixed-up life where I need to be. I'm going back to New York."

The next morning arrived bogged down in a thick, grey haze that hid the beautiful details of the plantation—its ornate columns, manicured lawn, the exactness of the finely laid cobblestone path. The haze thinned just enough that from the veranda Maudie could be seen at the edge of the road, standing with her back to a horse and buggy. Atop the buckboard, whip in hand, stiff-lipped and ramrod straight, a driver waited patiently for his passenger.

A minute later the front door swung wide, and Zoey bounded outside. She wore a simple pastel-blue cotton dress with the gold sash from her bedroom tied around her waist. From her neck a burlap sack swayed across her waist.

"Oh mercy, let's at least give you some pizazz," Maudie said, tugging a tidy bow into her sash. "Now, ain't that better."

Zoey smiled down on it. "I love it!"

"Now everything you're gonna to need is in that bag. And remember, when you get to the train depot, you go straight to the ticket station and tell 'em your name and they'll have your ticket ready. And when you get to New Jersey station, the first thing you do when you get off that train is find a man in a white linen suit. He'll be wear'n a black bow tie and carry'n a sign with your name on it. His name is Ned Sabel. He'll take you from there. You got all that?"

"Yes, ma'am."

Just then Mase came stumbling out the door with a large leather suitcase in tow. "Phew! I thought I was about to miss my flight," he wheezed.

Zoey did a double take at the baggage. "I don't think I can carry anything else."

"No worries. I got it."

"What do you mean?"

"Yeah, what exactly *do* you mean?" Maudie added.

"I'm coming with you!"

"No, you can't come with me."

"Why?"

"Be-because…"

"It's not safe, Zo. You wouldn't be able to defend yourself."

"Trust me," she said with the confidence her black-belt status afforded her, "I've picked up some skills over the past century. I'll be fine."

"You weren't fine when we found you laying on top of that ridge."

"Mase, seriously. I'll be alright."

He sighed. "Well, okay. But the moment I go back in the house I'm telegraphing Mr. Vanderson that you're on your way. Are you sure you don't want me to come?"

"You know I'd love to have you by my side, but this is something I have to do alone. And besides, you need to take care of your family here. You understand, don't you?"

"I guess I do," he said softly. Dropping his bag, he wrapped his arms around her. "I don't like it, but I understand." With a final hug he helped her into the carriage. "So when you get to the train station—"

"I've already told her everything," Maudie interjected.

"Oh—right. Okay then, so one last thing, when you get there, have Mr. *Vanderhoozy* telegraph us back immediately to let us know you got there safely. It should only take you about a day and a half." He closed the door. "Now remember, telegraph us immediately."

She leaned her head out the tiny window. "I miss cell phones, don't you?"

"Nah," Mase said with a grin. Then he waved his arm, and the driver cracked his whip.

The carriage pitched forward, carrying her down the path toward the pond as she waved her goodbyes. Drawing her hand back inside the buggy, the certainty of her decision turned as grey as the fog they were disappearing into.

With Willow Creek behind her, she opened the burlap sack she had been given and laughed aloud when she saw a jar of blackstrap molasses and a ham sandwich, knowing Maudie considered this a vital part of "everything she would need." The other contents made more sense though—a derringer pistol, which she had no idea how to use, and a wad of cash with strange markings she had seen only in history books.

The last item, hunkered into the corner next to the molasses, gave her the assurance she needed more than weapons or money. Without its pine box to denote its importance, one could have easily tossed it out as a misplaced, oversized pebble, but Zoey knew what it was. She raised it to her lips and kissed it.

Within an hour, the sun had burned away the dreary beginnings to the day, replacing them with the brilliant hues of a Monet-inspired landscape. The lazy clopping of the horse as it pulled the carriage through the countryside was a hard contrast to her harried, horn-blaring, crash course she had taken out of Manhattan on the day she had been killed.

Excitement and hope grew within her as she made her way to the Charleston train depot. It was only when she boarded that anxiety and fear joined her as unwanted travel companions. For the remainder of the day and into a restless night, her emotions railed against each other—one minute she was full of joyful expectations, then dread and uncertainty the next. Again and again, she mulled over Mase's words about love and how uncertain men were about it. What if he had it all wrong?

As the wee hours of the morning approached, her lack of sleep began to blur all negative thoughts into a surreal hue of positive anticipation, but by the time her train rolled into the New Jersey depot, that anticipation faded as anxiety came crashing back.

Stepping down onto the wooden platform, she was suddenly caught up in a wave of disembarking passengers. Lost in the crowd, she swung her head in all directions, looking for the man in the white linen suit and the black bow tie who was to take her to Boone.

"Miss Antonelli!" a voice penetrated the frenzied mass of travelers. "Over here, Miss Antonelli!"

She turned in circles, losing herself deeper in the crowd as she was swept away from where she had left the train. Tucking her chin to her chest and her bag under her arm, she leaned forward and began trudging through the chaotic horde. Suddenly, from out of nowhere a buffalo of a man in a long black coat barreled into her and knocked her to the ground, slamming her back against the broad planks and taking her breath away.

Several seconds passed as she lay gasping for air, the self-absorbed crowd passing her by, until a skinny girl in a tattered pink nightgown rushed to her side. As the girl stooped next to her, Zoey reached up toward the single gold crucifix dangling from the girl's right ear. At the same time a train whistle blared out three shrill notes. On the second one the girl volunteered a timid smile. On the third she was gone, leaving Zoey wheezing and trying to pull herself to her knees.

"Are you okay?"

She raised her head to find a middle-aged gentleman in a crisp white linen suit, his black bow tie and chalkboard sign with her name on it indicating help had arrived.

"I'm sorry about the big oaf who just plowed into you, but I've run him off. Here, let me help you up," he said, bending down.

"Are—you—Ned Sabel?" she pushed out in short breaths.

"Yes, and you must be Miss Antonelli."

"That's me. Thank you, Mr. Sabel," she said, brushing herself off.

"Please, call me Ned. Mr. Winslow has contracted me to escort you to Mr. Boone Vanderson's residence here in the city. Is that correct?"

"Yes," she said, turning her head back and forth, her mind suddenly preoccupied.

"Is there something wrong?"

"I can't find my bag," she said, dropping to her knees and scanning the surroundings from ground level.

"What type of bag was it?"

She jumped up and began racing back and forth through the crowd, repeatedly directing a worried eye his way. “It’s just a plain burlap bag, brown with a long, waist-length strap. It’s got everything in it!”

A half hour later, having combed the platform along with the rest of the depot, she surrendered her search.

Following an inquiry at the lost and found, Ned suggested that it had most likely been stolen. “If you don’t mind me asking, what was in it?”

“A little pistol, money, some food and a…”

“Don’t worry, Miss Antonelli, those things can all be replaced.”

She groaned, “Some can—but not everything.”

“Was it a lot of money?”

“I don’t know, I didn’t really check. But it wasn’t the money. It was the thing that could save my life.”

“Ma’am, you can always get another gun.”

“No, it wasn’t the gun. It was… oh, never mind. It’s gone.” She scanned the station one more time, coming to grips with the bag’s fate, her focus suddenly shifting to the reason she was back in New York. “Can we go see Boone now?”

“Of course, my coachman has our carriage just around the corner.”

With the theft behind her, she settled in for the hour-long ride to Boone’s house, Mr. Sabel providing commentary along the way as if she had never been to the city.

“… and this building was erected in 1802 and that bridge across the river, the one under construction, that’s going to connect us to Brooklyn. Folks say it’ll take ten years to complete.”

As much as she wanted to chime in on how many more bridges would ultimately tie into the city, she joyfully opted to mention Boone and how excited she was to see him. "Have you heard of Mr. Vanderson? He seems to know everyone. He even has—" Her attention suddenly dropped off as they rounded the corner.

"What is it, ma'am?" he said as his eyes followed hers down the street to Vanderson's house. "Is everything alright? You've turned a little pale."

Her nerves frayed as a thousand butterflies found their way to her stomach. Looking up to the bars on the window, to the gilded cage in which she thought she had been confined, she threw up her hand. "Can you hold up just a minute?"

Sabel leaned out the window. "Driver, stop the carriage please." He turned to her. "Miss Antonelli, the house is right there."

"I-I know." She sat with her fingers intertwined, grinding against one another, her chest heaving. "I just have to compose myself." She took three long breaths. "Okay, I'm ready."

After proceeding the remaining few yards, Sabel ran to the other side of the carriage. "Do you want me to come with you?" he said, helping her to the curb.

"No, no, I'm fine," she said through a nervous smile. A moment later she was on the front steps, about to place her hand on the knocker, when the door opened. A beautiful young lady dressed in a long flowing evening gown adorned with several pieces of heavy jewelry stood before her. "Oh, my heavens." She threw her hand over her heart. "You startled me. I didn't hear you knock."

"I-I didn't. I just walked up."

"My apologies, by the way, we're on our way to the theatre and are in a bit of a rush, but how can I help you?"

"Who're you talking to?" came a man's voice from inside.

"And you are?" the lady asked.

"Oh, it doesn't matter. I-I'm such a dunce. I'm at the wrong house. You see, I'm new in town and… Well, I'm sorry. Forgive me." She turned, lowered her head, and began running back to the carriage, fleeing the evidence of Boone's betrayal standing in the doorway.

"Wait!" came the man's voice again. "What house are you trying to find?"

She glanced over her shoulder to a short bald man in a tuxedo, his arm tucked under the woman's. She stopped. "Boone Vanderson's."

"He doesn't live here anymore," he said. "We moved in just yesterday."

"He sold it?"

"Got it for a song," the woman crowed. "Lock, stock and barrel—including all the furniture."

"Please, dear, you're gloating again." Turning his attention back to Zoey, he said, "Yes, ma'am, we bought it alright, but if you're wondering where he lives now, I'm afraid I couldn't tell you."

"That's alright. I'll let you get to the theatre."

As she approached the carriage, Mr. Sabel walked up. "I couldn't help but overhear. I'm afraid I'm at a loss now for what to do. This is the only address I was given."

"That's okay, I think I know where to find him. Do you mind taking me someplace else?"

He wrapped her arm around his. "May the journey continue."

Chapter 34

As they made their way out of the city, a row of dark clouds crept up the eastern horizon, lumbering their way above the city's low-hanging skyline. An hour into the countryside, the clouds had turned the clear blue sky into a steel grey ceiling.

"I hear this place is New York's biggest market," Sabel said.

Zoey stuck her head out the window and looked up at the darkening sky. "And the biggest mess too. Especially if those clouds let loose."

"Just dirt roads out there?" he asked.

"Not a cobblestone or brick to be found." She ducked back in. "See for yourself."

He stuck his head outside. "Well, I'll be, it's the size of a little city."

She held her hands in her lap, her fingers twisting her dress into tiny knots.

"And you're sure he's here?"

"I'm not sure of anything."

Just then the carriage came to a stop. "Which way, sir?" the driver called down.

Sabel shrugged. "Where to, Miss Antonelli?"

Leaning out the window, she stared down a wide dirt road lined with tents, lean-tos, and makeshift buildings. "This is the main street. Just keep going straight until you start seeing livestock pens. Look for a sign that says Vanderson's Pork and Poultry. It's next to a little rough-cut building, about the size of two sheds."

A long sigh followed her back into her seat as the sounds of merchants haggling with hopeful customers rose outside the confines of the carriage, their clamoring to make deals adding to her anxiety.

"Miss Antonelli?"

Her fingers returned to her dress, stretching and pulling it.

"Miss Antonelli?" he said louder. "Zoey!"

"Yes, oh—I'm sorry," she replied, releasing the mangled fabric.

"Are you going to be alright?"

"Yes, yes, I'll be fine." She turned back to the window, her excitement growing in anticipation of seeing him, though the air of the unknown still clung to her.

A few minutes later the carriage tipped sharply forward then back again as it came to an abrupt halt.

"Sorry about that, sir," the driver said. "I just about missed it."

Sabel leaned toward her. "Do you want me to come with you?" he asked, his tone revealing he was privy to more information about Boone than he had let on.

"Thank you, but I'm okay." She hesitated. "That's actually the second time you've asked if I wanted you to come with me. Is there a reason you should?"

"No, no, I—"

"You know something, don't you? I'm not moving until you tell me."

"Really, Miss Antonelli, everything is fine."

"I'm not going any further. Do you know something I should know?"

He pursed his lips.

"Mr. Sable, please just tell me. This may be the most important decision of my life."

"I'm sorry but I can't. I'm bound by client confidentiality."

"Now you have to tell me. Please. I've come all the way from South Carolina looking for something I'm hoping exists in a man I've misjudged since the day we met. Please, Mr. Sabel, what do you know? I need to know that I truly had misjudged him."

A moment passed. "You know, I have a daughter about your age. I'd want her to know for the exact same reason." He paused. "Oh, to hades with confidentiality. Part of my contract with Mr. Winslow was that before I delivered you to him, I was to do a background check on Mr. Vanderson."

"Who are you?"

"I'm a private investigator."

"Incredible," she said, shaking her head, thinking back on how many times Mase had looked out for her. "So what did you find out? Please tell me he's not a murderer or sex trafficker."

"No, ma'am, he's neither of those things. Oddly enough he's rather well respected and held in high regard for his efforts in fighting the latter. However—he's no saint either, or at least it appears he's not. His dealings with a man named Boss Tweed have had him under scrutiny for years. From loan-sharking to gambling, your Mr. Vanderson's darker dealings, which have made him rich, appear to involve only financial matters. But just to make it clear, he's never been charged."

"So he's been defrauding—or whatever you said—helpless people?"

He gave her a sideways glance. "Hardly helpless. It seems he has only one specific target market he works with—rich Southerners." He waited. "So do you still want to go in?"

"Is there anything else?"

"No, ma'am."

"Thank you for telling me. But I'm still going in."

"Are you sure?"

"Mr. Sabel, I know part of that story—not everything, but I know enough—and I know other things about his character. I also know now about the feelings he…" She paused. "Thank you again. I have to go now."

He nodded. "Okay, but I'm still going to wait here."

As she climbed out of the carriage, a slow, steady drizzle began to fall. She stood for a long while examining the tiny shanty where she had first met the man in the tall black hat, the man she had hated, the man that had twisted her feelings into something she could not explain, the man who somehow had managed to help pry her away from what she thought was her destiny.

Slowly she began walking toward the building, her nervousness rising in time with the increasing downfall. As the rain came harder, she hiked up her dress and continued, carefully placing each step to not lose her footing in the mud-soaked road.

From under the tiny overhang, she ran her hand through her hair, then with a deep breath, she rapped her knuckles against the door, shifting side to side as she waited.

From the other side of the building, from the far corner of the adjacent pen came a voice as strong and confident as she remembered. Her heart skipped a beat.

"Come here! I swear if you don't come here, I'll…" his voice faded into the growing deluge.

She stepped out from under the protection of the overhang, soaked head to toe, water streaming down her neck and onto her dress, now a darker shade of waterlogged blue. Like a wilting flower, her bow drooped below her gold sash, dangling dangerously above the muddy field through which she trudged, toward the man at the opposite side of the pen.

With his back to her, he stood taller than she remembered, his shoulders appearing broader in the attire of a common farmer—torn and tattered overalls bearing the stains of true labor. In front of him was a giant sow rooting her way back into the corner, wriggling her haunches in hopes of avoiding capture.

"That's it," Boone said, dangling a looped rope over her while slowly coaxing the animal farther back. "That's it… good piggy."

He gradually lowered the rope, moving it just past its snout, preparing to yank it back across her massive body, when suddenly Zoey hollered, "Run, Ulysses! Run!"

The animal squealed and bolted through Boone's legs. He slipped and slid across the mud, comically flailing like a newborn foal testing its legs for the first time.

"Who the—" he growled, jerking his head over his shoulder. Throwing the rope to the ground, he turned, his eyes flashing red as he took a step toward her. The rain and the wind whipped across them, their clothes thrashing against their bodies as they stood facing each other.

"Zoey! Is-is that you?"

"Why didn't you stay?" she cried out through the howling wind.

"What?"

"Why did you lock me in that room? Why were bars across the window?"

"Those bars were to keep people out, not in. It's the same reason I had Gibson lock your door."

"Why did you let Logan have that monster Dag join his caravan?"

He held out his hands, palms up, rain battering down on them. "I didn't know anything about that other guy. I only hired Logan to take you to Beaufort. I swear, I didn't know about anyone else."

"He drugged me and ripped my leg apart. He was a murderer who almost killed me!" Tears raced alongside the rain flowing down her cheeks.

"I don't know what happened," he said, spreading his arms. By degrees he approached her, cautious, fearful of her vanishing into the driving rain. "Why are you here?" he asked.

"Because Mase told me what you did and how you knew I loved him."

"If you love him, then why are you here?"

"But I don't. I thought I did, but I don't…"

"Zoey, why—are—you—here?"

She swallowed. "Because you came after me."

"That's it? You came all this way to thank me?"

"Of course, I want to thank you, but-but I have to know—why didn't you stay?"

"Because you said you loved Mase! It was in your letter. How could I come between that? You deserve to be happy. That's what I wanted. That's why I left before you came to."

"You'd rather see me happy than to—"

"Zoey, why—are—you—here?" he said taking a step toward her.

"Because!"

"Because why?"

"Because it's you I love! I love you!"

With the wind hurling about them and the rain beating down, he stood motionless, his eyes beginning to glisten, not from the rain but because she'd finally said the three words he had longed to hear since the moment they met. "You love me?"

She lowered her head, giving him a tender nod. "Yes," she said softly. She raised her palms to cover her mouth, then she pulled them down to cover her heart. "Yes! Yes! I love you!"

Taking her in his arms, he pulled her into him, pressing his lips against hers, kissing her again and again. The rain fell harder. Running her hands through his hair, she arched her head back, welcoming his mouth against her neck. Smiling, laughing, oblivious of the torrential downpour, she kissed him back. Hugging him, she buried her head in his chest.

"I was so wrong about you and so obsessed with something that never existed," she said. "I never saw how you… Can you ever forgive me?"

He pulled back. "Forgive you? There's nothing to forgive."

"So you believe me and all my ramblings—you believe I did come from the future?"

"I do. There's still so much I want to know… but yes, I believe you."

"And you don't think I'm crazy?"

"Well, I didn't say that," he smirked. Leaning into each other, their foreheads gently touched. "It's me who's crazy. I'm the one who actually waited a hundred and fifty years for you."

She pulled back a little, smiling as she blinked the raindrops away. He kissed her neck, then slowly inching to her ear, he whispered, "Come on, let's get Ulysses out of this storm before she catches her death."

The next morning the same roosters that had so rudely awakened her after her first night in the Vanderson Pork and Poultry performed their same annoying routine. Unlike that disastrous morning, instead of being hungover and afraid, she awoke invigorated, happy, and not alone. Next to her were Boone's broad shoulders, his bare muscular chest slowly rising and falling. She followed every curve of his torso up to his face, hungering to kiss him but withholding her urge for fear of disturbing the smile that rested upon his lips. Unable to restrain herself, she kissed his cheek. The corners of his mouth crinkled upward as his dimples deepened, sending a wave of desire through her.

"Good morning, Miss Antonelli," he whispered, his hushed baritone forming each word in perfect balance with the love she knew he had for her.

"Good morning Mr. Vanderson."

His arm moved lightly across her side, his hand slowly running up her shoulder, fingertips gliding up her neck and falling softly against her cheek. Gazing into her eyes, he hesitated, then he tilted his head and pulled her to him, kissing her forehead, then her cheek, teasing her until, with the weight of a butterfly, he pressed his lips to hers.

By noon the tiny porthole that served as a window was a solid pastel circle of blue. A beam of light passed through it, crossed over the curves of their bodies where they lay in the bed, and onto Zoey's gold sash where it ran unfurled across the hardwood floor. With the dusty hands on the cuckoo clock in the corner counting the hours, they passed the morning away experiencing the joy of their love like two moonstruck teenagers.

She ran her fingers through his thick mane. "I like your hair fluffy. It frames that manly jaw of yours like—" Angling her head toward the opposite wall, she said, "Did you hear that?"

A grunt, followed by the wall shaking suddenly sent her sitting upright.

"Shhh," he said, holding his finger to his lips, "we've been found out."

"Is that Ulysses out there?"

"The good general needs to be fed," he chortled. "Every day at noon she comes knocking."

Zoey laughed. "You'd think she was jealous by the way she's banging at it."

Leaning up on his elbow, he pulled her closer. "I've got to go into the city today. You'll join me, won't you?"

"Of course!" she replied with a bounce.

"I've got some business to attend to with Boss Tweed and I have to go by and pick up some things at my house."

"I thought you sold it?"

"Did you go by there before you came here?"

"Yes. The couple told me you sold it and everything in it."

"I did. I just need to get my revolver and some paperwork I forgot to get out of my desk. Then I've got to go see Tweed. You still want to come, don't you?"

"Of course. It'll be the perfect time to tell you about the future!"

"Fantastic," he said, twirling a strand of her hair between his fingers.

"I know we have plenty of time, but you should know that Tweed proves to be one of the most corrupt people in the history of New York. He's evil. In fact, within the year, he'll be in jail."

"I know," he said with an apologetic tone. "I've known for years. Not much at first, but then more and more." His head fell. "I was too weak to say no. I was doing his bidding and even trying to become more like him."

"Why didn't you leave?"

"I told you—revenge." His voice rose an octave. "Through him I was able to steal back from those who took my family from me. It was the only way."

"Whoever you did these things to, did you know they had been involved in what happened to your family?"

"No!" His breath grew heavy. "Can we just go?"

"I'm sorry," she said, watching him struggling to pull himself out of the past, regretting her inquiry and the pain she had inadvertently caused. "Yes, we can go." Easing the blanket from his fist, she kissed him on the cheek. "You're going to be amazed by how much things change over the next century."

"And the stone. You'll tell me all about it?"

"Of course. It's the main character."

Chapter 35

The rich array of autumn foliage proved the perfect backdrop for their journey into the city. With a cool breeze blowing in from the east, they wrapped themselves in a blanket, snuggling together in the open-air buckboard that had replaced the sleek black carriage from the first time they had ventured into Manhattan together.

Zoey rested her head against his shoulder. He was still in his overalls, and she moved his shoulder strap away from her cheek. "You didn't want to change for Mr. Tweed?"

"Nope." His answer came crisply. "Time he sees me for who I really am."

"And who is that, Mr. Vanderson?"

He smiled. "A man who finally has it all."

From the time they passed through the market gates to when they rolled into the city, she captivated Boone with her tales of the world to come, the advent of more wars, the inventions, the internet, her life as a journalist, and how she had met Paul Talbert, the man he knew only as Mase. When she began explaining the stones, he pulled the wagon to a stop.

"So you're telling me you thought the stone should have taken you forward in time rather than back?"

"Yes, I don't know why it didn't, but I'm glad it didn't."

"And if you used it again, it would take you to the future, like it did for your friend Mase?"

"I think so. That's what I was hoping for when I was on that mountain ridge."

"But it wasn't a real memory stone?"

"No." She hesitated. "I have a question for you. Do you really believe me? I know you say you do but do you really? I mean, it's so absurd. Listening to myself, I even find it hard to believe. Do you *really* believe me?"

"Yes, Zoey, I do. I'm never going to lie to you, I promise you that. Yes, I believe you."

"What was the turning point when you thought, 'Okay, she's not insane after all.'"

"Well, your ramblings all seemed rather sincere—crazy, mind you, but sincere. And then, of course, your prediction of the Chicago fire." He stopped as if holding back a laugh. "And then… there was the pink stripe in your hair."

Her lips skewed. "So my hair made you a believer?"

"Besides the ramblings and the fire, it was also your mannerisms, the way you spoke… just your air. You—you just seemed to transcend time."

"Nah," she laughed. "It was the hair."

He threw his head back with a raucous laugh. "That's what I'm talking about." He snapped the reins, sending the wagon back into motion. "Tell me again about what happens if someone places their hands on top of someone else's who's holding one of those stones."

Onto the cobblestone streets of Manhattan they rode, his chattering for information on the memory stone continuing all the way to the South Street Seaport.

"What are we doing here? I thought you had a meeting with Tweed."

"Tweed can wait. I thought we'd take one last trip around the harbor."

"Oh, I'd love that!" She squealed with delight. "But why does it have to be the last?"

"I'm selling it."

"But you *love* your boat."

He paused, reflecting upon the transaction. "True, but it was time."

She scanned the docks. "You must be happy about that sight."

"What's that?"

"Not a clipper ship in dock. Your entire fleet out making money over the whitecaps."

"Well, maybe for someone else."

"How's that?"

"Sold them all a couple weeks ago."

She stepped back. "Boone, what's going on?"

"Liquidation, my sweet, time-traveling maven. Sweet, redeeming liquidation."

Once out of dock, he navigated to a stretch of calm waters far enough into the harbor where only the gulls and water lapping against the hull could be heard. Releasing the sail, the boat floated idle. Leaning back, he took her in his arms and kissed her lightly while pulling a blanket around them.

"Aren't you going to miss her?" she asked.

"Miss who?"

"The *Lady Anne*."

"Of course," he said, though his tone was neither mournful or full of regret.

"You don't seem upset."

"It's just business."

"And selling off your fleet? Just business too?"

"Yep, just business." He leaned his head back and sighed. "Hear that?"

"Hear what?"

"The sea gulls, the sail waving in the wind, the water on the hull. Now *that*, I'll miss."

She rolled her head against his shoulder. Content in the blissful absence of chatter, secure in their embrace, they snuggled beneath the blanket, falling asleep as they slowly drifted back toward the docks.

"Oh wow," she said, waking to a setting sun. "We're almost back at the seaport and look how dark it's gotten."

"So it has," he said, rubbing his eyes.

"What time was your meeting with Tweed?"

"Seven. I'm having dinner at his home."

"That's gotta be soon."

He pulled a pocket watch from the top of his overalls. "You're right, that's in an hour."

"Then we've got to go," she said, retrieving a rope to bring the mainsail taut. "You'll need to change and get ready."

He placed his hand on her arm, taking the rope. "It's okay. I don't have anything to change into so we have time. He'll just see me when he sees me. I would ask you to come along but I know how you feel about him."

"I'll be fine just strolling around his neighborhood. What about retrieving your gun and paperwork at your old house?"

"It's on the way."

On the ride back to his house, they passed several streets lined with homeless people causing her to reflect on the drastic changes in her new love's attire, along with the sudden "liquidation" of his home, carriage, and beloved sailing vessels.

Unable to hold back any longer, she tiptoed into asking, "So do you have plans for that big influx of cash?"

"What cash?"

She grabbed her gold sash from the floorboard and began fidgeting with it. "I-I didn't want to pry because it's none of my business." She tied the sash around her waist, finishing it off in a nervous bow. "I was just curious is all."

He delighted in her innocent approach to the subject he knew was certain to come. "I was wondering when you were going to ask me about that."

"I'm sorry, I know I shouldn't ask."

"No, it's quite alright. I'd be asking too and, to be honest, a lot sooner than you did."

As they turned the corner onto his street, he brought the wagon to a standstill.

"Oh no," she said, raising her hands to her chin. "You're going to jail. I'm never going see you again!"

He rocked back. "No! Nothing like that."

She exhaled. "Oh, thank goodness."

"True, I've sold many of my possessions—to be exact, all my possessions except for the pork and poultry business—but I don't have the cash from any of it."

"You've already rolled it into other investments?"

"You might say that…"

"I'm confused."

"My investments are in other people's lives now."

"Now I'm even more confused."

His smile grew larger. "I think I like this new game."

"Oh, please just tell me."

In an instant his smile faded. "The reason there's no cash is that I've distributed it according to the scams and underhanded dealings I used to obtain it."

"Are you saying you gave it away?"

"What I'm saying is that I've returned it to the rightful owners." A somber cloud suddenly came over him. "It took me too long to realize that what I was doing was enacting revenge on innocent people. Deep down I knew I was wrong, but I was so consumed with hatred that I was numb to it. I was trying to ruin my enemies who weren't even my enemies. All along I was ruining my own life."

"What changed things?"

"Time, for one thing, but the other thing—the most important reason—was a conversation."

"With who?"

"A man dressed in dirty overalls, like the ones I have on but almost in shreds. He wasn't homeless, or at least I don't think he was, but I could sense he'd been through a lot in his life. Not so much by his clothes but something else. I—I can't explain it."

"Where'd you meet him?"

The color in his cheeks rose. "You know the place."

"Where?"

"Remember the church I took you to, the one I wouldn't go into?"

"Yes."

"After I left you in Charleston, I came back, more miserable than ever. I hated myself. I hated not telling you how I truly felt. I hated how long I had lied and cheated. I hated having seen the devastation I brought into other people's lives. I-I just couldn't take it anymore. I went into my office, pulled my revolver from my desk drawer, and was about to—"

"Oh, Boone, no!"

"Of course, I didn't go through with it. But afterwards I walked the streets. For hours I just walked, head down, not knowing where I was going, or even why I was walking. When I finally looked up, I was in front of that church. It was a Thursday evening. No one was going in or out, but the door was open. For some reason I just went straight in and sat in the farthest back pew." He chortled. "And of course, I had no idea what to do. I'd never prayed a day in my life except asking God for revenge. There I was, sitting, staring across the rows of pews into a dark, vacant pulpit. I'm not sure how long I was there before he sat down beside me."

"The man in overalls?"

He nodded. "For a moment it was awkward. All those seats and he sat down next to me. Who does that? So I started to get up and he held up his hand in a way that said, 'Don't leave.' Anyway, it stopped me. I can remember wanting to leave but I couldn't."

Her eyes widened.

"Without looking at me, he said the strangest thing. At least at that moment it was strange."

"What was it?"

"It was about forgiveness. He said, 'Forgiveness is a journey in time.' Nothing else. Just those six simple words."

"That's it?"

"That was it. Nothing else."

"What did you say?"

"I-I didn't know what to say. All that came out was, 'Excuse me?'"

"And then what?"

"He turned to me—and in a thousand years I'll never be able to explain it—but the warmth coming from him was like nothing I've felt before. I can only describe it as love—pure, joyful, unconditional love. Then he reached over and gently placed his hand on my shoulder."

"Didn't that freak you out?"

"Trust me, if that had happened with any other stranger, I'd have punched him, but I didn't. I actually welcomed it. It was like… when my father used to place his hand on my shoulder when I was upset."

"Then what?"

A tear rolled down Boone's cheek as his lip began to quiver. "He said, 'Your sins have been forgiven.'"

She leaned toward him. "Your sins?"

"I didn't know what to do, but what happened suddenly came easier than I had ever thought possible. I closed my eyes and for the first time in my life—I prayed. I said a prayer—a real prayer, thanking God for his grace, thanking him for lifting all the guilt and forgiving me for all my sins. I'm not sure what else I said, but I said it out loud and with a perfect stranger who had only said two vague, random sentences to me."

"What did the man say after that?"

Boone slowly turned his head side to side, a glow emanating from him. "Nothing."

"Nothing? That was it?"

"There couldn't be any more because when I looked back up—he was gone."

She threw her hand over her mouth.

"Gone—just gone," he said.

"Do you think…"

"I don't know what I think. All I know is right then and there I was determined to pay back everyone I had taken anything from. That's why I've sold it all. Every single person I defrauded or took advantage of has been paid back *and* with interest. And I confessed to all of them what I had done."

"Did any press charges?"

"Not one."

"Wow!"

"Incredible, isn't it?"

"Unbelievable!"

"You don't believe me?"

She laughed. "Sorry, bad word choice. Of course, I believe you." She grabbed his hand. "How do you feel?"

"Fantastic! For the first time in my life, I feel free. No more anger, no more guilt and no more sadness."

"And what now?"

"I get to go see Mr. Tweed and tell him I'm finished and that I'm settling for a life as a poor ole pig and chicken farmer."

Chapter 36

A minute later they were walking up to Boone's front door. The windows were dark with not a flicker from a lamp or a candle inside.

"I may have been a little too long-winded with my story," Boone said, knocking on the door. "If they're home, would you mind doing me a favor and waiting here for me? I'm sure they won't mind. I'll come back for the gun and paperwork later. This way you won't have to wander the streets while I'm at Tweed's."

As he was about to knock again, the door creaked open, just wide enough for the lady Zoey had met before to poke her head out from a dark hallway. "Who is it?" she said.

"Hello, Mrs. Alcott, it's me, Boone Vanderson and Zoey Antonelli."

"Oh, yes—yes, Mr. Vanderson."

"I'm sorry I'm a little late. Is your husband home?"

"He's…" She ducked her head back inside then reappeared a few seconds later. "He's, uh—detained."

"I was wondering if I could come back to do the paperwork and if you wouldn't mind if Miss Antonelli waited for me here?" He wrapped his arm around her waist. "With it being dark I thought it would be safer."

Zoey offered up half a smile.

"Just one minute," Mrs. Alcott said, disappearing again.

"Boone, why don't I just come with you? I don't think she wants me to come in."

"I just have this feeling you'd be safer here. Is that okay?"

"Of course it is," said Mr. Alcott, popping up where his wife had been, his forehead beaded with sweat, cheeks flushed red against the backdrop of the dark hallway.

Boone studied him for a moment. "Are you sure?"

"Oh, yes. It's quite alright," the man said through a stiff grin. "In fact, we welcome Miss Antonelli to wait here while you handle your business."

"I greatly appreciate that. It shouldn't take but an hour or so. It's just that I'm late and—"

"Don't think anything of it, Mr. Vanderson." The man ducked his head inside then quickly back out again. "By all means, please come in, Miss Antonelli."

She rolled her eyes back at Boone with an apprehensive gaze.

After kissing her on the cheek, he gave the bow on her sash a playful tug. "I'll be back in a wink."

As he climbed into the wagon, he convinced himself their lack of lighting was simply a personal preference. Flicking the reins, he set off, determined to make his stint at the Tweed mansion as short and painless as possible.

Back inside Zoey waited for her sight to adjust to her dim surroundings as Mr. Alcott bolted the door shut then locked it. Halfway down the hall a soft light floated from underneath the dining room's drawn curtains.

Mr. Alcott swallowed hard. "Follow me." As he parted the curtains, he whispered out the corner of his mouth, "Try to remain calm."

With the only light coming from a tiny candle on the edge of the table, Zoey hesitated. "Why are all the—"

"Hello, kitten." The words slithered from a shadowy corner across the room, striking her in the chest like a serpent's fangs. Hovering in the darkness above the opposite corner of the dining table, a tiny flick of light drew her attention to ten inches of a razor-sharp bowie knife pointed directly at her.

Centered on the other side of the table, Mrs. Alcott sat rigid, her mouth gagged, hands tied behind her back, bug-eyed with fear, sweat pouring from her platinum blond hair down her face in waves.

"Well done, Mr. Alcott," came the voice again. "Please retake your seat."

"I'm so sorry," Mr. Alcott muttered as he passed Zoey. Sitting next to his wife, a skinny girl in a dirty pink nightgown rushed up behind him. The dangling gold crucifix in her right ear glimmered, confirming she was the street urchin from the train depot. Unlike before, she refused to look at Zoey, choosing instead to go about her work of binding Alcott to the chair, then gagging him with a matching handkerchief, the same as the one shoved into his wife's mouth.

"What is this?" Zoey said, aiming her question to the corner from where the voice had come.

The strike of a match followed by a small incendiary burst threw light under the brim of a large floppy hat. Smoke billowed under it and rolled up around its edges, disappearing into the blackness.

She lifted her chin, teeth clenched. "I said, what—is—this?"

"I see our kitten hasn't lost her claws," came the unknown voice.

Her chest caved as the words sucked the breath from her lungs. Her memory returned her to the *Maria*, back to her tumultuous journey, praying it couldn't be.

From under the brim, a pale hand floated a stubby cigarette to invisible lips, a long drag igniting a flame that revealed the ghoulish features of a monster too foul for hell, resurrected to haunt her again.

"Dag? Is-is that you?"

The screech of chair legs across the wooden floor rocked her on her heels. Glancing to the knife, she flashed back to the man in the corner, watching his silhouette rise as he slowly moved behind the Alcotts. Like a tiny firefly, the hot tip of his cigarette jumped from one wick to the next of a three-candle brass candelabra, illuminating the room in a grim half-light, revealing the man holding the knife to be that of the buffalo who had knock her down at the train station. Cowering in the farthest corner was the girl in the pink nightgown. Standing slump-shouldered beneath his hat, head down, hands resting on the Alcotts' heads was the man controlling the room.

"You should've let me finish our little journey." His words oozed out, hissing their way to her. His chin tucked to his chest so that she could see only the top of his hat, he began rubbing the Alcotts' heads, as if petting a pair of house cats. "I'm just curious to know how long you were part of Vanderson's scheme."

"Why don't you just get on with it?" the man with the knife grumbled.

"Shut up, you idiot," Dag howled. "Just stand there and hold your weapon like a good boy."

Zoey's fighting senses suddenly came alive as she sized up the room for an attack strategy. With the man and his knife out of range and the table protecting Dag, she would have to wait. "What do you want?" she asked flatly.

Pushing his way between the Alcotts to the edge of the table, he lifted his head, the candlelight rolling across his ghostly skin, the veins along his temples pounding.

"Does anyone else know about our operation, besides you and your boyfriend?"

"I-I don't know what you mean or what you're planning but Boone will be back any minute and he's bringing friends."

"Ohhh, now that's rich!" he said, turning to the girl in the corner. "You hear that, Katy Ray? Missy here thinks her boyfriend's coming back with an army or something." He leaned across the table. "It's with my most sincere apologies that I must inform you that your Mr. Vanderson isn't coming back at all."

"Why wouldn't he?"

The corners of his eyes took on a devilish edge. "Because our boss is going to eliminate the problem."

"Your boss? Eliminate the problem? What're you talking about?"

"You really don't know anything, do you? You don't know that, like your boyfriend, I also work for Boss Tweed. Only difference is he trusts me. Your boyfriend—not so much anymore. You see, Tweed suspected your sugar daddy was siphoning off our inventory awhile back, so he put me on the case."

"You mean Boone was helping girls escape becoming sex slaves?"

"Ooohhh, wash your mouth, kitten! You make it sound so bad. *Soiled doves*, if you please." He leaned toward her. "Your boy had another name for our birds he was secretly letting loose. What did he call them, Katy Ray? Little finches, wasn't it?" He took a long drag from his cigarette, arching his head back, blowing smoke rings proudly into the air. "And you were actually the finch that tipped open the cage."

"What're you talking about?"

"You were the first of our would-be doves I began trailing that proved to Tweed his hunch was right. I would have snatched you on the street in New York that day, but you conjured that black magic fighting of yours."

"So then you trailed me all the way to South Carolina to kidnap me?"

"What can I say? Boss Tweed took a shine to you." He snickered. "Well, he took a shine to the money he thought he could make off you. When Tweed sets his mind to what he wants, he always gets it." His voice grew agitated. "So yeh, I had to lug that sickly little Birdie girl all the way to swamp-infested Charleston just to nab you out on the trail from that decrepit cowboy."

"Can't you just leave us be? Boone's giving up everything. He's going to tell Tweed that right now. He's out!"

"You're never *out*, kitten."

"But he is! I'm telling you he's sold everything. I'm sure the Alcotts told you they bought his house and everything in it. He's even sold his ships and—"

"Yeh, yeh, I know all that. Tweed's got men at the telegraph office that have been feeding us all his messages for over a month. Thanks to your Mr. Winslow's telegraph, I knew you were coming back to New York. So nice of him to include your train schedule too." A crooked smile appeared on his face. "Now that's *my* black magic."

"So if you know he's truly out. Why can't you just let us go?"

"I've done told you. You're never out. And when you cross Tweed, that's the end of the line. Speaking of which,

I'd say he's got him swinging from the end of one right about now. And as for you… well, it's time for us to finish our dance."

"Good, let's get on with it," said the man with the knife.

Dag took a long, frustrated breath, then walked toward him, his hand extended. "Give it to me!"

"Sorry, sir," the man said, relinquishing the blade.

Her heart sank as she watched Dag trade out the man's knife with a revolver.

"Keep that on her," Dag said, walking up behind Mrs. Alcott. Running his hand through her hair, he placed the knife against the side of her shivering neck. "Before we go any further, let's just see what kind of black magic you can conjure now."

"Why do you keep saying 'black magic'?" Zoey said, looking down on the blade and the small red line it had already produced against delicate skin.

"Because every time we've met, you've worked some sort of witchery. No girl can fight the way you did in the street that day. And you said you knew the power of the stone I took from that burial mound." His voice rose, each word a pain-filled exclamation. "Then somehow you managed to escape those savages, leaving me to pay the price! Nobody could have done that without some sort of magic—nobody!" Slinging his hat to the floor, the candlelight reflected off a jagged, six-inch swath of mangled scalp, blazing red with clumps of black scabs, a clotted line against his pasty white forehead, blood oozing from tiny patches of stringy blonde hairs that had somehow escaped the Indian's knife. "Pretty, ain't it," he snarled.

Zoey recoiled, forcing herself to maintain eye contact, afraid if she didn't, his manic intentions would explode.

Taking the knife from Mrs. Alcott's throat, he tapped it against his own ravaged skull. "All this loveliness, not to mention the pain, all brought on by you!" He lunged the blade toward her, the point centered at her heart. She faltered backwards as he performed another mock stab at her from across the table. "Take one more step, either backwards or forwards, and my man shoots. You hear that, boy? Shoot this witch if she takes one more step!"

"My pleasure," the big man said.

In an instant, Dag's voice reverted to a steely calm. "So, what I propose is you perform a little demonstration." Then in a manic outburst he yelled, "Katy Ray!" throwing his hand back toward the girl in the pink gown. A second later she was placing a wadded ball of burlap in his hand. With his other hand he rolled it out onto the table, then pulled it up in front of him, letting it dangle down by the straps tucked inside.

Her mouth fell open. "My bag!"

His lips curling up, he dove his hand inside, extracting the memory stone Maudie had given her. He threw the burlap across the table. "Your bag—my stone!"

She stood mesmerized. "That's mine!"

"Like I said. The bag's yours, the stone's mine?"

"You don't know what you have."

"Of course I do. This is the stone from the burial ground. The one you *stole* from me. The one that you used to escape with. The only thing is, I don't know how to use it." The knife's point swung toward her again. "That's *your* job. I need you to summon what's inside."

"You're insane!"

His chest heaved in tandem with a gravel-filled roar. "I'll show you insane," he said, moving the knife to Mrs. Alcott's forehead.

"Stop," Zoey yelled, reaching out to him.

With one hand pressing down against the blade, he dragged the knife across the blonde hairline. Blood poured down over Mrs. Alcott's face. Her chair rocked violently as muffled screams filled the room.

"No! Stop—please don't—"

A second later, his knife was scraping backwards as he dug his fingers under her skin, ripping her scalp from her skull as blood gushed down her dress.

"Give her the stone," Zoey shouted. "I'll show you its magic. For God's sake, give her the stone!"

"And then what?" His voice rose in childish anticipation of being given an unexpected gift. "What will it do?"

"She-she'll vanish. Just please give her the stone."

"That's it? What about me? What will it do for me?"

Zoey stared into Mrs. Alcott's bloodstained eyes, struggling for an answer that would save her life.

He hammered the butt of the bloody knife onto the table. "What—will—it—do—for—me?"

"Her hair! That's it—her hair," she said.

"Her hair?"

"It's almost the same as yours. If you give her the stone, she'll vanish, but what's hers will then be yours."

"I don't get it."

"The scalp they took from you will be restored. What's hers *will be yours*. You'll have powers too—you'll be able to see into the future, *you'll be rich* because you'll know the future. Just give her the stone!"

He stood mesmerized at the possibilities.

"Do it now though because if she dies without it in her hands, you won't get anything." Zoey breathed heavily, praying her combination of half-truths had found their mark.

With frenzied twists and turns, he began untying his mangled prisoner's hands from behind her back.

"Listen to me, Mrs. Alcott," said Zoey. "You have to hold onto the stone."

Her bloody head rocked back and forth amid softening moans.

"Don't let go of the stone, Mrs. Alcott. Whatever you do—don't let go!"

Chapter 37

Suddenly the room went silent as Mrs. Alcott's head slumped to her chest, hands hanging limply at her sides, palms open—empty. Slowly Dag's heavy breathing became audible as Mr. Alcott's muted cries for his wife mingled with the whimpers of the girl in the pink nightgown and the snickers of the man with the pistol.

Dag slammed the stone onto the table. "I missed it!"

"You're a fool," Zoey said.

Just then Mrs. Alcott's head swayed, a faint moan building in intensity from below the mangled remnants of a hairline.

Dag scrambled to put the stone in her hands only for it to fall to the floor. "Take it!" he screeched.

Grabbing both her wrists, he folded her hands onto the bloody pool in her lap, then slapped the stone onto her palm and forced her fingers around it. "Now hold it," he screamed into her ear.

Zoey pleaded, "Mrs. Alcott, you have to take the stone! Do you hear me? Please—take—the—stone!"

Dag squeezed her hand. "If you don't hold this thing, I swear I'll cut off your hand too."

Zoey watched his bloody fingers forcing Mrs. Alcott to take what she could not grasp. "Make her hold it. Yes, that's it—make her hold it!"

"What do you think I'm trying to do?"

"Keep *your* hand around *hers*! Just keep it there, don't let her drop it."

He leaned over the dying woman's shoulder, wrapping his hand around the one in which he had placed the stone.

Zoey inched forward, watching the perfect scenario play out, waiting for Mrs. Alcott's last breath to take her into the future while simultaneously vanquishing her nemesis along with her. Although Alcott would have no memories of the past, Zoey rationalized trading memories for life was the only choice.

"Why won't she die?" he screeched, placing his hand over her mouth. "Die, you mangy wench! Die!"

From deep within, a spark of final retaliation ignited as Mrs. Alcott bit through her gag and sank her teeth into the pale fingers across her lips. Dag jerked his hand away with a yelp. At the same time, she threw the stone over her shoulder and into his cheek, causing him to stumble backwards.

Zoey's fighting instincts kicked in as she assimilated every aspect of the situation. She watched him falling out of fighting range while the man with the gun shifted his attention toward his boss's debacle. Zoey had just enough time to kick over the candelabra and send the room into near darkness. With the only remaining light coming from a small candle on the edge of the table, she dropped onto her back. Using the floor as leverage, she placed her feet under the table and pushed upward, sending it and the lone candle across the room, into Dag and the Alcotts. With total darkness as the equalizer and chaos as a diversion, she crawled toward the curtains.

"Where'd she go?" said the man with the gun.

Dag unleashed a string of cuss words. "Alcott's out cold and his woman's dead." Another profanity-riddled tirade followed as he demanded Zoey reveal herself.

A brush of hair whisked over her forearm. She waved her hand blindly in the dark, and a second later small, trembling fingers found it. "Katy Ray?" she whispered. The hand pulled hers to a nodding head. Zoey pressed her lips to the girl's ear. "Follow me."

"Where are you, witch?" The strike of a match cast an evil glow across the lower half of Dag's face, Mrs. Alcott's blood smeared across his cheeks making him look like a demented clown.

Silently she pulled the girl through the curtains out into the hall. "This way," she said, blindly maneuvering to the back of the house, to Boone's office. Tugging the girl inside, she closed the door and turned the lock behind them.

"Why didn't we just run out the front door? This is all the way at the back," the girl whimpered.

"Front door's locked," Zoey said, groping her way through the darkness to the desk. She opened a drawer and rummaged frantically through it. "Got it."

The girl snuggled next to her, running her hand down Zoey's arm onto the cold barrel of the revolver Boone had come close to using to end his life. "Please save me."

"Shhh," Zoey said, pulling the girl behind the desk. "They'll be coming soon."

"Just use your magic," the girl pleaded.

"Katy, I don't have any magic. That man is just crazy."

"You have to use it."

"Listen to me now. We have to—"

"No!" Katy said, wresting the gun out of Zoey's hand and flinging it aside.

"Why'd you do that!"

"This is what you want," the girl said, pulling Zoey's fingers open. "Use this."

With no light to see what was being placed in her hand, Zoey still recognized its smooth, rounded edges. "You found the memory stone!"

"I found it when I was crawling across the floor. Now use the magic—please! I don't want to die and I-I can't go back doing what he was making me do."

From under the door a soft light etched across the floor from the candle Dag held as he paced up and down the hall. "Come on out, kitten," his voice slithered through the hallway.

She took the girl by the arm. "Listen to me. We have to find that gun."

"But we don't need it. You have the—"

"You don't understand. This stone is not—"

His voice outside the office door stopped her. "Give me the gun. You take the knife. I'll check the upstairs."

She pulled the girl to her, pressing the stone into her shaking hand. "No matter what happens, if you hold onto it, you're protected."

The girl returned a quivering smile. "What about you?"

"Don't worry about me," she said, untying the gold sash from around her waist then twisting the ends around her wrists. Flexing her arms outward, she tested the fabric's strength while monitoring the small crease of light coming from under the door. Moving shadows indicated the man with the knife lurked on the other side. "Stay right here and don't duck behind the desk. Let him see you, okay?"

"Are you sure?"

Zoey ran beside the door. "Yes, now just stay there." With her back against the wall, she waited.

A few breathless minutes later the handle jiggled, followed by silence. Bam! The heel of the big man's boot sent the door crashing open. Stomping to the middle of the room, he glared at the girl behind the desk. "Where's she at, Katy Ray?"

The girl cowered back into the corner, clutching the stone against her chest.

"I said, where—is—"

Whipping her sash over his head and around his neck, Zoey leaped onto his back, sending the enraged bull thrashing about the room, knocking over tables and lamps, sending chairs toppling, while she clung on, swinging like a loose sail in a tornado. The tighter she pulled the sash, the more violent the beast became. Thrusting his knife blindly back and forth over his shoulders, he sought to stab his way free. Suddenly his blade hit its mark and sliced across the left side of her face, ripping through her eye. She shrieked as the red-hot pain sent her crumpling to the floor.

The man staggered back against the desk, bent over and gasping for air.

"Stand up," a small voice came from the corner.

Glancing up, Zoey could barely make out through all the blood the blurred image of the girl in the pink gown, one hand still holding the stone, the other holding the revolver.

His chest heaving, the man rose, glaring into the gun's barrel. With no hesitation he walked up to her. "You know you're not going to use that thing."

"You'll never have your way with me or anyone else again." Her lips forming a quivering snarl, she started to pull the firing hammer back. Just as it clicked into place, the man whipped the back of his hand across her wrist and knocked the gun from her hand. As it slid across the floor, he lowered his head and began following her retreat into the corner.

Zoey staggered to her feet. Barely able to see through the bloody haze, she stood, grimacing through the pain. "Stop!"

Spinning back toward Zoey, the man glowered. "So you want to be the first?"

Suddenly the pain was gone. The sound of the man's boots trudging toward her morphed into the murmuring of a faraway crowd chanting her name. Instead of a soft mat and a stadium of adoring fans, she stood alone on hardwood planks in the middle of a dark room with her only supporter backed into a dark corner. In place of her signature pink patch over her left eye, a stream of crimson provided the advantage she had always afforded her opponents. With only half her vision, she watched as time stretched forward, allowing her to calculate her nemesis' every step, the position of the knife in his right hand, the rise and fall of his chest.

Stopping within a few feet of her, he looked her over. "Not much of a beauty anymore," he cackled.

She shifted her weight to the balls of her feet, inching her hands upward.

"Such a shame," he said. His brow twitched as he recoiled his knife, the telling action she knew he would take just before thrusting it forward.

Time suddenly flashed forward as she twisted her torso to the right, dodging the blade as it passed over her chest. With her left arm she locked his elbow while rocketing her knee into his groin. Pulling the knife from his hand, she spun around. In one sweeping motion she delivered a single slice of the razor-sharp metal across his jugular just as his knees hit the floor. With the thud of a bull elephant, he fell face-forward onto the floor.

For a moment she stood straddling him, confirming his death as blood puddled around her feet. Blinking away the impact of the gruesome event, she turned to the girl. "Come on—we've got to get out of here before the other one comes down." Pulling Katy out into the hallway, Zoey stopped, catching her breath as the searing pain from the blinding gash across her face rendered the long corridor a gauntlet of darkness. Only the glint of a streetlamp through the front door's window signaled their way to safety. Through clenched teeth, she grimaced. "Do you have the stone and the gun?"

"Ye-yes," the girl said.

Reaching down, Zoey found Katy's tiny hand gripping the revolver. "I'll take that," she said, calmly pulling it from her. "Keep the stone. And remember what I said about holding on to it." As the adrenaline of the attack continued to wear off, a river of fire ran across her face. Stifling the need to cry out, she suffered in silence while pushing the girl safely behind her. Pointing the gun blindly ahead, she clutched the girl by her gown and slowly began leading her to the front door.

The clamoring of feet rushing down the stairs stopped her. Katy threw her arms around Zoey's waist. The flickering streetlamp through the front door window suddenly disappeared, Dag's heaving frame obscuring its light and barring their only means of escape.

"Not so fast, ladies," he said.

Zoey waved her gun wildly in his direction, the combination of blood, sweat, and darkness preventing her from finding her mark.

A flame suddenly appeared, floating between ghostly fingers, igniting a candle on a small hallway table. Its light illuminated his revolver that had, unlike hers, found its mark.

"Don't move it. Don't you dare move," his voice screeched over her like fingernails against slate. "You're too far away to make the shot anyway and too blind to—"

Summoning all her quickness, she jerked her weapon dead center of the door, yanking the trigger, again and again and again. After the fifth time she staggered back, her body numb with horror as Dag stood wide-eyed, stunned by the weapon's inability to fire a single shot. Shaking with rage, he stepped toward her, squinted down the length of the gun barrel, then slowly squeezed the trigger.

"No," Katy screamed as she lunged in front of Zoey.

The blast from his revolver reverberated through the house as the girl's body collapsed across Zoey's feet. Falling to her knees, her head fell forward over Katy's limp body. "I told you to hold on to it!" she cried.

Suddenly the girl's eyes popped open. "Wh-what happened. Am I…"

Zoey pulled the girl's hand from under her nightgown. White-knuckled, her fist was wrapped around half the stone. The other half lay a foot away, a small chip knocked loose from Dag's bullet lay next to it.

The girl gleamed up at her. "I told you it was magic."

Zoey jumped to her feet as Dag clapped his hands. "I knew it had powers," he yipped. "I knew it!"

Zoey sank her fingernails into her palms, forming fists as solid as the rock that had saved the young girl's life. With only one way to escape, she'd have to go through him, and it had to be now while he was spellbound by the memory stone that had stopped his bullet from killing the girl. Lowering her head, she began to race toward him when suddenly she stopped, a smile raising her blood-stained cheeks.

Behind him, standing in the doorway, was Boone.

A twist of her nemesis' head drew her back to him, his attention no longer on the girl, the trance broken. His gaze, along with his revolver, now centered on her. His eyebrows pitched together. "Goodbye, kitten."

At the same time the bullet left Dag's barrel, Boone's fist crashed into the side of his jaw, knocking him unconscious.

Sprinting down the hall, he scooped Zoey up just as her knees began to buckle. He eased her to the floor, one of her hands against her chest covering a growing circle of red. "Oh, my dear!" He brushed her hair back, revealing the bloody gash across her face. "What has he done?"

"Your gun…" The words came soft and low, absent any signs of pain. "It had no bullets."

"I took them out after I tried to—"

She raised a hand to his lips. "Of course…" she said, her voice fading.

Sitting on the floor, he pulled her into his lap and rested his head against hers, rocking. "I-I have to go get a doctor. I have to—"

A tiny hand touched his shoulder. "No, you don't," Katy said.

"Who're you?"

"I'm nobody," she said, picking up the other half of the stone. Piecing them together, she placed them into his hand. "She just needs this."

Boone gaped at the objects. "Is this—"

"Make her hold it."

"Is-is this the stone?"

Zoey nodded.

As he gently laid the pieces across her open hand, she rolled her head toward the girl, her voice nothing more than a whisper. “My bag, I need you to—”

“You shouldn’t be talking,” Boone pleaded. “Save your energy—please!”

“I’m going to be okay.” Her eyelids fluttered. “Funny, I don’t feel any pain.”

Katy leaned over them. “What did you want me to do with the bag?”

“The money that’s in it. Use it to go…” She swallowed, waiting for the strength to continue. “Use the money to find Paul—I-I mean Mase Winslow. He’s a…” Her voice faltered into an inaudible mumble.

“He’s the owner of the Willow Creek Plantation in Beaufort, South Carolina,” Boone said.

“Find him,” Zoey continued in starts and stops. “Tell him everything. He’ll take care of you.” Her eyes closed then slowly opened. “You’re crying,” she said, raising her empty hand to wipe a tear from Boone’s cheek.

Pulling it to his lips, he kissed it then gently placed it over the one with the broken memory stone. “I’m not going to leave you.”

She looked down to where his hand rested over hers. “You have to let go.”

Tightening his grip, his tears fell onto their intertwined fingers. “I’m not going to lose you. I can’t!”

“If you don’t let go, the stone will take my memory. I won’t know you anymore.” Her eyes fell tenderly on his. “Our love will be lost.”

“No!” he said, shaking his head. “We’re meant to be together. You know we are. Wherever it takes us, we’ll—we’ll just fall in love all over again.”

With her breathing growing shallower, she said in a distant voice, "What if—we're separated?"

"Then I'll find you." He pulled her closer, kissing her cheeks as her blood and his tears fell silently across her chest. "I promise, I'll find you. No matter what it takes—I'll find you."

Cradling her in his arms, the shadow of a smile fell across her lips as he kissed her.

Katy stumbled back against the wall as she watched their bodies slowly fade away, a faint image of their embrace lingering for a moment then vanishing. Grabbing the bag, she ran down the hall, past Dag and toward the streetlamp to freedom.

For several minutes the only sounds within the house were the clickety clack of evening carriage rides emanating from the streets. Down the hallway to the back of the house, they floated. Several minutes passed before the sounds of sluggish footsteps worked their way to the vacant spot where Zoey and Boone had laid. A glimmer of the candle's light dappled across a faint hand as it stretched down to pick up the tiny remaining piece of the stone.

Chapter 38
(One Month Later)

A white fleck floated past the window. Mase sprang up off the floor, abandoning the tiny wooden blocks he had so proudly stacked in front of his baby boy. "Did you see that?" he said, scooping him up and hurrying to look outside. "Wow, it's come early!" His voice was full of exaggerated wonderment. "There's another one, and another!" He tucked the boy's blanket around him, pulling him closer. "That's snow, my boy—the first of the year."

While counting the flakes for his son, a knock came at the door.

"Who is it?"

"It's me, Mr. Mase," came a husky voice. "You got a visitor downstairs."

"Alright, tell them I'll be down in a minute." Placing the baby into his crib, he leaned over and kissed him on the forehead. "Daddy's going to come right back, and when I do, we'll count some more snow."

Upon entering the foyer, he found a young girl in a long winter coat, her back to him, peering out the window.

Hearing him behind her she spun around. "It's so beautiful."

"First snows always are," he said.

"No, I-I mean your house, the pond." She spread her arms wide. "The whole plantation."

He tilted his head. "And you would be…"

"Oh my, where're my manners. My name is Katy Ray."

"Pleasure to meet you, Miss Ray."

"You can call me Katy."

"How can I help you, Katy?"

She tugged on her coat's lapel, fidgeting with a button. "Well, sir, I'm not sure how to begin. I mean, you're going to think I'm crazy." She held out her hand, her voice rising. "I promise—I'm not crazy."

He motioned downward with an opened palm. "Just take it easy." He paused. "Did someone send you?"

Her head bobbed.

"Who?"

"A lady."

"What was her name?"

"I only know her first name. She saved my life."

"So—can you tell it to me then?"

"It was Zoey."

He swallowed. "Long dark hair? Pretty?"

"Yes…" she said, fading off, "she was very pretty."

"Where is she? Why didn't she come with you?"

"She couldn't."

"Why?"

"Because she—she's gone."

"Gone where?"

"I don't know."

"I'm sorry, miss, but I'm not following."

She nervously twisted her button until it popped off. Paying it no mind, she began wringing her hands together.

"You're not going to believe me, but she said you could help me."

"Ma'am, I promise I'll help in whatever way I can, but you have to tell me what's going on. Why don't you start by telling me why Zoey's not with you?"

"Because she disappeared, sir."

"Disappeared?"

"I knew I shouldn't have come." She grabbed the doorknob. "I-I'm sorry. This was all a big mistake. I'll go now."

"No! Wait!" He placed his hand on her shoulder. "Tell me what you mean by 'disappeared.'"

Her mouth went dry as she worked to gain her composure. "She-she was dying from a gunshot." She swung her head back and forth. "This is the part you won't believe."

"Go on."

"In her hand she had a stone."

His pulse quickened.

"But this wasn't a normal stone. This one had magic in it. I swear on my life, sir, this was magical. It was—"

"A memory stone!" Suddenly he was seeing through her to memories of when he had experienced his own miracle.

"You don't believe me, do you?"

With his hands together as if in prayer, he raised them until his fingers touched his lips. "Come with me. I think you and I have a lot to talk about."

Two hours later Mase and the young girl emerged from his office.

"Thank you, Mr. Winslow," she said, tears streaming down her face. "This is too kind. Are you sure?"

He took her by the hand. "Of course, I'm sure. Now I want you to go out to the smokehouse. It's on the other side of that big row of cedar trees down from the house. Maudie should be in there about now preparing for tonight's meal. Tell her you're going to be staying with us for a long while. She'll know what to do."

"Thank you! Thank you!" She turned toward the door then spun back to him, throwing her arms around his neck. "God bless you, Mr. Winslow!"

"Go on now. Maudie's waiting."

He chuckled, watching as she bounded down the front steps. After seeing her disappear among the cedars, he pulled the door shut then headed back into his office. Sitting down at his desk, he pulled out a small brown journal bound shut with a leather strap. As he dipped his quill pen into a gold-plated inkwell, a hint of a smile appeared, growing larger as he laid pen to paper. He hesitated a moment, pulling it away, letting it hover back over the page as he composed his thoughts. As the pen's tip found the page once again, his eyes began to glisten as he scratched out the beginning of his letter.

Dear Spoon…

(Modern day)

The soft white noise coming from the office's heating system coupled with the neon-blue hue emanating from the room's dozen computers was enough to lull anyone to sleep. If it weren't for the nature of the incoming calls and the frantic tapping of keystrokes accompanying the intensity of the conversations associated with them, the four investigators manning the night shift of Manhattan's missing person's division would be snoozing away.

A slender lady balancing five coffees on top of a box marked "Danny's Donut Hole" entered the room undetected. Except for one middle-aged lady hunched over her desk, squinting at a field of data scrolling across her computer screen, she was the only one not on the phones.

Tiptoeing her way behind her, the young girl leaned into the unsuspecting lady's ear and whispered, "coffee and donuts."

"Oh my!" the lady said, jerking back in her seat. "You sneaky little devil. You could've given me a heart attack." She eyed the box with a smile. "Considering your delivery, I think I'll forgive you. Thank you, dear."

"Has it been a busy night?" the girl said laying the box down.

"Pretty quiet up until about a half hour ago, then everybody's phone—except mine—lit up."

"Not a bad way to end your shift."

"It gave me some time to look into this report that came in about twenty minutes ago."

"The one you had your nose dug into just now?"

"Yeah. I've been trying to dissect it. There's a lot of information missing but I think we might have a high-profile case here."

"Really? Who is it?"

"I'm sure you know her. She's that journalist who works for the NYC *Chronicle*—the one with that really popular column—the one with the pink stripe in her hair."

"Oh yeah, they did that local news interest story on her because of her karate skills. She's the one who inspired the little girl who lost her eye. Zoey…"

"Antonelli."

"Yeah, that's it. Zoey Antonelli—I love her. So what leads you to believe it's her?"

"The data field for occupation only says journalist and location of residency only says New York City. I've already checked and there's only one Zoey Antonelli who's a reporter in New York and that's where she works. I've got to call the person who submitted it now though."

"But it's only six in the morning."

"I know, but he stated she's been missing for ten days."

"Oh no! That's way too long."

"I just hope the guy who filed it isn't some whack job."

"How about this? Since your shift is up, I'll take this over. As soon as the *Chronicle* opens, I'll give them a call to see if Miss Antonelli has been showing up for work. If she has, then the report's probably a hoax perpetrated by some anti-feminist who randomly picked a successful, attractive female to target his angst. To be honest, that's what it sounds like to me, especially since the *Chronicle* hasn't filed their own report."

"I hope it *is* a hoax. This city's pretty fond of that pink stripe of hair."

By noon that day an unseasonal wave of southern winds blew in, transforming New Jersey's Liberty State Park into a hyperactive epicenter of eager tourists bent on enjoying a day gazing out at the Statue of Liberty. Alongside the throng of visitors, Boone stood staring out into the harbor.

"Vanderson!" yelled a squatty man chomping on a cigar. "Would you quit gawking out there. You're giving Lady Liberty the heebie-jeebies."

"Heebie what?"

The man stomped up to him, tossing his mangled cigar in the trash can Boone was holding. "I swear, every time I turn around, you're someplace else."

"I'm sorry. It's just that I'm still getting used to it all."

"What's to get used to? A janitor picks up trash and throws it away and cleans toilets. Are you saying you're not smart enough for *that*?"

Boone curled his fist around the lapel of his blue custodial jumpsuit, wanting to rip it off and throw it in the trash can that had become his constant companion since being hired under the table for the only job a nineteenth-century refugee could obtain.

"The next time I catch you daydreaming, you're out of here!"

As the man stormed off, Boone glanced back at the great statue then across the bay to the colossal New York skyline. There his gaze remained, undeterred by the consequences with which he had just been threatened. "If it takes the rest of my life, I *will* find you."

On the opposite side of the harbor, an old man wrapped in a tattered blanket climbed out of an equally ragged tent. His frame, like the tent, was a loose connection of worn-out parts that had gradually eroded from a lifetime of weathering storms. Slow and steady, he ambled through the tiny community of similar dwellings, the residents of which remained inside, curled under pieces of cardboard, soiled towels, and other disregarded materials that could provide warmth. Squinting his eyes, he scanned the huge oaks and maples that helped shelter his mangy tent village.

"That way," came a voice, small and weak.

He turned to find a fellow tent dweller poking her head from around a tree.

"There," she said, holding a crooked finger to a clearing past the canopy of hardwoods.

The old man nodded his thanks. A few minutes later he was standing out in the noonday sun on a grassy bank bordering a walking path that weaved its way up to the South Street Seaport. The sun's rays glistened across the white-caps of the Hudson River, creating an endless horizon of shimmering diamonds floating atop the water.

The old man carefully eased his way to the ground. "Now that's a view," he said, trying unsuccessfully to cross his legs like the young woman beside him.

The scene's beauty was lost on her as she sat twisting her blue dress between her fingers. Her gaze locked onto the busy dock, her focus only on the cargo ships being loaded and unloaded.

"What're you looking at?"

She shrugged.

"Anything come to you yet?"

She shook her head.

"I brought this for you," he said, handing her one half of a Kit Kat bar.

"Thanks." She held it out in front of her, turning it from side to side.

"You eat it. It's a candy bar."

"A candy bar?"

"Yeah." He shoved the other half into his mouth. "You'll like it," he said through a muffled grin.

A moment passed as she sat nibbling away at the tiny chocolate delight. She nodded her approval.

"Have you thought about going to a hospital?" the man asked.

She tilted her head.

"I mean… well, you just don't look like you belong here. You must have had an accident or something. You've been here over a week now and, well, you seem lost.

Really, really lost. Don't you have any relatives or friends you can go to or call?"

Just then two policemen walked past in the direction of the docks.

"Hold on a minute," one said, pulling out a cell phone. A few seconds later he held it up to the other officer. "What do you think?"

"There's no pink stripe."

"No, but I'd bet my pension, *that's* Zoey Antonelli."

A Personal Note From The Author

If you read The Memory Stones I would like to say a heartfelt thank you for sharing your time with me. If you enjoyed it and have time to post an honest review, I would greatly appreciate it. And if you'd like to contact me directly, feel free to email me through my website below. I love making new friends!

For more info visit:
LewisPennington.com

About The Author

Lewis Pennington graduated from East Carolina University in Greenville, North Carolina with a degree in Graphic Design and Marketing. Upon graduation, he moved to New York City where he began his career with the now defunct Science Fiction Magazine Omni Magazine. After decades of navigating through the corporate marketing maze he is now focusing on his next chapter in life—providing readers with inspirational fiction. Lewis and his family live in Asheville, North Carolina.